PRAISE FOR
RALPH COMPTON

"Compton writes in the style of popular Western novelists like Louis L'Amour and Zane Grey . . . thrilling stories of Western legend."—*The Huntsville Times* (AL)

"Compton may very well turn out to be the greatest Western writer of them all. . . . Very seldom in literature have the legends of the Old West been so vividly painted."
                                    —*The Tombstone Epitaph*

The Sundown Riders

DEVIL'S CANYON

Ralph Compton

BERKLEY
New York

BERKLEY
An imprint of Penguin Random House LLC
penguinrandomhouse.com

Copyright © 1998 by Ralph Compton
Penguin Random House supports copyright. Copyright fuels creativity, encourages
diverse voices, promotes free speech, and creates a vibrant culture. Thank you for buying
an authorized edition of this book and for complying with copyright laws by not
reproducing, scanning, or distributing any part of it in any form without permission.
You are supporting writers and allowing Penguin Random House to continue to
publish books for every reader.

BERKLEY and the BERKLEY & B colophon are registered trademarks of
Penguin Random House LLC.

ISBN: 9780451195197

Signet mass-market edition / May 1998
Berkley mass-market edition / December 2019

Printed in the United States of America
22   24   26   28   30   31   29   27   25   23

Cover art by Hiram Richardson
Cover design by Steve Meditz

This work is respectfully dedicated
to my brother,
William F. (Bill) Compton.

THE IMMORTAL COWBOY

The saga of the "American Cowboy" was sparked by the turmoil that followed the Civil War, and the passing of more than a century has by no means diminished the flame.

True, the old days and the old ways are but treasured memories, and the old trails have grown dim with the ravages of time, but the spirit of the cowboy lives on.

In my travels—which include Texas, Oklahoma, Kansas, Nebraska, Colorado, Wyoming, New Mexico, and Arizona—there's something within me that remembers. While I am walking these plains and mountains for the first time, there is this feeling that a part of me is eternal, that I have known these old trails before. I believe it is the undying spirit of the frontier calling, allowing me, through the mind's eye, to step back into time. What is the appeal of the Old West, of the American frontier?

It has been epitomized by some as a dark and bloody period in American history. Its heroes, Crockett, Bowie, Hickock, Earp, have been reviled and criticized. Yet the Old West lives on, larger than life.

It has become a symbol of freedom, when there was always another mountain to climb and another river to cross; when a dispute between two men was settled not with expensive lawyers but with fists, knives, or guns. Barbaric? Maybe. But some things never change. When the cowboy rode into the pages of American history, he left behind a legacy that lives within the hearts of us all.

—*Ralph Compton*

Foreword

In 1821, William Becknell first opened a trade route from Independence, Missouri, to Santa Fe, New Mexico. It quickly became known as the Santa Fe Trail, and for more than seventy years—until the coming of the railroad—trains of pack mules and heavy freight wagons moved millions of dollars in goods to the western frontier.

But for some, Santa Fe was the "jumping-off place," the beginning of their quest for riches, for New Mexico was sheep country. In California there was a ready market for wool, and an abundance of horses and mules, which were in short supply in New Mexico. But following the war with Mexico—when Mexico ceded California to the United States—a series of changes began that eliminated commerce between Santa Fe and Los Angeles.

The discovery of gold attracted miners from as far away as England, China, and Japan, while California's ready access to the Pacific made its ports attractive to sailing ships from around the world. By 1855, goods muled in from Santa Fe were no longer worth the cost and the danger.

The country west of Santa Fe had little attraction, except for groups of Mormons who had settled in northern Utah, near the great salt lakes. But there were a few hardy souls who fought the land, the elements, and the Ute Indians to prospect for gold along the rivers of south central and southern Utah. The land, as one old prospector put it, "warn't good fer nothin' but holdin' the world together." There was cactus, scorpions, rattlesnakes, cougars, and grizzlies. Men sweated by day and froze by night. The land was laced with a variety of canyons and arroyos that flooded during cloudbursts, and when dry, provided excellent cover for hostile Utes with ambush on their minds. In the mountains, the weather was as unpredictable as the land was dangerous. Within a matter of hours, men could be drenched by cloudbursts, pelted by hailstones, or frozen by sleet and snow.

In the glory days, when traders risked their lives to reach gold-rich California, there were no wagons west of Santa Fe. There were only pack mules, and with good reason. The terrain was such that a wagon might be forced to travel for miles just to avoid a deep and dangerous arroyo. But miners—snowed in for the winter in the mountains of southwestern Utah—seldom owned enough pack mules to freight in needed goods, and removing gold ore by mule was a slow, dangerous process. That, and the fact there was a continual lack of mules in New Mexico. A good mule, when one could be had, sold for as much as two hundred dollars.

Some miners, desperate for a means of freighting in goods and freighting out gold ore, sought out teamsters who were bold enough to take their wagons into the treacherous mountains. Men who armed themselves with Bowie knives, repeating rifles, and Colt revolvers. These men, who fought hostile Indians, outlaws, the elements, and the land itself, were the first mercenaries. These were the *Sundown Riders,* blazing a trail ever westward.

L.A. Hensley

Prologue

Santa Fe, New Mexico. August 1, 1870.

"It ain't hard to spot a galoot that's spent all his days lookin' at the stinkin' end of a mule," said the big man with a black, bushy beard. "His face gits to lookin' just like that mule's behind."

He sat across the table from Faro Duval, a teamster from Independence, Missouri, who had just won his fourth pot and ended the game.

"Juno Shankler," said the barkeep, brandishing a sawed-off shotgun, "you ain't startin' no fight in here. Git up and git out."

Faro's fellow teamsters—Shanghai Taylor, Tarno Spangler, and Dallas Weaver—had their backs to the wall, their hands on the butts of their Colts.

"Faro," Dallas said, "back off. He makes a move, we'll fill him full of lead. Lay down that scattergun, barkeep. If anything's to be settled, we'll settle it outside."

"You got it, mule jockeys," said Shankler. "One at a time, by God, or all at once."

"I stomp my own snakes," Faro said. "If anybody needs help, it'll be you."

Slowly the barkeep lowered the shotgun, as Faro

backed his chair away from the table and got to his feet. When he reached the door, he nodded to his three companions. While Faro stood there, his hand on the butt of his holstered Colt, Shanghai, Tarno, and Dallas filed out of the saloon. Faro then stepped out, closing the door behind him.

"Don't be a damn fool, Shankler," said a patron who had seen the play. "You're callin' out an *hombre* with the bark on. He ain't like the glory-hungry kids you're used to."

"Mind your own damn business, Hugo," Shankler said.

Shankler stepped out the saloon door onto the boardwalk. Faro leaned against a hitch rail on the other side of the street. Faro's three companions stood aside, out of the line of fire. Shankler hitched up his gun belt and tilted his hat over his eyes.

"There's still time to back off, Shankler," said Faro.

"I could say the same fer you," Shankler said. "I just don't think you're man enough to take me, bucko."

"When you're ready, then," said Faro.

Shankler drew first, and his gun was only half out of his holster when Faro's lead hit him just above the left pocket of his shirt. He stumbled back against the saloon door and it opened, allowing him to collapse on the floor. Men who had been watching out the window of the saloon gathered around.

"Old Juno's been askin' fer that," somebody said. "He's always been long on guts an' short on judgment."

"Somebody git the sheriff," said the barkeep. "I

want his carcass took out, an' I ain't wantin' it said he was shot in here."

The sheriff arrived in due time. He was in the saloon only a few minutes when he went looking for Faro Duval. Faro had remained standing where he had been when he had been forced to shoot Shankler. His three companions had moved in behind him.

"You got witnesses a-plenty," said the lawman. "I'm Sheriff Easton. Who are you?"

"I'm Faro Duval. These are my partners, Shanghai Taylor, Tarno Spangler, and Dallas Weaver. We're not wanted and we're not huntin' anybody. We drove in four wagon loads of freight from Independence, and we'll be goin' back there, soon as we scare up some freight to take with us."

"I'm some relieved to hear that," said Easton. "There's others around here that's of the same mind as Juno. I'd not want them testing you."

"That's entirely up to them," Faro said. "I take no pleasure in killin' a man, but some won't settle for anything less."

"Then take my advice and stay out of the saloons," said the lawman.

Easton started back to the saloon just as a tall man in miner's clothes stepped out on the boardwalk.

"Wait up, gents," he said. "I want to talk to you."

Faro and his companions waited, and when he was near enough, the stranger spoke again.

"I'm Levi Collins. I gathered from what I heard that you men are teamsters."

"We are," said Faro. "We just brought four wagon loads of freight from Independence, and we're lookin' for some freight bound for there. I'm Faro Duval, and my partners are Shanghai Taylor, Tarno Spangler, and Dallas Weaver. What can we do for you?"

Collins rested his eyes on each of them for a moment, liking what he saw. They stood over six feet, Faro and Shanghai with dark hair, while Tarno and Dallas had hair the color of wheat straw. To a man, they were dressed like cowboys, from their wide-brimmed hats to their undershot, high-heeled boots. Collins judged them all less than twenty-five, and all four carried tied-down Colts. Collins spoke.

"It's near suppertime. I'm buying, if you'll listen to what I have to say. I may have some work for you."

"You don't look like an *hombre* needin' four loads of freight hauled to Independence," said Dallas.

Collins laughed. "To the contrary, the hauling I have in mind will take you west, but the reward will be great."

"We'll listen," Faro said, "but I won't promise any more than that."

"That's all I ask," said Collins.

He led the way to a cafe, and men were already pointing to Faro as a result of his having gunned down Juno Shankler. They took their seats near the back of the cafe, and Collins spoke again.

"You're mighty sudden with a pistol, Mr. Duval. Do the rest of you . . ."

His voice trailed off, for the eyes of the four men had suddenly grown cold.

"I . . . I didn't mean that like it probably sounded," said Collins. "What I should have said is that the journey I am about to propose will take us through Ute country, and how handy a man is with a gun could mean the difference between living and dying."

"We manage to protect ourselves and our freight," Tarno Spangler said.

"Yes," said Shanghai Taylor, "and in case you're wondering, we can carry our weight with Winchesters, too."

Collins laughed. "That's exactly what I was wondering. I don't have to tell you that, during an Indian attack, it's important to pick off as many as possible before they get in close with their arrows."

"Now that you've got our attention," said Faro, "why don't you lay the rest of your cards on the table?"

"I aim to," Collins replied. "Isaac Puckett, Felix Blackburn, Josh Snyder, and me have a gold claim on the Sevier River, in southwestern Utah. We're lookin' for teamsters with the sand to wagon in supplies, and when we have enough ore, haul it out."

"Whoa," said Dallas. "I seem to recall there was once a trade route through there, to California. That country's got more canyons and arroyos than Kansas has prairie dogs, and it's nigh impossible for anything to get through there, except mules."

"If we was goin' all the way to California, I'd have to agree," Collins said, "but takin' care, a good teamster can get a wagon as far as our claim on the Sevier River."

"Givin' you the benefit of the doubt," said Faro, "how far would that be?"

"Five hundred miles," Collins replied.

"My God," said Shanghai, "and there's hostile Utes between here and there?"

"Entirely too damned many," Collins said. "The canyons and arroyos, when they're not flooded, are prime prospects for an Indian ambush."

"For a gent hopeful of hirin' teamsters, you ain't painted a very rosy picture," said Tarno.

"I didn't intend to," Collins replied. "I'm not one to mislead a man."

"So far," said Faro, "that's the biggest thing in your favor. As a rule, we don't look for work that appears easy. If it was, either it wouldn't pay worth a damn, or everybody would be clamorin' for it. Pay-wise, what are you offering?"

"A thousand dollars a man for all of you," Collins said.

"If we was just haulin' in your supplies, then turnin' around and bringin' out your ore, that's a fair price," said Faro, "but from what you've said, you have considerably more than that in mind. Am I right, when I say you have yet to work the mine, before there *is* any ore?"

"You are correct," Collins said. "Before I come here to buy supplies and to try and hire some teamsters, my partners and me reckoned we'd have to sweeten the pot. Here's what we come up with."

From an inside coat pocket, he removed a sheet of paper which he unfolded and gave to Faro. After studying it, he passed it around the table to his three companions. Each of them read it, and Shanghai passed it back to Collins. Faro spoke.

"You're offering a quarter-share of your claim to us, for our services, then."

"That's right," said Collins, "and them services

would include takin' the time for us to work the mine, to produce some ore. You'd likely be there until spring, at least."

"*Madre mía,*" Dallas said, "and how are we supposed to keep ourselves occupied for all them months?"

"You likely could shorten that time, if you help us work the claim," said Collins, "or if that don't appeal to you, there's hostile Utes to be shot."

"By God," Tarno said, "you *do* make it sound interesting. Was it just me, I'd likely go along with you, but these other *hombres* . . ."

"These other *hombres* have another question," said Faro. "How do we know we won't break our backs on a hard-scrabble claim for a year, shootin' hostile Utes in between, only to have this claim come up dry, without enough gold to fill a tooth?"

Collins laughed. "I expected that."

He looked carefully around, and when it appeared nobody was watching, removed a small canvas sack from his coat pocket. He then removed his hat, and turning it upside down on the table, dumped the contents of the sack into it. There was a dozen or more hunks of rock, each of them shot full of thin veins of gold. Faro hefted one, and found it predictably heavy.

"My God," Tarno said, "that'd put the *Lost Dutchman* to shame. There's more?"

"Yes," said Collins, "and to answer your next question, we don't know exactly how *much* more."

"I've done some prospectin' in my time," Shanghai said, "and mostly there's just two kinds of gold to be found. There's dust and nuggets, generally washed down from a higher elevation, and you may poke around for the rest of your days, without findin' the source. Then there's the other kind—like this—that's been dug from a vein."

"Yeah," said Dallas, "but that vein may pinch out after a few feet."

"That's always a possibility," Collins conceded, "but this comes from just one of many such veins."

"If there's more of this," said Faro, "you have a bonanza. Have you registered the claim and had the ore assayed?"

"No," Collins replied, "and I have my reasons. We don't want to start a gold rush, because we don't know where this claim will take us, and fightin' the Utes is plenty bad enough, without havin' to shoot claim jumpers. We figure to work the claim for a year. If there's plenty more gold, then we'll register the claim and stick with it until she runs dry. But as you can see, it's rich enough that a year's worth of diggin' can set us all up for the rest of our lives."

The waiter arrived with their food, and Collins quickly swept the gold-laden hat off the table and into his lap. Collins had said just enough, and they proceeded to eat. Not until they were drinking final cups of coffee did anybody speak.

"Collins," said Faro, "if there's more gold where that came from, the proposition you just made us is beginnin' to seem worth the risk. I'm speaking for myself, now. Each of my *amigos* will make his own decision."

"Count me in," Shanghai said.

"Same here," said Tarno.

"I'll go," Dallas said, "but if it turns out this claim's been salted, just to lure us into haulin' supplies five hundred miles through the devil's backyard, then I'll get mean."

Collins laughed. "I don't blame you, my friend, but you have nothing to worry about. Do you think I'd be spending every dollar we own for supplies, and then hauling them five hundred miles into the mountains, if there wasn't some reward?"

"He has something there, Dallas," said Faro. "Collins, do you honestly believe you'll need four wagon loads of supplies to last a year?"

"Yes," Collins replied, "and I just hope that'll be enough. We have four pack mules and our horses, and there are your teams. They'll need grain at least twice a week, maybe every day, when snow flies."

"Maybe you're right," said Faro. "Besides our teams, we each have a horse."

"We're likely to need one wagon just for shells for our Colts and Winchesters," Tarno said. "All the gold in Utah won't be worth a damn, if them Utes attack and we discover we just opened our last tin of shells."

"I'm taking all that into account," said Collins. "There's virtually no game, especially in winter, so everything will have to be freighted in."

"One thing bothers me," Faro said. "There's always a bunch of *hombres* around the saloons and mercantiles that take an almighty lot of interest in other folks' business. When you take to buyin' supplies and ammunition by the wagon load, that's bound to arouse the curiosity of somebody. Like you said, a man don't spend that kind of money, unless he's got ideas of recoverin' it, with interest. I'd not be surprised if we don't have to ventilate some claim jumpers *pronto.*"

"I hadn't considered that," Collins said, "but you could be right. We're going to need maybe a wagon load of dynamite, and that's enough to stir up some interest."

"My God, yes," said Tarno. "That's enough dynamite to blow up all of Utah."

"It won't be too much," Collins said. "When you see the claim, and what we must move to reach the gold, you'll understand. Now, to prove my good intentions, I want all of you to fill in your names as one-quarter owners to our strike."

"I reckon we'll have plenty of time for that," said Faro.

"No," Collins insisted, "I want all of you to begin thinking of yourselves as owners."

"Have it your way," said Faro. "You're a trusting man, Collins."

"To the contrary," Collins said, "I prefer to think of myself as a good judge of character. I watched you playing poker in the saloon. The man who taunted you—that you had to shoot—had been cheating. You could have called his hand, shot him, and been without fault, but you didn't. Not until he forced you, and even then, you didn't want to kill him. It takes a man to forgive a lesser man his faults, to accept his insults without returning them in kind."

"All of us were with General Lee," said Faro, "and we've seen enough dying to last us a lifetime. I'd never shoot a man for shootin' off his mouth, but when he pulls a gun, he'd better be almighty fast, because that's where my patience ends. Now when do you aim to start buyin' those supplies?"

"First thing tomorrow," Collins said. "Maybe I can get to the mercantiles before the hangers-on show up."

"We'll look for you there, then," said Faro. "Soon as you've made your best deals, we'll start loadin'. I hope you have no preference as to loading, because we do."

"You have the experience," Collins said. "Load the wagons as you see fit. I have only one request. Allow some room in each of the wagons for some dynamite."

"I reckon you have a reason for that," said Faro.

"Yes," Collins replied. "It'll be a rough trail, and explosives can be touchy. If all the dynamite's on one wagon, and it blows, then we're all out of dynamite."

"We're also minus a teamster, his teams, and a wagon," said Tarno.

"Yes," Collins said. "That too."

Sante Fe, New Mexico. August 2, 1870.

Collins started with four barrels of flour, and one was loaded on each wagon.

"I hope one of your *amigos* can make biscuits," said Shanghai. "None of us is worth a damn at it."

"You're in luck," Collins said. "Perhaps I should say *we're* in luck. Felix Blackburn, one of my partners, once was a cook in New Orleans."

"Cooked for one of them fancy hotels, I reckon," said Tarno.

"No," Collins said. "He killed a man over a saloon girl and spent two years in jail. He learned to cook while he was there."

"Sounds like our kind of *hombre*," said Dallas. "After the war, we was all goin' back to Texas and rustle cattle, but the varmints wasn't worth nothin' unless they was drove all the way to Kansas, to the railroad."

Collins laughed, uncertain as to how much of what he was hearing was guarded truth, or simply cowboy humor.

"I'd suggest you save the dynamite and ammunition until last," Faro said. "That's the two things that'll likely stir the most interest. We ought to be as close as we can to pullin' out of here before anybody begins to wonder what we're up to."

But as the day wore on, it soon became apparent that four wagons simply would not accommodate all that Collins considered necessary.

"He's figurin' on an almighty lot of dynamite," said Shanghai.

"Too damn much dynamite," Tarno agreed.

"But we can't be sure of that," said Faro. "He's familiar with the claim, so we'll have to concede that he knows what he's doing."

"One thing he's figured all wrong," Dallas said. "We need a fifth wagon."

"Well, I hope he has an answer to that," said Faro, "because I don't. Even if we *had* the wagon, we have no mules, and we all know there's none for sale."

"Well, hell," Tarno said, "let's give up this fool idea of goin' to Utah after gold ore. We could get rich, drivin' mule herds from Independence to Santa Fe."

"You should have thought of that yesterday," said Faro. "We've given our word."

"Yeah," Dallas said, "and there'll still be a mule shortage in Santa Fe next year."

"We either tell Collins he's a wagon shy, or let him figure it out for himself," Tarno said. "What's it gonna be?"

"I'll talk to him," said Faro. "Maybe he can cut back on something."

But that was the last thing Collins had in mind.

"I don't want to question your judgment," Collins said, "and I don't doubt it when you say we're running out of wagon space, but we'll need everything I'm planning to buy. I have the money to buy a wagon, necessary harness, and teams, and I've been a teamster in my time. See if there's a wagon and teams for sale anywhere in Sante Fe."

Faro visited every stable and wagon yard to no avail. He was about to return to the mercantile and tell Collins the situation was hopeless, when he rode past a saloon. Behind it was a wagon, with mules hitched to it. Faro dismounted and entered the saloon. It was midday, and there were few patrons.

"There's mules and a wagon out back," said Faro. "I'd like to talk to the owner."

"That's me," said a man who had all the earmarks of a professional gambler. "I'm Hal Durham."

"I'm Faro Duval, and I need mules and a wagon. There's none to be had, except for yours. Are they for sale?"

"I'm afraid not," Durham said. "Sorry."

It was his right not to sell, but Faro didn't like the looks of him. He was dressed all in black, like an undertaker or circuit-riding preacher, and on his feet were gaiters, instead of boots. His flat-crowned black Stetson had a silver band encircling it, there was a flaming red sash about his middle, and a silver watch chain draped over one side of his vest.

"God," said one man to another, "the medicine show must be comin'. Damned if the dancin' bear ain't already here."

His companion flipped the brim of Durham's hat, and when it fell to the floor, put his foot on it. The pair of them laughed.

"I'll ask you only once," Durham said. "Pick up my hat, dust it off, and place it on my head."

"Haw, haw," said his antagonist. "When hell freezes."

Durham's right hand moved like a striking rattler, and when the brass knucks struck the other man's jaw, he went down like a clubbed steer. His companion reached for his gun but he wasn't quick enough. The brass knucks slammed into his jaw, and he crumpled to the floor.

"Here," the barkeep shouted, "no fighting in here."

Friends of the two felled men were trying to revive them.

"Hey," somebody said, "these gents is got busted jaws. Look how they're hangin'."

"I ain't takin' no responsibility for this," the barkeep shouted. "Somebody git the law in here."

Sheriff Easton arrived, studied the situation, and turned to the barkeep.

"He done it, Sheriff," said the barkeep, pointing to Durham.

"Done what?" Easton demanded. "I didn't hear no shots."

"Busted their jaws," said the barkeep. "Maybe kilt 'em."

"The two on the floor started it, Sheriff," Faro said. "This *hombre* slugged them."

"You again," said Easton. "What's your stake in this?"

"I told you I was leaving town," Faro said, "and I am. I needed another teamster, and I'm hirin' this gent. He'll be leaving town as I do."

"Him?" the lawman said. "He's a teamster?"

"Hell," said the barkeep, "he's a jackleg gambler, and he ain't a very good one. Lock him up, Sheriff."

"I can't see he's violated any law," Easton said. "You aim to press charges?"

"Well, I . . . "

"If he's leavin' town," said the sheriff, "that's good enough for me. What about it?"

"You heard the gentleman," Durham said haughtily. "I am working for him. Shall we be going, sir?"

"Yes," said Faro. "We have wagons to load."

The two men on the floor sat up, shaking their heads. The unruffled Durham stepped out the door, and Faro followed.

Chapter 1

"You take a lot for granted, my friend," Durham said, when he and Faro had left the saloon. "I told you the wagon and mules aren't for sale."

"I seem to recall you having mentioned that," said Faro, "so I got you an invitation to leave town. Then, when you're far enough out in the brush and cactus, I'll just shoot you and take the teams and wagon."

Durham laughed. "A man after my own heart. It takes one with unconventional ways to appreciate them in another. Not that I care a damn, but why the urgent need for my wagon and teams?"

"My three pards and I have taken on a hauling job requiring five wagons," said Faro. "There's not a wagon or mule to be had in all of Santa Fe."

"I wouldn't know about that," Durham replied. "I acquired my teams and wagon while I was in Texas. A friendly wager turned serious, and I relieved a gentleman's financial embarrassment by accepting his mules and wagon."

"You're a gambler, then," said Faro.

"Any objection to that?"

"I reckon not," Faro said. "I set in on a game occasionally. It's a cut or two above stealing."

"A man wins too often," said Durham, "and it leads to a misunderstanding. There was an unfortunate soul killed yesterday evening, over a game, I hear."

"Yeah," Faro said, "I heard about that. Every man has his price, Durham. What will it take to separate you from that wagon and mules?"

"Like I told you," said Durham, "they're not for sale. When I leave here, I'm going on to California, and I'll be needing them."

"Really?" Faro said. "What do you know about the country west of here?"

"Nothing," said Durham.

"Then you should," Faro said. "It's all but impassable, even for experienced teamsters, and you'd be better off with a good saddle horse."

"Oh, I have a horse," said Durham. "He follows the wagon on a lead rope. I kind of like the wagon."

"Durham," Faro said, "this hauling job of ours will take us five hundred miles west of here. In the old days, that used to be a trade route to California. What would it take for us to hire the use of your wagon for a load of supplies as far as we'll be going?"

"I'd have to think about it," said Durham. "A loaded wagon would slow me down."

"Oh, hell," Faro said, "the damn wagon *empty* will slow you down to a crawl."

"I'll consider it, then," said Durham. "When will you be leaving?"

"At dawn tomorrow," Faro said. "We'll be at the

mercantile a while longer, should you change your mind."

Durham said nothing, and Faro left him standing before one of the many saloons in Santa Fe. A man who had been following Faro and Durham came on down the boardwalk, and ignoring Durham, entered the saloon. Durham waited a moment, making sure nobody was watching, and then entered the saloon.

"A bottle," Durham said to the barkeep.

Taking his bottle, Durham looked around the dim interior of the saloon. It was still early, and there were only two or three other patrons. The seedy-looking stranger who had entered ahead of Durham sat at a corner table, and Durham sidled over there. Without a word, he hooked a chair with his foot, dragged it out, and sat down. The other man eyed him, took a pull from his bottle, and said nothing.

"There's four of 'em, Slade," said Durham, "and all I was able to learn is that they're haulin' four wagon loads of supplies five hundred miles west of here."

"Exactly where are they haulin' 'em?" Slade demanded.

"Somewhere along what used to be a trade route to California," said Durham. "They're needing teams and another wagon. They tried to buy mine, and when I refused to sell, this Faro Duval wanted to hire the use of the teams and wagon for as far as they're going."

"Damn it," Slade said, "you should have sold 'em the teams and wagon. You could always take 'em back, after the ambush."

"I have my reasons for not selling the teams and wagon," said Durham. "I said that I'd consider hiring

the wagon and teams to them, and when they've unloaded their goods, go on to California from there."

"Well, at least you done somethin' right," Slade
said. "Now track 'em down and make a deal. I want to
know where they're goin', and why. It's your rig, so in-
sist on handlin' the teams and wagon yourself."

Durham drained his bottle, got to his feet, and left
the saloon. His relationship with Slade and his four unsavory companions had come about purely by chance.
The outlaws had robbed a bank in Tucumcari, and had
ridden their horses to death, just ahead of a ten-man
posse. Durham's wagon and approaching darkness was
all that had saved them from a rope. Durham had
closed the puckers of the wagon's canvas, and the outlaws had hidden inside. By traveling all night, Durham
had lost the posse, and had found himself part of a
band of outlaws. At first it seemed a daring, hell-for-
leather thing to do. But now he wasn't so sure. Nearing thirty, he had lived by his wits since he was ten.
Truthfully, he had acquired the wagon and teams in
Amarillo, but only because the McCutcheon sisters
had staked him with the understanding he would take
them with him to California. He had stood them up,
and he had little doubt they'd be getting even. He was
unsure only of the time and place, and having been in
Santa Fe almost a week, he was becoming more uneasy by the day. The more he thought of Mamie and
Odessa McCutcheon, the more the rugged country to
the west appealed to him. Returning to his wagon, he
mounted the box and drove to the mercantile. Faro,
Tarno, Dallas, and Shanghai ceased what they were

doing. Levi Collins came out of the store as Durham stepped down from the wagon box.

"I've decided to let you use my wagon," Durham said.

"Bueno," said Faro. "What are your terms?"

"I'll handle the teams," Durham said, "and I want you to stake me with enough grub and supplies to get me to California."

"Collins," said Faro, "you're paying. What do you think?"

"We can live with that," Collins said.

"It's a deal, then," said Faro. "Durham, these are my pards, Shanghai Taylor, Tarno Spangler, and Dallas Weaver. Levi Collins, here, is the gent hiring our wagons."

"I'll leave the wagon here for loading," Durham said. "When you're done, move it out with your own wagons. Where will you be for the night?"

"In that vacant lot across from the wagon yard," said Faro. "A couple of us will be standing watch all night."

"I'll see you there in the morning," Durham said.

As Durham started back toward the business section, his worst fears became reality. On the opposite side of the street, Mamie and Odessa McCutcheon stepped out of a café and started down the boardwalk. Durham bolted for the first available sanctuary, which was a dress shop. Ignoring the startled old lady who owned it, he hurried out a back door into an alley. Repeatedly looking over his shoulder, he hurried back to the lodging house where he had taken a room. Gathering his few belongings, he slipped out the back door. Darkness was still four hours away, and keeping to narrow alleys and byways, he managed to reach the saloon where he had left Slade. This time, Durham didn't bother ordering a drink, but went directly to Slade's table.

"You're gettin' mighty damn brave," Slade said, his eye on Durham's traveling bag.

"I made the deal for the wagon," said Durham. "We leave tomorrow morning."

"We'll be a few miles behind you," Slade said. "Don't waste no time findin' out where they're bound, and why."

Durham nodded. It galled him, having a two-bit outlaw talk down to him like he was a hired hand. He took a back alley route to the edge of town, and for the lack of a better place, took refuge in the shade of a thicket, resting his head on his traveling bag. When it was dark enough, he would join Faro Duval's outfit, and sleep under the wagon.

"He's a sure enough dude, if I ever saw one," Shanghai said, when Durham had gone. "What in tarnation is he doin' out here, with mules and a wagon?"

"Likely one jump ahead of his past," said Tarno. "Never seen a gambler yet that there wasn't enough skeletons in his closet to start a graveyard."

"We don't question his past, unless it catches up to him and begins causin' us grief," Faro said. "I doubt there's a man on the frontier who hasn't left somethin' behind that he ain't exactly proud of."

"Amen to that," said Collins. "Whatever his reason for having teams and a wagon, and whatever his reason for being here, it's our good fortune."

"I'm wonderin' why he's takin' a wagon to California through such god-awful country as this," Dallas said. "Hell, he could have gone north to Cheyenne and rode the old Union Pacific the rest of the way."

"Let's get his wagon loaded next," said Collins. "Then we'll begin loading dynamite and ammunition."

The loading went smoothly, as Collins allowed the teamsters to pack the goods so that the loads wouldn't shift on the inclines and down slopes. When all the wagons were loaded, Collins drove Durham's wagon with the others to the lot across from the wagon yard.

"This is next to our last chance at town-cooked grub for maybe a year," Faro said. "Some of us will have to stay with the wagons while the others eat."

"The four of you go ahead," said Collins. "When you return, then I'll eat."

Faro and his three companions sought out a café and enjoyed a meal with plenty of hot coffee. It was just getting dark when they returned to the wagons, and found Durham there.

"I decided to bunk with the rest of you," the gambler said.

"There's grain for your mules in your wagon," said Faro. "Go easy on it, as long as there's decent graze."

Durham said nothing. His mind was awash with questions, the most bothersome one being how he was supposed to learn the purpose of this journey. If Slade and his outlaws ambushed the teamsters and seized the wagons, the most they could expect would be a few hundred dollars' worth of supplies. Of course, the mules and wagons would add to the spoils, but Durham suspected that Slade had in mind something far more profitable. So far, Durham had been told nothing but the possible destination. For all he knew, this Collins was a Mormon, freighting supplies in for the winter, but there was something that didn't quite fit. When Durham had left Tennessee in 1855, St. Louis newspapers had been full of tales of difficulties with Mormons along the Oregon Trail. They were an independent, self-sufficient clan, inclined to have their own teams and wagons. Turning his mind back to Faro Duval and his teamster partners, it didn't seem likely they would have taken on loads of one-way freight through five hundred miles of desolate, mountainous terrain. Not unless there was more at stake than just teamster wages.

"By God," said Durham, under his breath, "Slade may just be right. There's plenty I haven't been told, and much more than meets the eye."

Faro and his companions were up before dawn.

"Our last chance for town-cooked grub, gents," Faro said, "but we can't all go at the same time. Somebody must stay with the wagons."

"I'm not hungry," said Durham, remembering that the McCutcheon sisters were somewhere in town. "I'll stay with the wagons."

"So will I," Levi Collins said. "I've some last-minute business, and I'll attend to that when I go eat."

Collins sat down, his back to a wagon wheel, and lighted his pipe. Durham took up a similar position at the next wagon, his eyes on Collins.

"I noticed a considerable supply of dynamite in my wagon," Durham said.

"A man's always needin' dynamite in mountain country," said Collins. "Keep tight rein on the teams, and don't take your wagon over no sudden drop-offs."

"You got supplies enough to last a year," Durham said.

"Yep," said Collins. "This territory to the west is hell when the sun's shinin'. When the snow flies, that ain't no time to go lookin' for grub."

"As unsettled as the country seems, I suppose there are Indians," Durham said.

"Yep," said Collins. "Utes. Hostile as hell. They'll be sendin' a welcomin' committee before we're across the San Juans. You had any experience, Indian fightin'?"

"Some," Durham replied. "I was riding from Mobeetie, Texas, to Fort Worth. A band of Comanches attacked us in Indian Territory."

"You wasn't alone, then," said Collins.

"No," Durham said. "I was with a company of soldiers."

"No soldiers out here," said Collins. "Likely not a white man between here and California, except maybe them Mormons, in northern Utah."

"I thought you might be one of them," Durham said, growing bolder.

"No," said Collins. "My daddy was a Presbyterian, and in more civilized society, then I reckon I'd be one, too."

"You're fortunate, finding teamsters willing to haul your goods," Durham said. "Most of them have freighted in goods from back east, and are looking for loads that'll take 'em home."

"Yes," said Collins. "I have been fortunate. There are some good men on the frontier. But there are others who'll take your pay, eat your grub, and then betray you at the drop of a hat. I've experienced both kinds."

Durham looked away, for he didn't like the way the other man's eyes bored into his own. Nothing more was said until the four teamsters returned.

"Have the wagons ready to roll in half an hour," Collins said.

Durham set about harnessing his teams, aware that, compared to the others, he was slow and clumsy. Before Collins returned, a horseman approached. It was Slade, and he appeared not to have the slightest interest in the wagons. It was Slade's way of reminding Durham he had made a commitment to the outlaws, and Durham swallowed hard. Once he took the trail with these teamsters, he became a Judas, bound to betray them without even a promise of the traditional silver. But if Faro Duval and his partners ever discovered his underlying purpose in traveling with them, he was more than a little certain they would kill him without a qualm. Yet if he failed to deliver the information Slade was demanding, he would be just as readily shot dead by the outlaws. It seemed his only other option was to remain in Santa Fe, or strike out on his own, neither of which was possible. His wagon was loaded with goods that didn't belong to him, and if he ran like a scared coyote, he'd have only his horse and saddle, and a couple of changes of clothes. He dared not remain in Santa Fe, for he had no money for a stake at the gambling tables, and a pair of furious women were looking for him. Thanks to his involvement with the McCutcheon

sisters, he'd been forced to leave Amarillo without ply-
ing his trade at the poker tables. He hadn't gone hungry only because Slade and his gang had used some of
their ill-gotten gains to buy grub. Grimly, Durham finished harnessing his teams. Silently he cursed Slade
and his outlaws, the McCutcheon sisters, and finally,
himself.

"You got more faith in that tinhorn cardsharp than I
have," said Hindes, one of the Slade outlaws. "Thanks
to him and his wagon, we lost that damned sheriff's
posse. Right then, we should of rid ourselves of
Durham. Then we'd own the teams and wagon, and we
wouldn't be dependin' on a varmint that's likely to
double-cross us, first chance he gits."

"Hindes," Slade said, "don't waste your time
thinkin', 'cause you ain't equipped for it. If you hadn't
shot that bank teller, we might have escaped clean.
Now, damn it, his family is offerin' a thousand dollars'
reward, and the bank's matchin' it. Thanks to the tele-
graph, there's already wanted posters on us here, and
they're likely everywhere else, too."

"So what if these wagon loads of supplies ain't
nothin' more than settlers diggin' in for the winter?"
Withers said. "We'll be ridin' all over hell for nothin'."

"Yeah," said Peeler. "What do you aim to do with
five wagon loads of grub, if that's all there is?"

Kritzer laughed. "We could hole up in the mountains
until the law gives up on us."

"I've been givin' some sensible thought to this
whole thing," Slade growled, "which is a hell of a lot
more than the rest of you can claim. With prices on our

heads and every jackleg lawman on the frontier likely lookin' for us, we can run but we can't hide. There's a chance we might escape to California, and that's the direction these wagons are goin'. If Durham lets us down, or if they ain't a damn thing but five wagon loads of grub to be had for our trouble, we'll be halfway to California. What we got to lose?"

"I reckon that makes sense," said Hindes, "but I still don't like this Durham. I say it's foolishness, expecting him to work with us. Hell, he'll sell us out."

"Oh, I don't think so," Slade said. "What do you reckon them teamsters would do to our friend Durham if he spilled his guts and told 'em he's one of us?"

Withers, Peeler, and Kritzer laughed, and there was little Hindes could do, except join in.

Mamie and Odessa McCutcheon had found a lodging house near the stable where they had left their horses. The hostler had only stood there with his mouth open, for while the pair were unmistakably well-endowed females, they were dressed as men. Each of them had a revolver sagging from a tied-down holster, and before leaving their saddles, each drew a Winchester from a saddle boot. Leaving the Winchesters in their room, they went to a café to eat. They ignored the stares of men, settling down at a table.

"You'd reckon this bunch of peckerwoods never seen a pair of females before," said Mamie, "way they've aimed their eyeballs at us."

"Leastwise, not a pair like us," Odessa replied. "Wait'll tomorrow, when we invade the saloons."

"I'm wondering if a no-account gambler's worth it,"

said Mamie. "What spooked him, anyhow? I didn't say nothin' about him puttin' a ring on my finger. Did you?"

Odessa laughed. "No, but I kind of . . . implied . . . that you and me, it's always been share and share alike. What more could a man want, for God's sake?"

"That's likely what spooked him, then," said Mamie. "He wasn't man enough to keep up with either of us, and when you suggested we share the varmint, it purely scared hell out of him. There wasn't enough of him to go around, and he figured it out. Like Ma used to say, the worst thing you can do is put a man's pride to the test."

"Well, it was you that come up with the idea of the three of us travelin' to California in a damn wagon," Odessa replied, "and you that give him the thousand dollars."

"I said nothing about a wagon or teams of mules," said Mamie heatedly. "I said get a nice buckboard and a team of horses."

Odessa laughed. "Among all his other faults, Durham don't know a buckboard from a wagon, or a horse from a mule."

"He owes us a thousand dollars," Mamie said, "and that's worth trackin' him down. We had nothin' keepin' us in Amarillo, with all the family gone except for us. We won't be no worse off in California. Or even here."

The waiter had arrived, and was waiting patiently, regarding them in awe. Both women had long hair, black as a crow's wing, and flat-crowned Stetsons were secured by leather thongs under the chin. The sleeves of their flannel shirts were rolled up to the elbows, and their arms, hands, faces, and necks were burned as brown as an old saddle. When Odessa suddenly spoke to him, the waiter jumped.

"Youngster, bring us a pair of steaks medium-rare, some spuds, onions, some kind of pie, and plenty of coffee to wash it all down."

"Yes, ma'am," said the startled waiter, hustling away.

Men who had witnessed the arrival of Mamie and Odessa, and the intimidation of the waiter, grinned at one another, but nobody laughed.

Santa Fe, New Mexico. August 3, 1870.

Levi Collins mounted his horse and led out. Faro Duval was on the box of the first wagon, while Durham's wagon was fifth. He ground his teeth in silent anger. While nobody had said anything, it was obvious his dubious abilities as a teamster were in question, and they weren't going to chance his slowing down the caravan. He dared not fall behind, once they were in Ute country. Levi Collins dropped back, riding alongside Faro's wagon, so they could talk.

"We'll be travelin' northwest," Collins said, "followin' the Rio Chama for the first hundred miles."

"Plentiful water, then," said Faro. "Is it like that all the way?"

"Pretty much," Collins replied. "There's rivers aplenty. We'll be crossin' the Dolores, the San Juan, and the Green. There's numerous creeks and springs, as well. I reckon that's one of the few good things that can be said for southern Utah. There's plenty of water."

"Since you've been this way before," said Faro, "you must have some idea as to when we can expect trouble from the Utes."

"Not really," Collins replied. "They seem to favor the mountain passes of the San Juans, but when the trade route between Santa Fe and Los Angeles dried up, the pickings kind of played out. Some of the more aggressive bands have taken captives here along the Rio Chama, near Santa Fe."

"Captives?"

"Yes. In the old days, before the Spanish gave up California, captives were often sold to captains of sailing ships," said Collins. "Bandits and renegades from California bought the captives from the Utes, bartering horses and mules."

"California's been part of the United States for more than twenty years," Faro said. "Are they *still* that uncivilized?"

Collins laughed. "I've never been to California, but I suspect there is much of it that hasn't changed since the days of Spanish domination. I know from experience, however, that the Utes are hostile as ever. We've had to keep at least one man on watch both day and night, and they still caught us unawares a time or two."

"Then your partners won't have accomplished much, while you've been gone."

"No," Collins admitted. "In fact, we considered all of us going to Santa Fe, but these Utes know of the mine. While they couldn't or wouldn't work it, they might well have led claim jumpers to it. For a price, of course."

"They sound like a downright troublesome bunch," said Faro.

"They are," Collins said. "They were bad enough, on their own, but they've absorbed the hellish ways of the no-account renegade whites they've dealt with over the years."

After two hours on the trail, Faro halted the caravan to rest the mules, and found, not to his surprise, that Durham's wagon had fallen behind. He was waiting when Durham finally reined up his sweating teams.

"We'll be traveling through Ute country, Durham," said Faro. "Lagging behind the rest of the wagons could cost you your scalp."

Durham laughed. "Your concern for my scalp is touching, Duval."

"Then I'll just lay the cards on the table," Faro said coldly. "I don't care a damn for your scalp, but your wagon's carryin' a fifth of our goods. For that reason, I don't aim to risk havin' Utes burn the wagon and rustle the mules."

"It's still my wagon and my mules," Durham snarled, "and damn it, I won't stand for you talking down to me."

"Now, you listen to me, slick," said Faro, his cold blue eyes boring into Durham's. "As long as you hold up your end of the deal, I'll respect your position as owner of these mules and the wagon. That means trailing with the rest of the wagons. Continue falling behind, endangering the wagon, the teams, and the freight, and you're comin' off that wagon box, permanent."

"By God," Durham bawled, "you have no such authority."

"On the frontier," said Faro, "authority belongs to the man who can back it up. Not a man in this outfit would fault me if I shot you dead and left your carcass for the coyotes and cougars. But I wouldn't want you thinkin' I'm that uncivilized. If you can't or won't keep that wagon up with the others, I'll pull you off that box and have Levi Collins take the reins."

"The hell you will," shouted Durham. "You agreed I could handle my own wagon."

"The hell I won't," said Faro, "and just so I don't break my word, you won't own the wagon or the teams. I'll have Collins pay you a fair price. Then you can mount your horse and go anywhere you damn please, at a slow walk."

Faro turned and walked away. Durham's hand rested on the butt of the Colt he kept beneath his coat, but the rest of the teamsters were watching him. Slowly he relaxed, and when Faro gave the order for the wagons to move out, Durham was careful not to allow his wagon to fall behind.

Mamie and Odessa McCutcheon created a sensation when they began invading saloons. The barkeeps were speechless, while some men stared and others laughed. After visiting three saloons, Mamie and Odessa had learned nothing. The fourth, however, was the one in which Durham had knocked two men unconscious. When Mamie and Odessa entered, their attention was drawn to a painting mounted behind the bar. It was of a reclining, naked female, leaving nothing to the imagination. The McCutcheons eyed it with interest, and it was Odessa who spoke.

"Too much belly on her."

There were half a dozen men in the place, and one of them laughed. But the barkeep seemed suddenly struck dumb.

"You behind the bar," said Mamie. "We're lookin' for a gamblin' man dressed all in black, like a turkey buzzard. Goes by the name of Durham. He been in here?"

"Y . . . yes, ma'am," the barkeep stammered. "Started some trouble, and the sheriff told him to git out of town."

"When was this?" Mamie demanded.

"Two days ago," said the barkeep. "He was leavin' with some teamsters."

Without another word, the McCutcheons left the saloon and stood on the boardwalk.

"He's likely gone by now," said Odessa.

"No matter," Mamie said. "We'll ask around town. Somebody will know if there's been wagons takin' the trail. We'll just saddle up, and when the time and place is right, give old Hal one hell of a surprise."

Chapter 2

Faro kept the wagons moving until near sundown, for the Rio Chama provided plenty of water. After unharnessing his teams, Durham did nothing, and nobody seemed to expect anything of him. Levi Collins soon had a supper fire going, and when the teamsters had unhitched their teams, they set about preparing supper.

"There'll be rain before morning," Collins predicted.

"That won't slow us none," said Shanghai, "unless there's some sloughs ahead. Long as there's high ground, we can move on."

"Yeah," Tarno said, "unless that high ground gets too high. On steep slopes, after a good rain, that mud can get slick as goose grease. Mules' hooves and wagon wheels slip and slide."

"Once we reach higher elevations," said Collins, "there'll be mostly rock. Maybe even rock slides. You'll have to take it slow, maybe detourin' around ruts and drop-offs that could bust a wheel or axle."

"That's why there's a pick and shovel in each of our wagons," Faro said. "Sometimes in rough country, you can lose a day avoiding a particularly bad stretch.

Sometimes, with all of us pitchin' in, we can make it passable in a couple of hours."

"Pick and shovel work is one thing I don't like about the teamstering business," said Dallas. "I told my daddy when I left the farm, I wasn't ever layin' my blistered hands on another pick or shovel."

Faro laughed. "I recollect sayin' somethin' like that, myself. Ain't it funny how life plays tricks on a man, so he ends up eatin' more crow than bacon and beans?"

"I hope," Durham said, speaking for the first time, "that where we're goin', and our purpose for goin' there is worth pickin' and shovelin' our way through these mountains."

"We think so," said Collins, choosing his words carefully. "It's you that's bound for California. I reckon you'll have to decide whether pickin' and shovelin' another seven hundred miles by yourself is worth your reason for going."

It was the perfect answer, but rather than allow the exchange to continue, Faro Duval quickly changed the subject.

"Starting tonight, we'll take turns standing watch. There's six of us, and I'd suggest we have only two watches. Three of us can take it until midnight, and the remaining three can take it until dawn. I'll take either watch, but I prefer the second."

"So do I," said Collins.

"I want the second watch," Durham said.

"That settles it, then," said Faro, "unless Shanghai, Tarno, or Dallas objects."

There were no objections, and at dusk, Faro, Collins, and Durham each spread their blankets be-

neath one of the wagons. They would have barely six
hours to sleep. Prior to dousing the supper fire, Shanghai, Dallas, and Tarno refilled their tin cups from the
big black coffeepot. The wind being from the west,
they hunkered downwind from camp, so that their conversation might not be overheard.

"By God," said Tarno, "that Durham's got somethin' up his sleeve besides some extra cards. He wants
to know almighty bad where we're headed, and why."

"Yeah," Dallas agreed, "but he ain't got the guts to
come right out and ask."

"He's no fool," said Shanghai. "He can't get too
nosy without tippin' his hand. Hell, we ain't fools, neither, and he can't let us know he's all that interested."

"But we *do* know," Dallas said, "and it's almighty
important that we learn why he's so interested. Sometimes it's the way of thieves to throw in with you, eat
your grub, and all the while, be takin' your measure.
Then, when the time's right, the rest of 'em show up,
their guns blazing."

"It purely looks like we're into that kind of situation," said Shanghai, "but it makes me wonder how
they worked it out so slick. The same day we come up
one wagon shy, this mouthy cardsharp shows up with
mules and a wagon. I don't believe for a minute he
aims to go on to California. That's to give him his excuse for trailing with us."

Durham had purposely spread his blankets beneath
the farthest wagon, so that his movements wouldn't
rouse Faro Duval or Levi Collins. Somehow he had to
learn why these wagon loads of goods were being
taken into mountains infested with hostile Utes, and

since Levi Collins was bankrolling the whole thing, Collins should have some answers. Finally, when he could hear Faro and Collins snoring, Durham rolled back his blankets and got to his knees. From beneath his coat he drew a .32-caliber Colt pocket pistol and began crawling slowly toward the wagon where Levi Collins slept. Clouds were being swept in from the west, but there was sufficient starlight for Durham to reach the sleeping Collins. Coming in behind the wagon, he could see Collins's head resting on his saddle. Raising his Colt, Durham slammed its muzzle into the back of the sleeping man's head. Collins only grunted once, and Durham feared he hadn't struck hard enough, but there was no movement. He might have only two or three minutes, at best, and Durham had to settle for quickly going through Levi Collins's coat. The first thing his seeking hands found was the canvas sack in which Collins carried the ore samples. Durham, smart enough to realize it was some kind of ore, seized a hunk of it, just as Collins groaned. He started to club Collins again, but the teamsters on watch were downwind, and had heard Collins. Clouds had swallowed up the starlight, and it was all that saved Durham. He was barely in his blankets, breathing hard, when Collins groaned louder. Faro was nearest, and the first to respond.

"Collins, what's wrong?"

"We heard him," said Dallas, as he and his companions came on the run.

"Something . . . somebody . . . knocked me in the head," Collins replied.

"Durham," Faro demanded, "where are you?"

"In my blankets," said Durham, trying to sound sleepy. "Why?"

"Somebody just slugged Collins," Faro said.

"And you're thinking it might have been me," said Durham.

"The possibility had crossed my mind," Faro said grimly.

"Maybe he whacked his head on a wagon wheel," said Durham. "I just now hit my own, when I sat up."

"No," Collins said, speaking for himself, "somebody deliberately slugged me."

"Might have been a thief," said Tarno. "See if you're missing anything."

Collins crawled out from beneath the wagon, and taking hold of a rear wheel, managed to stand. He rummaged through all his pockets.

"Nothing is missing," Collins said.

"We heard you groan," said Shanghai. "Maybe that scared him away."

"Question is," Faro said, "if it was an intended robbery, how did the thief know to go after Collins? Why not Durham or me?"

"Hell, we're not more than twenty miles from town," said Durham. "You think Collins bought five wagon loads of goods without somebody making note of it? We were followed, and Collins was figured to be the one with the money."

"That's not bad reasoning," Collins said. "From now on, I'll sleep with my pistol in my hand."

"I think we'll have to do a better job securing the camp," said Faro. "If you were a target once, you could be again. Shanghai, Tarno, Dallas, it's up to you to see that there are no more attempts like tonight."

"Well, hell," Dallas said, "we wasn't looking for trouble, except from the Utes, and it is just a few miles back to Santa Fe."

"Now you know different," said Faro. "From here on, take nothing for granted. This should be proof enough that we have more to concern us than just the Utes. The deadliest and most effective defense is to secure your own camp, and then shoot anything moving in the dark. Collins—you and Durham—once you take to your blankets, are to remain there until time to begin your watch. *Comprende*?"

"Yes," Collins said, "although that seems a little extreme."

"Damn right it does," said Durham. "You expect a man to drink a pot of coffee and then hold it for six hours?"

"I don't expect a man with brains God gave a prairie dog to *drink* a pot of coffee, *knowin'* he's got to hold it for six hours," Faro said. "The rule stands."

"You gents better get what sleep you can," said Tarno. "Second watch is less than two hours away."

"Yeah," Shanghai said, "we can stand here and jaw the rest of the night, and it won't change a thing. Come first light, we can look for tracks."

But the rain Collins had predicted arrived before dawn. Faro had equipped each of the wagons with a canvas shelter that could be erected behind the wagon, providing a dry area for a cook fire and the preparation of a meal. By crowding it a little, the men were able to get out of the rain to eat their breakfast and drink their coffee.

"I'm not accustomed to this convenience on the trail," said Collins, "but I appreciate it. You know, a man can ride all day with rain blowin' in his face and pourin' off the brim of his hat down the collar of his shirt, but when it's grub time, he don't want that rain in his grub or in his coffee. I've never understood that."

Faro laughed. "A small victory for mankind. Rain could drive a man crazy, if there wasn't some escape from it. Even if it's only while he's eatin' his grub and drinkin' his coffee."

They took the trail, with a chill wind from the west whipping rain into their faces and causing the mules to balk. The rain ceased after two hours, but ominous gray clouds hung low, blocking the sun. In their wet clothing, the wind seemed unseasonably cold. Not until late afternoon did the skies clear, allowing a timid sun to emerge. Levi Collins had ridden on ahead, and when he returned, he loped his horse alongside Faro's wagon.

"Up yonder, maybe three miles," Collins said, "there's a broken ridge runnin' parallel to the Rio Chama. It'll shelter us from the wind. Might be a good place to hole up for the night and dry out."

"*Bueno,*" said Faro. "Ride back and tell the others."

The ridge provided welcome relief from the chill wind, and though it was still early, the teamsters unharnessed their teams. In the "possum bellies"— cowhides slung beneath each wagon—there was dry wood, and soon there was a roaring fire going. Men gathered around, seeking to dry their sodden clothing before dark. It was as good a time as any for Faro to talk to them.

"Tonight—and every night from now on—the three of us who are sleeping will stay close to one another. No sleeping under different wagons. That attack on Collins last night might have been avoided, if Durham and me had been closer. From now on, we will be."

"From what I've heard," Durham said, "that won't stop Indians."

"Indian trouble will come soon enough," said Faro, "but our visitor last night wasn't an Indian. Instead of slugging Collins unconscious, an Indian would have slit his throat. We have white men—probably outlaws—stalking us."

"That makes no sense," Durham scoffed, "unless there's something far more valuable in these wagons than the supplies you loaded in Santa Fe."

"What you've said makes even less sense," said Dallas. "How does anybody learn what might be in the wagons by slugging Collins?"

"Well," Durham said, "there's bills of lading, I suppose."

"Yes," said Collins, "and they're in my coat pocket, where they were last night. But I can assure you, there are no secrets to be found within them. You—or anyone else—had an opportunity to watch the wagons being loaded."

Durham said no more, for he was treading on dangerous ground. During the day, he had studied the piece of ore he had taken from Collins, and even to his inexperienced eye, the threads of gold set his heart to pounding. Now that he knew the secret purpose of the expedition, his devious mind began considering ways of dealing himself in, while eliminating Slade and his outlaw companions. Of necessity, Slade must be convinced these wagon loads of goods were to sustain some distant colony through the winter, and nothing more. The sooner Slade could be contacted and convinced of the futility of further pursuit, the more likely that he and his men would ride back to Santa Fe in search of other pickings. With that thought in mind, Durham made his first move right after supper.

"Durham," said Faro, "where are you goin'?"

"Some private business," Durham said, "before your shoot-anything-that-moves order kicks in at dark."

"Risky, goin' out alone," said Faro.

"Your concern is touching," Durham said, "but if I needed one of you to go along and hold my hand, I'd have asked."

"Ask and be-damned," said Tarno Spangler. "None of us is that kind."

The rest of them laughed, and Durham went on, satisfied that they wouldn't follow. Slade had come much closer to camp than Durham had expected, and when suddenly the outlaw appeared, Durham was startled.

"Well," Slade demanded, "what have you learned?"

"Nothing of any interest to you," said Durham, hoping he was lying convincingly. "All I've learned is that these supplies are for the winter, and that they're going to settlers in southern Utah. I've seen what's in the wagons, and there's nothing but some ammunition and grub."

"You lie," Slade snarled. "I had Withers watchin' through a glass, and he seen cases of dynamite bein' loaded. Enough dynamite to blow Utah into the Pacific Ocean."

"Well, hell," said Durham, "I wasn't there for the actual loading of the wagons. All I could do was look in through the puckers, and I couldn't afford to seem too interested."

"You'd better *get* more interested, and you'd better do it quick," Slade said. "There's more to this than supplies bein' hauled in for the winter. If you don't come up with some information we can use, we'll lay an ambush, gun everybody down, and figure it all out for ourselves."

"And you'll learn nothing," said Durham desperately. "If there's anything to be learned it'll have to come from them, but not if they're dead."

"I'm not the patient kind," Slade said, "especially when I think I'm bein' strung along. I don't make threats, either, so you can take what I said about that ambush as gospel. To the last man, Durham. By God, to the last man."

Slade turned and walked away, the finality of his words ringing in Durham's ears. He had been told, in no uncertain terms, that if an ambush became necessary, he would die with the others. Durham fought down the tremors of fear that crept up his spine, gritting his teeth and clenching his fists. He knew, as surely as if the outlaw had spoken the words aloud, that if he betrayed the valiant men with the wagons, he would never share any of the spoils. His reward would be a lead slug, probably in the back. It strengthened his resolve, and as he made his way back to the wagons, his devious mind dealt him an inside straight. He would double-cross Slade, and his double-cross would be the granddaddy of them all.

Sante Fe, New Mexico. August 4, 1870.

Mamie and Odessa McCutcheon had no difficulty discovering which way the wagons had gone. At the mercantile, they loaded their saddlebags with supplies. They then mounted their horses and rode northwest, along the Rio Chama.

"Five wagons," Odessa said. "We're on the right trail."

"That storekeeper was right helpful," said Mamie. "He remembered them teamsters was needin' a fifth wagon. Just in time, with no mules or wagons for sale, they come up with one."

"It's all the better for us," Odessa said. "If Durham's throwed in with experienced teamsters, maybe the Indians won't burn our wagon and eat our mules."

"What we don't know," said Mamie, "is where these wagons are going. I can't imagine being stuck somewhere between here and California, in Indian country, with only Durham. Can you?"

Odessa sighed. "It *does* strain the imagination. I'm thinking, if these teamsters are fair men, they'll allow us to return with them to Santa Fe, bringing our mules and wagon. For that matter, perhaps we can sell the teams and wagon to them, for the thousand dollars we gave Durham."

"Oh, God," Mamie said, "to recover our mules and wagon, I hope we don't have to tell them *everything.*"

"That he compromised our honor, and that if he hadn't run out on us, we'd have willingly gone with him, allowing him to compromise it some more?"

"Especially *that,*" said Mamie. "Oh, what is that damnable fault in females that leads them to make fools of themselves over no-account men?"

"It goes with the territory," Odessa said. "What *else* is a woman goin' to make a fool of herself over?"

They were only a few miles from town, when Odessa reined up.

"What is it?" Mamie asked.

"Tracks," said Odessa. "Horse tracks."

"Durham had a saddle horse," Mamie said, "and it's likely tied behind the wagon. The other teamsters may have horses too."

"No matter," said Odessa. "There's tracks of four horses that are on top of all the other horse, mule, and wagon tracks. Four riders are followin' the freight wagons."

"Not necessarily," Mamie replied. "Since Durham took everything we had to give, you have become unnaturally suspicious."

"Look at this ground," said Odessa. "There are no permanent ruts, so this has never been a wagon road. There are no tracks except those made by the five wagons, their mule teams, the led horses, and the horses of the four riders following. Except for what we can see right now, there might not have been anybody through here for a hundred years."

"So?" Mamie said. "That proves exactly what?"

"That these four horsemen didn't just *happen* this way," said Odessa. "They're following the freight wagons."

"Oh, damn it," Mamie said, "you're impossible. I don't wish to discuss it further."

"Have it your way," said Odessa, "but I think those teamsters are about to encounter some unexpected trouble, and I won't be surprised if Hal Durham is neck-deep in it. Why else has he thrown in with them?"

"Oh, God, I don't know," Mamie said, exasperated, "but I hope he has. Perhaps one of them will shoot him."

"I laid it on the line to Durham," Slade told his outlaw companions. "If he don't soon come up with some information we can use, we'll ambush the lot of them, and figure it all out for ourselves."

"I think you just played hell," said Hindes. "You're givin' Durham all the reasons he needs to double-cross us. Now he's likely to throw in with them teamsters, to save his own hide."

"I got to agree with Hindes," Withers said. "They ain't been on the trail long enough for Durham to learn much."

"I'm agreein' with Hindes and Withers," said Peeler. "Damn it, this was all your idea, plantin' Durham in their camp. Now that he's there, give him time to play out his hand. If he double-crosses us, we can shoot him when we bushwhack the others."

"I'll buy that," Kritzer said.

"So all of you are lined up against me," said Slade

bitterly. "By God, we should have split up after Hindes shot that bank teller in Tucumcari."

"We ain't wantin' to split up," Withers said soothingly. "Hell, can't we disagree with you, without you wantin' to ride off and quit?"

"Yeah," said Kritzer, "this is no time to fold. Usin' Durham may not be a bad idea, but you're goin' at it wrong."

"Thanks," Slade said. "Why don't *you* tell me how I should go at it?"

"I will," said Kritzer defiantly. "After we hit that bank in Tucumcari, Durham saved our hides. You made him one of us, you been usin' him ever since, but you ain't promised him a damn thing."

Hindes laughed. "Slade's promised to shoot him if he don't come through for us."

"My point, exactly," Kritzer said. "If a man's takin' a risk, he's got a right to expect some reward."

"Yeah," said Withers, "and bein' shot ain't exactly a reward."

"I reckon I been overlookin' that," Slade said. "I'll loosen the reins a mite, and maybe convince Durham he's one of us. We got just a little over two thousand dollars from that bank job in Tucumcari. Each of us would of had five hundred, but bein' fair, we got to cut Durham in. Five men thins the pot down to four hundred for each of us. Next time I meet Durham, I'll see that he gets his share."

"What the hell?" Hindes bawled.

"That wasn't exactly what we had in mind," said Peeler.

Withers and Kritzer said nothing. Slade laughed.

*   *   *

When Durham returned from his meeting with Slade, he looked grim. While nobody said anything, Shanghai, Tarno, and Dallas eyed the gambler suspiciously.

"Remember," said Faro, "when you sleep, spread your blankets near one another. We don't know how soon the Utes will discover us, and I reckon they'd like nothing better than finding us sleeping under separate wagons."

Faro had seen to it that the wagons were in the open, away from underbrush or trees that might leave them partially or fully in shadow. The three men on watch were moving constantly, coming together only occasionally for brief conversations. It was near midnight when Faro heard movement.

"Durham!"

"Damn it," said the gambler, "I have a cramp in my leg. I need to stand."

"Not near as bothersome as a bullet through the head," Faro replied. "Stay put."

"It's time for us to begin the second watch," said Collins. "We might as well get up."

"Please, Mr. Duval," Durham said, "since I'm on second watch, is it all right if I get up, too?"

"Careful, Faro," said Dallas. "Next thing, he'll be wantin' you to go to the bushes with him, and hold his hand."

Shanghai and Tarno laughed.

"That's enough," Faro said angrily. "The three of you get to your bedrolls. Durham, you get the hell out of yours."

"Yes, Daddy," said Durham meekly.

Faro silently cursed Durham for his sarcasm, and his three companions for using it as a source of cowboy humor. He barely spoke to Collins or Durham throughout the second watch, as he wrestled with a troublesome question. What *was* Hal Durham's game?

Fortunately for Slade and his companions, they made their camp well away from the river, in the surrounding brush. Being in no hurry, lest they catch up to the wagons, they slept well past dawn. So it was that when they heard approaching horses, they hadn't yet started their breakfast fire. They watched from cover as Mamie and Odessa McCutcheon rode past, obviously following the wagons. Suddenly, Odessa reined up. When she spoke, they heard her clearly.

"Them four varmints that was followin' the wagons has left us."

"Like I told you," Mamie said, "they likely wasn't followin' the wagons at all. They just turned off somewhere and went their way."

"Well, I think they were," said Odessa, "and I'm of a mind to double back and see how far it was they left the trail."

"Oh, come on," Mamie said. "Don't go looking for trouble. God knows, there's always enough, without scratching and digging for more."

They rode on as Slade and his companions looked at one another in wonder.

"Who in hell are *they?*" Kritzer wondered.

"That pair of females looks tough enough to go huntin' cougars with a switch," said Withers.

"Yeah," Peeler said, "and they been trackin' us. At least, one of 'em has."

"By God," said Hindes, "I never seen a female whose tongue wasn't thonged down in the middle and loose at both ends. When they catch up to them wagons, you think that nosy old pelican won't tell them teamsters they're bein' trailed?"

"Maybe not," Slade said. "You heard her. She didn't notice where we rode off, and up ahead they won't find our tracks."

"I purely don't like bein' bogged down in somethin' I don't understand," said Kritzer. "Where does these two fit in, and why are they followin' them wagons?"

"God," Withers said, "they was carryin' tied-down pistols, with rifles in their saddle boots. I never seen a woman carry that much artillery."

"I'd bet my horse and saddle they can use it, too," said Peeler.

"We'll go on," Slade said, "and I reckon we'll find out what business they got with them wagons."

"Don't none of you forget," said Hindes. "There's always the Utes."

Chapter 3

The night had passed uneventfully, and following a hurried breakfast, the wagons took the trail. The terrain had grown progressively rougher, and teams crept along slowly as teamsters sought to avoid drop-offs and large stones that might crack, allowing the full weight of the wagon to lurch against a single wheel. But before the caravan had been on the trail an hour, there came that sound they all dreaded: the sickening, shattering crunch of a ruined wagon wheel.

"Well, by God, that don't come as no surprise," said Tarno Spangler as he swung down from his wagon box.

Durham's wagon reared back in an unnatural position, for nothing remained of the left rear wheel except the hub with its shattered spokes. Durham still sat on the wagon box, the reins in his hand.

"Get down," Shanghai said in disgust. "We ain't jackin' the wagon up with you settin' on it."

Faro was looking at the huge stone over which the broken wheel had tried to cross. The stone had rolled, allowing the wheel to slide off and slam into the solid rock beneath it.

"Durham," said Faro, "this could have been avoided. There was room for that wheel to pass without even touching the stone that caused the break. Were you asleep?"

Durham had climbed down from the wagon box, and he faced Faro defiantly.

"Hell, I can't see every rut and rock in the trail," he snarled.

Faro's patience had run out. He brought his right all the way up from his boot tops, and his fist slammed against Durham's chin. The gambler's feet left the ground and he hit the rocky ground on his back. He sat up, blood dripping from the corners of his mouth.

"When you take the reins," Faro said grimly, "it's your responsibility as a teamster to see every rut and rock in the trail. Now get up. You have work to do."

Tarno and Dallas removed the spare wheel and wagon jack from Durham's wagon.

"Remarkable insight, loading the spare wheel and the jack behind the freight," Collins observed.

"It's the first and most important thing a teamster learns," said Faro. "To do otherwise would be like slidin' your Winchester into the saddle boot empty, and lockin' all your shells away in a trunk."

To Durham fell the dubious honor of jacking up the sagging rear of the wagon. With a huge hub wrench created for that purpose, Faro broke loose the hub of the shattered wheel and removed it. Within an hour, the wagon was again ready for the trail. Durham had already mounted his wagon box when the two riders appeared. Every man had paused, his hand near the butt of his revolver, but they all relaxed when it became obvious their visitors were women. Durham dropped the reins and was about to leap from the box when Odessa McCutcheon spoke.

"Mr. Durham, you just stay right where you are, so's we can keep an eye on you. Slide down off that box, and I'll part your hair with a slug."

"Ma'am," said Faro, "since you obviously have an interest in Durham, I reckon you'd better tell the rest of us who you are, and what you want."

"We're the McCutcheons, from Amarillo, Texas. Mr. Durham, here, took a thousand dollars from us. He was to buy a team of horses, a buckboard, and take us with him to California."

"He compromised our honor," said Mamie, "and then sneaked off without us."

Shanghai, Tarno, and Dallas had been watching Durham's face, and could control their mirth no longer. Slapping their thighs, they howled with laughter. Faro was distracted for a moment by the outrageous conduct of his companions, and that was almost enough. Hal Durham had drawn his Colt from beneath his coat when, with a suddenness that surprised them all, Odessa McCutcheon drew her Colt and fired. The slug slammed into Durham's right shoulder, and his weapon clattered to the wagon box.

"Damn you," Durham shouted, clutching his wounded shoulder.

"Get down," said Faro, "and take off your coat and shirt. I reckon we'll have to patch you up, since these ladies seem to have plans for you."

"While that's being done," Collins said, "I believe we should establish the ownership of this wagon and these mules. After all, there's a fifth of my goods in the wagon. Ladies, I am Levi Collins. These teamsters are Faro Duval, Shanghai Taylor, Tarno Spangler, and Dallas Weaver."

"I'm Odessa McCutcheon, and this is my sister, Mamie. We've told you all that we . . . all that's decent . . . to tell. Has this skunk took any money from you for the wagon and the mules?"

"No," said Collins. "He offered us the use of the wagon and mules for as far as we'll be going, in return for enough supplies to take him on to California."

"In Santa Fe, we were told the territory between here and California is very rough, and inhabited by hostile Indians," Mamie said. "Do you believe it's possible for a wagon to get through?"

"I understand it's twelve hundred miles," said Collins, "and we're only going the first five hundred. A good teamster, taking his time, can get that far. Beyond that, I can't say."

"Mamie and me kind of like the idea of goin' on to California," Odessa said. "Will you make us the same offer of supplies to California, for use of the wagon and teams as far as you aim to go?"

"Yes," said Collins, "and gladly. We were desperate for another wagon. Will you be taking Mr. Durham with you?"

"I wouldn't take them to a dogfight if they was guests of honor," Durham shouted.

"Durham," said Dallas, "you shut your mouth, or I'll leave your damn wound open and bleeding."

"Mr. Durham promised us a trip to California," Odessa said, "and I think it only fair that he honor that promise. God knows, he hasn't honored anything else."

"Yes," said Mamie, "he should be an experienced teamster by the time your freight is unloaded from the wagon. Then Mr. Durham can take it on to California, and us with it."

"After all you've been through," Collins said, "you'd trust him not to do you harm?"

"We don't trust him as far as we'd trust a sand rattler," said Odessa. "He can't do a thing to us he ain't done before, and the difference is, this time, he won't get any help from us. One bad move, and we'll leave the varmint hog-tied upside down over a slow fire."

Faro laughed. "I do believe the ladies can take care of themselves."

"The deal's off, Collins," Durham snarled. "I ain't takin' this damn team and wagon no farther. Especially not to California."

"You made a deal, Durham," said Faro, "and we're holding you to it. In return for your services, you'll be allowed enough supplies to get you to California. Whether or not you choose to go is entirely up to you."

"We'll pay our way for as long as we're with you," Mamie offered. "We can do all the cooking."

"Yes," said Odessa. "In Texas, we cooked for cow camps during branding."

"I can't speak for anybody but me," Dallas said, "but that's music to my ears."

"Yes," shouted Shanghai and Tarno, in a single voice.

"I won't say no to that," said Faro, "but this promises

to be a long, hard ride. Could be especially rough on you ladies."

"Then don't *think* of us as ladies," Odessa said. "We grew up in Texas, with cowboys and bull whackers. There ain't nothin' any of you can say or do that we ain't heard said or seen done a dozen times."

"There are hostile Ute Indians," said Collins.

"No matter," Odessa said. "Are they worse than hostile Comanches?"

"I doubt it," said Faro. "Collins, I think they're as well equipped for this trail as any of us. The two of you have rifles in your saddle boots. Can you hit what you're shootin' at?"

"Anything crawlin', walkin', runnin', or flyin'," Odessa said. "Need some proof?"

"I don't think so," said Faro. "Your word's good enough for me."

Dallas had bandaged Durham's wound, and was helping him into his shirt and coat. The gambler's ears perked up when Odessa spoke to Faro.

"We found somethin' that might interest you. For a good long ways, four horsemen was following you. Maybe half a dozen miles back, they veered off, and we didn't see their tracks again."

"We don't *know* they were following you," Mamie said. "Odessa *thinks* they were."

"I was through here a week ago, riding to Santa Fe," said Collins, "and there wasn't a sign of a track. This isn't the kind of country men travel without some definite purpose."

"Exactly what I was thinking," Faro added. "Collins, when we move out tomorrow, I'd like for you to take my wagon for a while. I'd better have a look at our back trail. All of you back to your wagons. We're moving out."

"I can't handle the teams with a hurt arm," said Durham.

"Then get off the box and get on your horse," Odessa said. "I'll take over the wagon and teams, but I refuse to ride the box with you."

The men watched with considerable amusement as Durham climbed down from the box and untied his horse from behind the wagon. Odessa climbed to the box, took the reins, and clucked to the teams.

"A remarkable woman," said Collins. "Mamie, are you as adept as Odessa?"

"Of course I am," Mamie said, "but don't tell her."

"The rest of you hang back here for a while," Slade said, after the McCutcheon sisters had ridden on. "Them females is bound to catch up to the wagons, and when they do, I aim to be close enough to see what happens. I'd like to know how they fit into all this."

Slade rode up to a higher elevation from which he could see the river without being seen. He then followed the ridge, but before he could see the wagons, he heard a shot. He kicked his horse into a fast gallop, and by the time he could see the wagons, Durham was removing his coat. Even from a distance, Slade could see the bloodstain on the shoulder of the gambler's white shirt.

"Damn him," Slade said under his breath. "Done some fool thing, got himself plugged, and likely learned nothin'."

While Slade couldn't hear the words, all the activity below was sufficient to hold his attention. He watched Dallas attend to Durham's wound and saw him again climb up to the wagon box. Finally, there was another exchange of words, and Durham was replaced on the wagon box by one of the newly arrived women. The wagons again took the trail, and on his horse, Durham followed the fifth wagon. Shaking his head, Slade rode back to join his impatient companions, uncertain as to what he should tell them.

The rest of the day passed uneventfully, and even with the time lost replacing a wheel on Durham's wagon, Faro estimated they had covered almost twenty miles. At first, he'd had his doubts about Odessa Mc-Cutcheon's ability to handle the teams, but Odessa had proven herself as adept as any man. Moreover, when they reined up at the end of the day, Odessa was the first to have her teams unharnessed. While she was so involved, Mamie got a supper fire started. Shanghai, Tarno, and Dallas happily pointed out the locations of the food, the two coffeepots, and other utensils. The lot of them watched in amazement as Mamie and Odessa prepared supper in record time.

"And to think," Dallas said, "if it wasn't for Durham, we'd still be doin' all our own cooking."

"Yeah," said Tarno, "life's a mixed blessing. The same rain that makes a man's crops grow turns into a flood and washes 'em all to hell and gone."

"Changin' the subject," Shanghai said, "I reckon it'll be easier on the ladies if they're both on the first watch."

"You ungrateful varmint," said Dallas, "why should they stand watch at all? Odessa's on the wagon box, likely from now on, and they're doin' all the cooking. You want they should tuck you in?"

"That would be nice," Shanghai said. "I reckon they done considerably more than that for Durham, the no-account bastard."

"No more such talk," said Faro, who had been listening. "You don't discuss a lady's reputation, no matter what you've heard or suspect."

"Nothin' bad intended," Shanghai replied. "I'd be some flattered if either of 'em would look at me twice."

"They're a mite old," said Tarno. "They must be near twenty-five."

"Hell," Dallas said, "ain't you heard? Good wine gets better with age."

The conversation ended when Mamie banged a tin cup against the bottom of a pan. Supper was ready.

"Mama mia," Shanghai said, as they dug in. "I can't believe this is the same grub we was eatin' before these ladies took to cookin' it."

"Me neither," said Dallas. "It was always particularly bad when it was your turn to cook."

"Well, you wasn't any great shakes, yourself," Shanghai growled.

"Shut up and eat," Odessa ordered.

They shut up and ate. Faro laughed.

"Ladies," said Faro, when supper was over, "we have two watches. The first one from dusk to midnight, and the second from midnight to dawn. The men on watch have orders to shoot anything that moves, so there will be no moving around at night. I realize it may be some . . . inconvenient, but we don't know when the Utes will discover us."

"I told you we growed up in Comanche country," said Odessa. "We fully understand the need for that rule, and after we've turned in, we won't be up wanderin' about. Just be sure you don't spread your blankets on the down slope from me. You might get soaked in the flood."

"I don't aim to sleep the whole night, with everybody else standing watch," Mamie said. "I'll stand the first watch. We can dig a fire pit, keep the fire burnt down to coals, and I can keep a pot of coffee hot."

"Well, if you can do that for the first watch," said Odessa, "I can as well or better for the second. You got any objection to that, Mr. Duval?"

"None," Faro said. "I welcome all the help I can get. First night out, some varmint got into camp and slugged Collins."

"White man," said Odessa, her eyes on Durham. "An Indian would of slit his throat."

"That's what we figure," Faro replied, "and those four sets of tracks you found seem proof enough."

"We've shot Comanches by the light of the moon," said Mamie. "White renegades ain't all that different."

With Mamie on the first watch, and Odessa on the second, they said little, kept coffee hot, and their guns ready. The night passed uneventfully.

"Makes you wonder," Dallas said next morning, "why some decent *hombres* ain't long since dropped a loop on them two. What in tarnation did they ever see in Durham?"

"Many a decent *hombre* rode off to war and never returned," Faro said. "How many of our *amigos* did we leave at Shiloh, Gettysburg, and Missionary Ridge?"

"Too many," said Shanghai, "and them that survived—like us—returned to a land on the ragged edge of starvation. Every day I'm alive, I thank God we had the sense to go to Independence and become freighters."

Mamie and Odessa had breakfast ready in record time. When they were preparing to move out, Odessa harnessed the mules to Durham's wagon, climbed to the box, and took the reins. Nobody questioned her, and Durham saddled his horse. Collins had tied his horse behind Faro's wagon and had mounted the box. Faro rode his horse alongside the moving wagon for some parting words with Collins.

"I should catch up to you in a couple of hours," Faro said. "I aim to ride back as far as I must to intercept those tracks and see where they lead."

Collins nodded, and Faro rode away, aware that Durham was taking particular notice of his going.

As a precaution—aware that the McCutcheon sisters were now part of the teamsters' outfit—Slade and his companions no longer followed the trail the wagons had taken.

"Damn it," Hindes complained, "we don't *know* that them females said anything about seein' our tracks. This is a fool idea, ridin' through the brush, with limbs swattin' us in the face, and thorns rakin' us over."

"We don't know that they *didn't* tell of seein' our tracks," said Slade. "This way, we can find out for sure. If them teamsters suspect anything, one of 'em will be ridin' along the back trail, lookin' for our tracks."

"If they *do* come lookin' for us, it proves one thing," Kritzer observed. "It tells us this is more than just a load of grub to get some settlers through the winter."

"Damn right," said Slade. "There's more at stake here than five wagon loads of grub, and Durham's done somethin' to arouse their suspicion. He got on the bad side of that pair of females in a hurry."

"Maybe he's a ladies' man, and they followed him from somewhere," Withers said.

"Oh, hell," said Peeler, "he'd have had to know them before he fell in with us. If he come from Amarillo, like he said, that means they follered him from there. How does a man *do* that?"

Hindes laughed. "We missed out on the big money, gents. We should of stripped the varmint down, opened a freak show, and sold tickets."

"Quiet, damn it," Slade said.

Faro Duval reined up, listening. Each of the outlaws had quickly seized the muzzle of his horse to prevent a betraying nicker. They were downwind from the approaching rider, and they watched as Faro continued along the back trail.

"There it is, by God," Slade said softly. "There's a hell of a lot more to this than we can see, or they wouldn't be scouting the back trail."

"He won't have any trouble findin' where we moved off into the brush," said Kritzer, "and when he finds the ashes of our fire, he can trail us from there. Let him learn we're ridin' parallel to the trail the wagons is takin', and he'll *know* what we're doing."

"Yeah," Hindes said, "and if they got any sand, they won't wait for us to make our move. They'll come *lookin'* for us. You got any ideas, Mr. Slade?"

"As a matter of fact," said Slade, "I have. It'll take him a while to find where we left the trail and figure out what we have in mind. We're going to get ahead of the wagons. So far ahead, they won't know *where* we are, and they won't dare send just one rider to look for us."

"That's as good as tellin' 'em we got an ambush in mind," Hindes said.

"Then you come up with somethin' better," said Slade, with a snarl.

"Back off, Hindes," Kritzer said. "That's not a bad idea. We don't know for sure just where these wagons are goin', and until we have some idea, gunning everybody down in an ambush would be foolish. They'll know an ambush is comin', but they won't know when or where. We'll still have an edge."

"Depends on how you look at it," Peeler said. "Somewhere ahead, there's hostile Utes. I reckon *they'll* have the edge."

"It'll be up to us to stay out of their way," said Slade. "It ain't often they get a shot at five wagon loads of grub and goods, and I'm gamblin' they won't pass it up."

Hindes laughed. "You shouldn't never gamble, Slade. I've seen you raise on a pair of deuces."

"I'm ridin' on," Slade gritted. "Any of you that ain't

got the sand to follow, now's the time to split the blanket."

Slade kicked his horse into a lope, and one by one, his three companions followed.

Faro found where the four horsemen had veered off into the brush and made camp for the night. From there, instead of returning to the Rio Chama and following the five wagons, the four riders kept to the brush, seeking a higher elevation.

"From here," Faro said aloud, "they might have seen the McCutcheon sisters ride by, and suspected their tracks had been noticed. For that matter, they likely saw me followin' the back trail."

Faro followed the faint trail only a little farther, until the strides of all four horses lengthened into a fast gallop. Were they—aware they were about to be discovered—trying to get ahead of the wagons and ambush them before Faro returned with a warning? Down the slope he galloped his horse, and free of brush and low-hanging limbs, rode hard to catch up to the wagons. Durham was the first to see him coming, and he did nothing. But on the box of the fifth wagon, Odessa McCutcheon heard the urgency in the hoofbeats of the approaching horse.

"Rein up," Odessa shouted, reining up her own teams.

The other four wagons halted, and men came off the high boxes, Winchesters in their hands. Faro dismounted, holding the reins of his lathered horse as it tried to reach the river.

"You found 'em," Odessa said.

"Yes," said Faro, "and after leaving our trail, they spent the night in the brush. From there—sometime this morning—they rode to a higher elevation. They had to see me as I rode the back trail, and now they're somewhere ahead of us."

"So we got an ambush to look forward to," Shanghai said.

"Eventually," said Faro, "but not yet. I thought they might be planning to cut down on you before I could ride back and warn you. Since they didn't, they're going to keep us spooked, if they can, by always bein' somewhere ahead."

"When bush-whackin' bastards are stalkin' me," Shanghai said, "I don't get spooked. I get mad as hell. Let's leave these wagons where they are, saddle our horses, and ride the varmints down."

"I'm ready," Tarno shouted.

"So am I," said Dallas.

"No," Faro said, "they may be expecting that. Many a man, mad as hell, has been shot dead as hell, because he walked or rode into a trap. Besides, as long as they're ahead of us, they can blunt the attack of any hostile Utes looking for a fight."

"Sound thinking, my friend," said Levi Collins.

"If they're anything like Comanches," Mamie McCutcheon said, "they might pass up this other bunch, and come after the wagons. Quanah Parker and his Comanches dearly love to loot wagons. Especially when there's weapons and ammunition to be had."

"From what I've seen of Utes," said Collins, "they'll come after whoever is the first to show up. To their way of thinking, they can scalp these four renegades, and *still* waylay these wagons."

"Which gets us back to the possibility the Utes may take care of these *hombres* that appear to be stalking us," Faro said.

"I believe these men following us are not all that concerned with the freight aboard the wagons," said Collins. "If they were, why not attempt to take the wagons *now,* before we're hundreds of miles into the mountains?"

"They suspect that where you're going, there's something more valuable than what's in the wagons," Odessa said, "and right now, they're not sure just *where* you're headed. Until they are, they can't afford to murder us all."

"That sums it up very well, madam," said Collins. "When I was slugged, our first night on the trail, my attacker was seeking to learn where we are going, and why. Since he obviously learned nothing, it appears to have made them all the more determined that there is some treasure at the end of the rainbow."

"They just ain't sure where the end of the rainbow is," Dallas said.

"Exactly," said Collins, "and I don't look for them to become dangerous until they're convinced they can complete the journey without us."

"Yeah," Tarno said, "but we don't know *when* they're likely to make that decision."

Durham laughed. "I'll be watching all of you sweat. I got nothing to lose."

"Oh, but you have," said Odessa. "If we get ambushed, and it looks like we're all out of luck, I'm saving my last slug for you."

"I think, from here on," Faro said, "we'll have to scout the trail ahead. Not just for signs of these horsemen who are stalking us, but for hostile Utes as well. Collins, if you'll continue to take the reins for me, I'll scout ahead every morning. I'll ride at least as far as the wagons are able to travel in a day."

"Certainly I'll take over the wagon for you," said Collins, "but it strikes me that you will be taking all the risk."

"Maybe," Faro said, "but it's a risk someone has to take. I don't believe these riders who are stalking us will give away their game just to ambush one man, and I think they'll alert us to a possible attack by Utes by acting as bait. As long as they're somewhere ahead of us, the Utes will have to deal with them first. Any conflict between the two groups will warn us. Now that these four riders are ahead of us, it's important that they stay there. I'll be trailing them, makin' sure they don't double back."

"A good day's run is twenty miles," said Dallas. "If you aim to ride that far ahead, and one of those bunches decides to go after you, the rest of us won't be able to get to you in time to help."

"I understand that," Faro said, "but if either group gets in a position to ambush us, we must know in time to mount a defense. If we're grouped, and they come after us all at the same time, they could wipe us out in a single volley. Behind your wagons, each of you has a horse on a lead rope. Keep those horses saddled, and if you should hear shooting somewhere ahead, then mount up and come a-runnin'.'"

"For what purpose?" Durham demanded. "You've already admitted that if everything goes sour and you're attacked, the rest of us will be too far behind to help you."

"Durham," said Faro, "if I ride into an ambush, that doesn't necessarily mean the rest of you are free of it. If I'm attacked, you may not arrive in time to help me, but there's a chance I can stand them off until the rest of you can swing in behind them, or flank them. You can only defend yourselves against an ambush by having something or somebody to attack. A group attacking one man will attempt to surround him, and that brings them out into the open. You won't get a better chance than that."

"It's time we had an understanding," Durham said. "I agreed that you could use the wagon and the teams, but I don't recall promising to help defend you against hostile Utes or outlaws."

"Suit yourself," said Faro, "but as long as you're part of this outfit, you stand to be shot just as dead as any of us."

"Then I don't choose to be part of this outfit," Durham said. "Not unless I'm told where we're headed, and what's in it for me, once we get there."

"You've been promised sufficient supplies to take you on to California," said Collins, "and that's all you have any right to expect."

"That's right," Faro said, "and we reserve the right to withdraw *that* offer, if you're unwilling to help us defend the wagons against Indians and outlaws. You're welcome to saddle your horse and ride on, but you get nothing."

"Damn you," said Durham bitterly. "Damn all of you."

He said no more, but neither did he mount his horse and ride away.

"Now," Faro said, "if you'll stay with the wagon, Collins, I'll trail those four *hombres* and see that they don't have any mischief planned somewhere ahead of us."

"Very well," said Collins.

The teamsters mounted their wagon boxes, Collins returning to Faro's wagon. Durham mounted his horse, his hate-filled eyes on Odessa McCutcheon, as she climbed to the box of what had been his wagon.

"I'm not finished with you," Durham snarled.

Odessa laughed. "You got that turned around all wrong, gamblin' man. You was more than finished with Mamie and me when you left Amarillo like a scairt coyote. The truth is, we ain't finished with you. You should have rode out while you had the invite."

Chapter 4

Faro had no trouble trailing the four riders, and it soon became obvious why they did not attempt to hide their trail. When Faro judged he had ridden more than twenty miles, the trail continued. The outlaws were counting on any pursuit being limited because of the possibility of bushwhackers. If the pursuers got too far ahead of the wagons, they ran the risk of being ambushed by Indians or outlaws at a point too distant for their companions to join them. Just on the chance the outlaws might have doubled back, Faro rode ten miles north without finding any sign. He then returned to the place he had left the trail of the outlaws, and rode ten miles south. There were no telltale tracks, so he rode back to meet the oncoming wagons. Levi Collins saw him coming and reined up. It was time to rest the teams. All of them—including Durham—gathered around to hear Faro's report.

"I rode a good twenty miles without getting close to them," Faro said, "and then to north and south, without finding any sign they'd doubled back."

"What do you think it means?" Collins asked.

"They're not ready to bushwhack us," said Faro,

"and by staying far enough ahead, they don't figure we'll force a fight."

"They're figurin' that right," Dallas said. "Best defense against an ambush is to ride the varmints down, before they're able to find cover and dig in."

"Damn them," said Shanghai, "they got us between a rock and a hard place. They'll be knowin' we can't afford to leave the wagons and all of us go after them, nor do we dare split our forces."

"In that case, Faro," Collins said, "since we're still in danger of Indian attack, I think your scouting ahead every day is a needless risk."

"Maybe," said Faro, "but we need to know that these riders are still far enough ahead of us to rule out an ambush. We can't be sure of that, unless I trail them. As for Indians, that's a risk I'll have to take."

"I can do some of the scouting," Collins said.

"That's generous of you," said Faro, "but I can handle it."

Tarno laughed. "Faro ain't much for blowin' his own horn. What he won't tell you is, for four years, he was a scout for John Mosby."

"My God," Collins said, *"The Gray Ghost.* Please do your own scouting, Mr. Duval."

The wagons moved on, covering another fifteen miles before reining up for the night. Durham had kept his silence, mulling over what Faro Duval had said about the outlaws and their obvious intention of staying far ahead. Durham wondered if the outlaws had been near enough to have heard the shot, and if they had witnessed his fall from grace. He had to believe they had washed their hands of him, for now there was no way he would be able to rendezvous with Slade. That meant when the outlaws decided an ambush was in order, Durham would be just another target in the sights of their rifles. Double-crossing Slade was no longer a possibility. Like it or not, he must cast his lot with these teamsters, if he was to survive. To that end, immediately after supper, he began mending his fences. Going to Faro Duval, he spoke in as friendly a manner as he could.

"Duval, I've been doin' some thinking, and I owe you and Mr. Collins an apology. The deal I made with you in Santa Fe was legitimate, and I was wrong, trying to back out of it. If we're attacked by Indians—or anyone else—I'll take part in the defense, and I'll do my best. I'll take over the wagon again, if you wish."

"Far as I'm concerned," said Faro, "your apology's accepted."

"Mr. Duval speaks for me, as well," Collins said.

"Well, there don't neither of you speak for me," said Odessa McCutcheon. "I like this teamsterin', and I reckon I'll stay with the wagon."

"Since it's your wagon," Durham said, "I can't argue with that."

"Praise be to God," said Mamie, "he's admitted it."

Durham's apparent repentant attitude did much to lighten the mood of the camp, but Mamie and Odessa McCutcheon still viewed the gambler with distrust. It was a fair night, with moon and stars, and during the first watch, Mamie McCutcheon took the opportunity to speak to Shanghai, Tarno, and Dallas.

"Durham's got a lyin' tongue. Don't believe nothin' the little sidewinder says, and if Duval or Collins will listen to you, warn them. He knows them outlaws was trailin' you for some reason, and he's makin' peace so's he can hang around and find out why."

"You don't have to convince me," Dallas said. "I still think he's the varmint that crept up and slugged Collins."

"I think so, too," said Shanghai, "but there's no proof."

"There might have been," Tarno said. "We should have searched the varmint."

"Without givin' away any secrets," said Mamie, "could he have taken something from Collins that might tell him where these wagons is goin', and why?"

"My God, yes," Dallas said, recalling the little sack of gold ore. "He could have taken part of something that wouldn't have been missed."

"He done it, then," said Mamie.

"I believe you're right," Shanghai said. "I wish you'd talk to Faro."

"Odessa will do that," said Mamie. "The varmint's slick as calf slobber, and we purely don't believe for a minute he's reformed. He's just waitin' for a chance to turn somethin' to his advantage, and he'll back-shoot any one or all of us, if he has to."

"Faro can fool you," Tarno said, "and I think Collins is deeper than he looks. I won't be surprised if they're thinkin' like you and Odessa. Whatever Durham has in mind, I can promise you, he won't get the jump on all of us."

Mamie laughed softly. "I didn't think so. You *hombres* has been over the mountain and seen the bear. The kind of men we knowed in Texas before the war."

The night wore on. Shanghai, Tarno, and Dallas felt some better for having talked to Mamie McCutcheon. Odessa seemed even more forceful, and they had little doubt that the outspoken woman would be equally convincing to Faro Duval and Levi Collins.

The Sevier River, southwestern Utah.
August 6, 1870.

"My God," Isaac Puckett groaned, "don't them Utes ever let up? If we had dynamite, and Levi was here, we still couldn't work the claim."

"That's been botherin' me some," said Felix Blackburn, feeding more shells into his Winchester. "Levi's been gone near three weeks, and we ain't accomplished a damn thing."

"I ain't been much help," Josh Snyder said, "layin' here with a stiff shoulder and sore arm. I can't even comb my hair left-handed."

"I wouldn't complain too much," said Blackburn. "You could have took that Ute arrow in your belly, or through a lung. Besides, it might have been Isaac or me, instead of you."

"Yeah," Puckett said, "and we'd best all lay low, because we got no more whiskey for fightin' infection. At least, not until Levi brings us supplies from Santa Fe."

"I got all the confidence in the world in Levi," said Snyder, "but we got to face the possibility that he never got to Santa Fe, that these damn Utes got to him first."

"Well, hell," Blackburn said, irritated, "why don't we just surrender to these Utes and let 'em have their way with us? If Levi don't bring us some ammunition, we'll soon end up throwin' rocks."

"Don't be talkin' agin Levi," said Puckett. "I reckon he'd of backed off and let either of you go, instead of him, if you'd wanted to. If you aim to lay here and sweat over what might go wrong, chew on this for a while. I'd bet my share of the claim that Levi made it to Santa Fe. What concerns me is that he may not find a teamster in all of Santa Fe with the sand to risk comin' into these mountains."

"We give him the authority to swap a quarter of the strike, in return for wagons and mules, if he has to," Snyder said.

"True," said Puckett, "but there must be some limit as to how far a man will go for gold, or the promise of it."

Blackburn laughed. "Damn right. Was I in Santa Fe, knowin' what I've learned about these Utes, I'd think long and hard about takin' teams and a wagon into this godforsaken country. For a quarter claim, a half claim, or a full claim. All the gold in the world ain't worth havin' an arrow drove through your brisket."

Blackburn had raised up just a little, so that the crown of his hat was visible above a boulder behind which he had taken cover. Suddenly an arrow whipped the hat from his head, and he fired.

"Get him?" Puckett inquired.

"No, damn it," said Blackburn. "I should have saved the ammunition."

"I think that's their game," Snyder said. "They know they're no match for our rifles, but they also got to suspect there's a limit to our shells. I think the varmints tempt us to shoot, even when we ain't got a chance of hittin' one of 'em."

"I wish you hadn't brought that up," said Puckett. "There's a little more than two hundred rounds for each of us, and we'll be out of ammunition for our Winchesters. Two more weeks, and if Levi don't show, we're dead men."

Durham continued to ride behind the last wagon, and when disaster struck, it was he who first became aware of it.

"Indians!" the gambler shouted.

Odessa was the first to rein up her team. Seizing her Winchester, she stepped off the wagon box and dropped to the ground, as arrows began to fly. The nearest cover was a windblown pine behind which Hal Durham had already crouched, firing his Winchester. In the seconds it took Odessa to fire twice, two Indian ponies galloped away, riderless. Each of the teamsters had bellied down, with or without cover, and their rapid fire took its toll. Their losses had been too great, and the attacking Indians wheeled their horses and rode back the way they had come.

"They're finished," Faro shouted. "Anybody hurt?"

Nobody had been hit.

"Durham," said Collins, "that was fast work."

"Yes," Faro said. "That's the way you stay alive in Indian country. Our Winchesters can cut them down before we're within range of their arrows, but only if we see them in time."

Durham said nothing. Odessa McCutcheon eyed

him with as much distaste as ever. But Faro had something more to say.

"We've been concerned with Indians ahead of us. Now we know there's just as much danger from our back trail. Durham, I want you to continue riding behind the last wagon, and sing out when you see anything or anybody suspicious. Collins, if you'll take over the wagon for a while, I'll scout ahead."

The teamsters mounted their wagon boxes and again took the trail. Faro rode ahead, and Durham loped his horse alongside Odessa McCutcheon's wagon. He grinned at her.

"You heard him," Odessa snapped. "You're to ride behind the wagon, so's I don't have to look at you."

"Pardon me if I don't take Duval seriously," said Durham. "He's so concerned with possible Indian attacks from behind, why is he riding ahead? So the rest of us can get shot full of arrows?"

"Durham," Odessa said pityingly, "you'd have to go to school and study some, before you could work your way up to ignorant. The big attack, when it comes, will be from up ahead somewhere. They struck from behind, hopin' to rattle us."

"You know so damn much about Indians," said Durham spitefully, "why don't you just keep one eye on the teams, and the other on the back trail?"

"Durham," Odessa said, drawing her Colt, "if you don't drop back behind this wagon so's I don't have to hear you or look at you, I'll shoot you."

For emphasis, she cocked the Colt, and Durham slowed his horse, allowing the wagon to move ahead.

*   *   *

"From that shootin'," Hindes said, "I'd say that bunch with the wagons has had 'em a taste of Ute. Ain't it funny, us ridin' miles ahead, and the Indians strikin' them from behind?"

"You'll likely be laughin' out of the other side of your mouth, 'fore we're done," said Slade. "I've had some experience with Utes, and it just tickles hell out of them to do what you ain't expecting. Just when you think they're behind you, they'll start bloomin' like yucca on a rise ahead of you."

"It's the God's truth," Kritzer said. "The Comanches are treacherous as hell, but they can't hold a candle to the Utes for pure cussedness. Once was, they'd sell their captives into slavery. Now I hear they'll burn you at the stake, just to hear you scream."

"It's enough to give a man the creeps," said Withers, "knowin' they're up here somewhere, never knowin' when they'll strike."

"My God," Peeler said, "if they're already striking, what'll they be like, as we ride on deeper into their stompin' ground?"

Slade laughed. "Anybody that's gettin' cold feet, feel free to just ride on back to Santa Fe. But keep in mind, them Utes is somewhere behind us. You could end up fightin' 'em all by your lonesome."

"Great God Almighty," Kritzer groaned, "them that's behind us ain't the problem."

The four outlaws reined up, speechless. On the rise ahead of them a dozen mounted Indians had appeared. Behind them, an equal number waited.

"They got rifles, by God," said Hindes, "and if my

eyes ain't failin' me, the varmint with that bunch up ahead is a white man."

"If we're aimin' to make a move," Withers said, "now's the time."

"No," said Slade. "They're armed with rifles, and we're within range. We'll wait and see what they have in mind."

The white man rode to meet them, and they could only stare, for his face had been horribly mutilated. His right ear was missing, he wore a patch over his left eye, and a long, hideous scar ran from just above his good eye to the corner of his mouth. His lips had drawn downward into a perpetual leer. There were other scars on his face and neck, and they all contributed to his overall terrible appearance. As in the days of old Mexico, across his chest were crossed bandoliers of shells. Two Colts rode in a *buscadera* rig, and under his arm was a Winchester. He laughed, and then he spoke.

"Feast your eyes, *amigos*. Have you ever seen a man so ugly? My Ute *compañeros* call me Perro Cara. That's Dog Face, in English."

"I won't say we're pleased to meet you," said Slade, "with them Utes behind you. I'd like to know why you're stoppin' us. What do you want?"

"The Utes don't care a damn why you're here," Dog Face said. "They'd as soon kill you and be done with it. Me, I'm different. Convince me there's a reason why any of you should go on livin'. Make it worth my while, and I'll speak up for you."

"We stuck up a bank in Tucumcari," said Slade,

"and a man was killed. We're on the run. Is that reason enough for you?"

"No," Dog Face said. "You varmints has been pussyfootin' around them wagons ever since they left Santa Fe. You could of already ambushed 'em and took their freight, if you had that in mind. Now what are you *really* after?"

"Why the hell should I tell you *anything*?" said Slade. "You'd root us out, and take it all for yourself."

"Then I reckon you'll just have to take your chances," Dog Face said ominously. "If you don't speak up *pronto,* I'll have the lot of you shot out of your saddles."

"Damn it," said Slade, "for now, you win."

Carefully, from his shirt pocket, he removed the small chunk of gold-laced ore that Durham had taken from Levi Collins. He tossed it to Dog Face, and he held it close to his good eye. He whistled long and low, and his free hand had dropped to the butt of one of his Colts. Slade and his companions swallowed hard, expecting the worst. Suddenly Dog Face laughed, and then he spoke.

"I reckon I'll let you live. For a while, anyhow. I got to warn you, though. These Utes is distrustful of whites. If they catch you tryin' to sneak off agin my wishes, they'll kill you. Now all of you ride on ahead of me, and don't even think about pullin' a gun. I can give any man of you a start, and still kill you."

When all the Utes came together, Slade and his companions swallowed hard, for there were more than two dozen. But that wasn't the worst of it. When they eventually reached the camp in a distant canyon, there

were more Indians, as well as two more renegades of
the same stripe as Dog Face.

"My God," Hindes groaned, "there must be fifty of
'em."

Slade and his men reined up, dismounting when
given the order.

"Now," said Dog Face, "tell us your names."

Slade spoke first, and the others followed.

"My *amigos* is Sangre and Hueso," Dog Face said,
"an' don't let their friendly faces throw you. They'd as
soon slit your throats or gut-shoot you as look at you.
But stacked up to these Utes, them an' me is the best
friends you got. Keep that in mind."

Sangre and Hueso said nothing, but their evil faces
spoke volumes. Sangre had little pig eyes, not a hair on
his head or face, and without his boots, wouldn't have
stood even five feet tall. But he made up in girth what
he lacked in height, and he carried two Colts in a *buscadera* rig. The butt of a third revolver and the haft of
a Bowie were barely visible above his wide belt.
Hueso was all the name implied, his bones being the
most prominent parts of his anatomy. He was gangling,
standing more than a foot taller than Sangre, and he
had the look of an albino. He might have been skinned,
rendered, and his hide stretched back over his bones.
On his right hip was a butt-forward, thonged-down
Colt, and on his left, a sawed-off shotgun. Every Ute
was armed with at least a Winchester, while some of
them had revolvers shoved under the waistbands of
their buckskins. They were truly a formidable bunch,
and Dog Face laughed.

"We heard shootin' a while back," Slade said. "Did you and this bunch of Utes attack them wagons?"

"No," said Dog Face. "We can take the wagons anytime. Like I told you, I knew all that grub an' supplies was bein' freighted in for some reason, an' now I know what that reason is. I reckon we'll just do what you *hombres* was doin'. We'll foller along, until we know where them wagons is headed. The grub an' goods will satisfy the Utes, leavin' the gold for Sangre, Hueso, an' me."

"Gold?" Sangre and Hueso shouted in a single voice.

"Yeah, gold," said Dog Face. "I was gettin' around to tellin' you."

He tossed the hunk of gold-laced ore, and Hueso caught it in a bony hand. It took but a moment for the greedy pair to comprehend. Their hands on the butts of their guns, they turned hard eyes on Slade and his companions.

"We don't know where it is," Slade shouted.

"Back off," said Dog Face. "He ain't lyin'."

"If we're follerin' the wagons to the gold," Sangre gritted, "what'n hell good is these varmints?"

"Yeah," said Hueso, we ain't splittin' with them."

"I'll decide who we split with, an' who we don't," Dog Face said. "I broke both of you bastards out of a California jail, because I owed you, but by God, I don't owe you no more."

It seemed Slade and his companions might have a small advantage, and Kritzer spoke.

"Why can't we throw in with you? The law's after us, and we got nowhere to go."

"I'll study on it," Dog Face said.

"While you're studyin'," said Sangre, "study on this bunch double-crossin' you when the time's right."

"I aim to," Dog Face said, "an' since you brung it up, don't you and Hueso go gettin' ideas. I been double-crossed before, but the bastards ain't around to brag on it."

The unsavory duo glared at Dog Face, hatred in their eyes, and Slade laughed. There was no honor among thieves, and they all knew it, but Dog Face was no fool. Playing on the obvious hostility between his own companions and Slade's outfit, either faction would find it difficult to double-cross or shoot him in the back. The fact that Slade and his men had not been relieved of their weapons made the situation perfectly clear to Sangre and Hueso.

"Now that we understand one another," said Slade, his eyes on Dog Face, "how is it that you got some of these Utes with you, but not the others?"

"There's different factions of 'em within these mountains," Dog Face replied. "I took me a squaw within this bunch, and I led the men over Cajon pass, into California. As you can see, the *Californios* provided us with fine horses, weapons, and ammunition. The Utes ain't forgot, an' that's somethin' that can't always be said of a white man."

As he spoke, his eyes were on Sangre and Hueso. From their expressions, it appeared his suspicions of the pair were well-founded.

"If you don't get along with all the Utes," said Hindes, "what's to stop all the others from jumpin' in ahead of us, killin' the teamsters, and takin' the wagons?"

"They ain't got the firepower," Dog Face said. "Winchesters cut 'em down before they git within range with bows and arrows. That bunch that attacked the wagons a while ago, half of 'em died, without once drawin' blood."

The Utes had gone about their business, paying no attention to Slade and his men. It was encouragement enough for the new arrivals, and they set about unsaddling.

"We got some grub," Slade said, "but not enough to make much difference, with all these *hombres.*"

"We're obliged," said Dog Face, "but it won't matter. It's summer, and there's plenty of game in these mountains. Come winter, we'll drift west, toward the Great Basin."

There was a stream along the floor of the canyon, with the western rim overhanging enough to provide shelter. Slade and his companions released their horses and dragged their saddles beneath the rim. There being little else to do, the outlaws stretched out, heads on their saddles, and lighted quirlys.

"A fine damn mess," said Hindes sourly. "Now what'll we do?"

"We'll keep our mouths shut," Slade replied. "Especially you. Spoutin' off could get us all shot dead."

"There's worse things than throwin' in with this bunch," said Withers. "At least, we ain't likely to be bushwhacked by Indians."

"Hell, we're surrounded by 'em," Peeler said. "Let

somethin' happen to this ugly varmint, Perro Cara, and we're dead as last summer's cornstalks."

"That's why we're gonna do whatever it takes to keep him alive," said Slade. "At least for a while. We're going to make ourselves useful to him."

Hindes laughed. "The mark of an honest man. Never back-shoot or double-cross a gent, as long as he's useful."

Somehow it rubbed Slade the wrong way, and with his hand near the butt of his Colt, he spoke.

"Hindes, you open your mouth one more time, and I'll kill you."

Despite the fact the first Indian attack had come from along the back trail, Faro didn't give up scouting ahead. This time, rather than scouting only as far as he believed the wagons could travel in a day, he rode much farther. While there was some personal risk, he wanted to see just how far ahead the outlaws were. He reined up quickly, for suddenly there were tracks of a dozen unshod horses. The riders had advanced until they had come together with other riders of unshod horses, and the lot of them had traveled west. Faro followed cautiously, and only when the riders were strung out enough could he again see tracks of shod horses. *Five* shod horses! He rode a little farther, just to be sure his eyes hadn't deceived him, but the tracks were there. Wheeling his horse, he rode back to meet the wagons. Seeing him coming, they reined up to rest the teams and climbed down from their wagon boxes.

"There's trouble ahead," said Faro. "These *hombres* I've been trailin' rode off with Indians. Two dozen or more, if I'm any judge. One of the bunch is ridin' a shod horse."

"Could be a white renegade," Dallas Weaver said.

"That's what I suspect," said Faro.

"There was no sign of any conflict, then, when these four men met the Indians," Levi Collins said.

"None that I could see," said Faro, "and that's puzzling. Two bunches of Utes caught these four *hombres* between a rock and a hard place, but there was no sign of a fight. It seems they all rode away together."

"Pretty mean odds, four men against that many Indians," Tarno said. "I reckon they done the smart thing."

"I ain't too sure of that," said Shanghai. "Hell, I'd as soon go down shootin' as to be rode off to an Indian camp and burnt at the stake."

"There's one factor we're not considering," Faro said. "The rider of that fifth shod horse may be a renegade white. If he is, it could account for those four being taken alive."

"Yes," said Collins, "and he may have taken them alive, seeking to learn why they've been dogging us. If all this was Indian related, I can't believe they wouldn't just come after us with a large enough force to kill us all and take the wagons."

"That's more the Indian way," Faro agreed, "so you may be right. There may be a white renegade calling the shots, but what can the four men he captured tell him about us and our destination?"

"From what I know," said Odessa McCutcheon, "one of them four varmints likely took somethin' from Mr. Collins that led 'em to suspect where you folks is goin', and your reasons. Don't you reckon them four would swap that information for their lives, if they had any choice?"

"By God, she's right," Dallas said. "There's nothin' worse than a bunch of Indians led by white outlaws."

"But we've already been attacked by Indians," said Mamie McCutcheon, "and they all came after us along the back trail."

"All Indians won't necessarily be part of this renegade bunch," Faro said. "That means we're subject to being attacked by God knows how many different bands."

Hal Durham listened in dismay, his pitiful plans to double-cross Slade's bunch crumbling before his eyes. Even now, Slade and his companions might be dead, and while Durham didn't care a damn for them, it complicated things for him. Strong on his mind was the hunk of gold ore he had given Slade. Men had killed for less than the promise within that piece of rock, and the killers would be somewhere ahead. Durham swallowed hard.

Chapter 5

The rest of the day passed uneventfully. After supper, before the first watch began, Faro had something to say.

"Collins, I have a plan that requires a case of that dynamite."

"There's plenty," Collins said. "What do you have in mind?"

"I want it capped and fused," Faro said. "With seven- to ten-second fuses. You'll keep a few sticks in your saddlebag, and I want some on every wagon box."

"There's oilskin in the first wagon," Collins said.

"*Bueno,*" said Faro. "See that the dynamite is wrapped to stay dry, and each of you had better use a bit of that oilskin to wrap a few matches. We already know we're facing a large number of men, and the time may come when we find ourselves surrounded. A few well-placed sticks of dynamite could even the odds."

"An ingenious plan," Collins said, "and I didn't even consider that, while purchasing the dynamite."

"The important thing is, we have it," said Faro.

"Since we're on the second watch, I reckon you and me had best fuse and cap that dynamite after supper. It'll cut into sleepin' time a mite, but I'll feel better when it's ready."

"I'll help, if you like," Durham said.

"Let the little varmint," said Odessa. "Maybe he'll blow himself up."

"I reckon Collins and me can handle it," Faro said. "We'll need to save the dynamite for Utes and outlaws."

The others laughed, but Durham did not, and Faro didn't like the look in the gambler's eyes. After supper, Collins broke open a wooden case of dynamite, and with Faro helping, they capped and fused the explosive. Collins dug into the first wagon and came out with the oilskin. With his knife, he cut a section of it into two-foot squares, and in these, sticks of capped and fused dynamite were wrapped. The teamsters watched approvingly, for it was a tactic that might well save their lives. Durham had already taken to his blankets in preparation for the second watch, while Odessa McCutcheon hunkered with the rest of the teamsters, drinking coffee. While Mamie stayed with the first watch, Odessa had remained with the second, if for no other reason than because her continual presence irritated Hal Durham. While the two appeared to hate each other's guts, Faro Duval was not convinced. Odessa had begun spending most of the watch with Levi Collins, and Collins had done nothing to discourage her. In fact, he seemed to relish her attention, and began returning it, with interest. One evening after supper, before the first watch began, Faro took his suspicions to Mamie McCutcheon.

"Mamie," Faro said, "I need a woman's advice, and I must ask you not to repeat anything I'm about to say."

"I am flattered, Mr. Duval," said Mamie, "and I just love secrets. I presume it somehow involves Odessa and her . . . ah . . . activities on the second watch."

"It does," Faro said. "Not so much what she's doing, as her reasons for doing it. Am I wrong to doubt that Odessa and Durham don't actually hate each other?"

Mamie laughed. "You are a strange man, Faro Duval. To answer your question, I'd have to say no. I fear Odessa is as much attracted to Durham as ever, and is perhaps using Mr. Collins in an attempt to revive Durham's interest in her."

"Damn," said Faro. "Do you think she can?"

"Frankly, I don't know," Mamie replied. "From what I've seen of Durham, I doubt it. To support my reasoning, I'd have to tell you some unflattering things about Odessa and myself."

"I won't ask you to do that," said Faro. "You're entitled to your private lives."

"That's kind of you," Mamie said, "but when one's life touches that of a two-legged skunk like Durham, something always gets lost in the stink. There are some women who, although they don't realize it, find a flawed, low-down man most appealing. If they lose one, they'll find another. Odessa and me, if there was any hope for us, should have been married before the war. When it ended, the few men who came home were crippled, sick, and bitter. The last thing any of them seemed to want was a twenty-five-year-old woman whose best years were behind her. Is it any wonder that a slick-talking, fancy-dressed varmint like Durham could turn a woman's head?"

"One of you, I can understand," Faro said, "but how . . . ?"

Mamie laughed. "Oh, he spent a week with Odessa, before he came after me."

"You gave in to him, knowing he'd taken advantage of your sister?"

"He didn't explain it that way," said Mamie. "He sort of . . . accused her of taking unfair advantage of *him.*"

It was Faro's turn to laugh, and Mamie blushed.

"Sorry," Faro said. "What did Odessa do?"

"She jumped on me," said Mamie. "She called me a whore, and some other words that I didn't know *she* knew."

"If she blamed you," Faro said, "then why did she come after Durham with fire in her eye and a Winchester in her hand?"

"Not to kill him," said Mamie, "despite what she says. She was furious, not because he took the thousand dollars from her, but because he ran out on us. She was counting on going to California with him."

"That's hard to believe," Faro said. "Don't you know, when a man's proved he's a sidewinder, he ain't likely to change? If Odessa and Durham *had* got back together, where would you fit in?"

"I was going to save her from him, if I could," said Mamie. "I thought if I was there, always around, he'd leave her for me. How many times must that happen to her, before she gives up on him?"

"You don't believe that," Faro said. "You already told me there's women who lose one no-account varmint, only to go lookin' for another. So you and Odessa came west, plannin' to share this slick-tongued gambler."

"Damn you," Mamie cried, "how dare you . . ."

"Quiet," said Faro. "This is a touchy enough situation, without involving all the others in it. So you came west with Odessa, not to even the score with Durham, but to continue what he had started, back in Amarillo."

"Yes," Mamie said, refusing to look at him, "but you must understand the terrible predicament in which we found ourselves. We were considered fallen women, disgraced in a town where we had grown up. In the churches, sermons were preached, condemning us as sinners bound for hell-fire. Don't you see? Anything— even a checkered life with a slick-talking gambler— would have been better than what we faced at home."

"I reckon I can understand that," said Faro, "but where does that leave you now? Do you still believe Durham will be taking the pair of you to California?"

"Oh, God," Mamie said, "don't ask me that. I don't know. Odessa and me talked some about taking our teams and wagon and returning with you to Santa Fe, but I don't know that she wasn't just creating false hopes. When we've gone as far as you intend going, I'm not sure Odessa won't try to push Durham into taking us on to California."

"Do you think that was Durham's only reason for throwing in with us, to escape you and Odessa?"

"I . . . I don't know what you mean," said Mamie.

"Then I'll spell it out for you," Faro said. "I had my doubts about Odessa when she kept insisting we were being followed by outlaws. You've heard her admit that she believes those men are concerned with where we're going, and why. Is it too far-fetched to believe that this Hal Durham has the same ambition?"

"I suppose not," she replied in a small voice.

"Then maybe Odessa's interest in Levi Collins accounts for more than just stirring up jealousy in Durham," said Faro. "Suppose Collins tells Odessa where we're going, and why? It appears to me that would get her back in solid with Durham. Would she go that far?"

"Damn it," Mamie cried, "I don't know. Why don't you ask her?"

She stomped angrily away, and Faro doubted he'd have to say anything to Odessa, for she dropped her tin cup and went after Mamie. The others—especially Collins—looked at him long and hard, but Faro said nothing. If Odessa or Collins took issue with his doubts and suspicions, let them approach him. Almost immediately after the second watch began, Collins did.

"Mr. Duval," said Collins, "I understand you do not look favorably on my interest in Odessa Mc-Cutcheon."

"Wrong, Collins," Faro said. "I don't look favorably on her interest in *you,* because I believe her interest goes considerably beyond what you expect. I think she's still neck-deep in her affair with Hal Durham, and that she aims to swap him something *he* wants, in the hope of rekindling his interest in her. Have you told her where we're bound, and why?"

"My business arrangement with you does not entitle you to pry into my personal life," said Collins stiffly.

"It does, when your personal life threatens the lives of us all, and the success of this expedition," Faro said coldly. "Now answer my question. *Have you told Odessa McCutcheon where we're bound, and why?*"

"No, damn it," said Collins irritably, "but I can't say that I won't."

"Collins," Faro said grimly, "I can't make you shut your mouth, but I can sure as hell make you wish you had. If you breathe a word of our purpose and destination to Odessa or Durham, our deal with you is off. We'll unload four of these wagons, leaving every damn bit of goods and grub on the ground, and return to Santa Fe."

"By God," said Collins, his face livid, "you wouldn't . . ."

"I would, and I will," Faro replied, his voice dangerously calm. "I want your promise of silence. Do I have it?"

"You have it," said Collins, choking out the words.

Faro said no more, and Odessa McCutcheon wasted no time in joining Collins. Durham realized something was afoot, and when the gambler laughed, Faro turned on him.

"Come now, Duval," Durham said, "there's enough of her to go around. Let the man take his pleasure. Tomorrow, he may be shot full of Ute arrows, and missing his scalp."

"Durham," said Faro, "one day I'll catch you dealing from the bottom of the deck, and when I do, it'll be your last deal."

Durham laughed again, but with a little less confidence. Faro turned away.

"I saw Duval talking to Mamie, and then to you," Odessa McCutcheon said, "and I've a feeling it involves me."

"No," said Levi Collins, a little too quickly. "It has to do with Durham. Duval doesn't trust the man."

"He shouldn't," Odessa said. "I've told him that from the start."

"How do *you* feel about Durham, Odessa?"

For a long moment she said nothing, and even in the starlight, he could see the anger in her eyes. When she finally spoke, her voice dripped with fury.

"So *that's* how it is. Duval believes I'm in cahoots with that snake-in-the-grass, slick-dealing gambler, and he's talkin' against me."

"Nobody's accused you of anything," said Collins. "We all know you and Mamie are here because of Durham, and that you once had plans of traveling to California with him. I think all of us are entitled to know what you and Mamie intend to do once these wagons have gone as far as we intend to take them."

"We intend to return to Santa Fe with Duval and his men," Odessa said. "Remember you still have our wagon loaded with your goods. Would you prefer to unload it, so that we can return to Santa Fe immediately?"

"Of course not," said Collins angrily. "You know that's impossible. I suppose I'll have to tell you what's bothering Duval, and what's bothering me."

"Please do," Odessa said coldly.

"You're an attractive woman, Odessa Mc-Cutcheon," said Collins, "and I'd be lying if I said I'm not flattered by your attention. But damn it, you were so smitten by this Durham that you followed him here, all the way from Texas. How am I to know that you're free of him, that you aren't out to learn confidential information from me, and pass it on to him?"

"I reckon the confidential information you're referrin' to is where you're takin' these five wagon loads of grub and goods, and your reasons for takin' 'em there," Odessa said.

"That . . . that's it," said Collins uncertainly.

Odessa laughed. "You don't have to tell me nothin', Mr. Collins. Stop me, if I got it all wrong. Somewhere in this godforsaken country, you made a strike. Silver or gold, but I'm bettin' it's gold. Usin' that—or the promise of it—you've convinced Duval and his friends that freightin' in your goods is worth the risk. Am I right, so far?"

Collins was aghast. "How did you . . . ?"

"You have pick-and-shovel hands, Levi," Odessa said, "and there's enough dynamite on these wagons to level every mountain between Santa Fe and the big water. I ain't told Durham a thing, but you can be sure he knows as much as I do. He's crooked as a sand rattler, but that don't mean he's stupid. Now you and Duval take your suspicions and leave me the hell alone."

She turned away, leaving him standing there with conflicting emotions, feeling like the fool she apparently thought he was. He was only mildly surprised when Faro Duval spoke to him from the darkness.

"I reckon you heard it all," said Collins.

"Most of it," Faro admitted. "I may have underestimated her, and where a woman is concerned, that's the worst possible thing a man can do."

"Thanks to you," said Collins, "I played the fool. In spades."

"Maybe not," Faro said. "You had the sand to confront her with your suspicions, and she'll respect you for that. Take her advice and shy away from her. You'll have to play out the hand before you'll know if it's you or Durham. If she's interested in you, then she ain't likely to change, but if she throws you down for Durham, then you've been out of the game since the first draw."

"What's done is done," said Collins gloomily. "If the purpose of our journey is all that obvious, what are we to do now? I'm not convinced that Durham wasn't one of that original band of outlaws. Now that they've been captured, he may have devised some kind of plan of his own."

"Speaking of Durham," Faro said, "where is he?"

"I have no idea," said Collins. "We'd better find him."

But Odessa McCutcheon found Durham first. He and Mamie were under one of the wagons, but the blankets didn't save them from Odessa's fury. A two-gallon coffeepot still simmered on a few coals from a dying fire. Odessa seized the coffeepot, removed the lid, and flung the contents on the hapless pair beneath the wagon. Bawling like a cut bull, Durham rolled out, wearing only his socks. Mamie followed, wearing even less. The moon had risen late, and as Mamie

stood there cursing Odessa, she left nothing to anybody's imagination. The entire camp was awake, and
they all just stood there while the naked Mamie
shouted at Odessa. But Odessa wasn't finished. She
cut loose with a right, and it caught Mamie on the chin.
She fell back against the side of a wagon, and after
catching her breath, went after Odessa like a wounded
cougar. They went down in an ignominious tangle of
arms and legs, Mamie shrieking in pain when her bare
behind landed in what was left of the fire.

"My God," Collins said, "shouldn't we do something?"

"We are," said Faro. "We're minding our own business. If you want to get involved, then jump in."

But Collins did nothing. He and the teamsters allowed the struggling women to thrash around until
they were exhausted. Mamie was first to stagger to her
feet, and without a word, stalked off into the darkness.
Odessa followed.

"Well, by God," Dallas Weaver said in awe, "what
about that?"

"Those of you whose time it is to sleep," said Faro,
"get back to your blankets."

"Some of us better go after Mamie and Odessa,"
Tarno Spangler said. "We don't have any idea what
these Utes is like. They may be just waitin' for a
chance like this."

"I'm aware of that," said Faro wearily. "This is our
watch, so it'll be up to Collins and me."

"There's Durham," Shanghai Taylor said. "What do
you aim to do about him?"

"Nothing, tonight," said Faro. "If the Utes want the

son of a bitch, they can have him. Way I feel right now, if they're of a mind to burn him at the stake, I'll light the fire."

Fearing retaliation from the teamsters, Hal Durham had concealed himself in a thicket not far from the wagons. From there, he could see Mamie and Odessa coming.

"You're stark naked," Odessa snapped. "Where are you going?"

"I don't know," Mamie snapped. "Anywhere away from you."

The very last thing Durham wanted was to encounter either or both the women, so he slunk down as far as he could get. He wanted only to sneak back into camp and retrieve his clothing when he felt it was safe for him to do so. Suddenly, from the shadows of the trees, two Indians emerged. Each of them seized one of the women, and Durham heard the sodden thunk as the captives were silenced with blows to the head. As suddenly as the Indians had appeared, they were gone, taking Mamie and Odessa with them. Durham didn't move, knowing he was in for it. Indirectly, he was to blame for the women being abducted and didn't relish facing any of the outfit. Especially Faro Duval. He soon heard Faro and Collins coming.

"Not a sign of them," Collins said, "and they couldn't have gone much farther. We'd be able to see them crossing that clearing up ahead."

"Yes," said Faro, "and that's bad news. With our weapons, these bands of Utes know we have them outgunned, and this is just the kind of opportunity they'd be looking for."

"Moonset is less than an hour away," Collins said, "and with most of this terrain in shadow, we don't stand a chance of finding any tracks tonight."

"We don't dare search for them in the dark," said Faro. "It's a good way to get ourselves ambushed. We'll have to wait for first light."

"We are going after them, then," Collins said, his relief obvious.

"Yes," said Faro. "Whatever else they are, they're white women. They deserve better than torture and death at the hands of hostile Utes."

"What are we going to do about Durham? This is basically his fault, you know."

"I know," Faro said, with a sigh. "If we can't rescue Mamie and Odessa, we may need him on the box of that fifth wagon. Otherwise, I'd say we draw lots for the pleasure of gut-shootin' him."

Durham listened with some relief. Some of the teamsters—doubtless one of them Faro Duval—would search for the women. It would be an ideal time for Durham to make his way back to the wagons. That he would be cursed and reviled, he had no doubt, but it didn't bother him in the slightest. He had been involved in far more shameful episodes, and he recounted some of them with pride as he awaited the dawn.

Mamie and Odessa McCutcheon awoke to find themselves belly-down across the bare backs of Indian ponies on lead ropes. Their hands and feet were securely bound.

"Damn you," Odessa shouted, "where are you taking us?"

Response was immediate. One of the mounted Indians dropped back and slugged her into unconsciousness with a club. Mamie had been about to add her shouts to Odessa's, but thought better of it as she beheld the painful results. Already, her head thumped like the beating of a drum. With some regret, she recalled her latest experience with Durham, and most of all, the things she had told Faro Duval regarding Odessa. Now she stood just as guilty as Odessa, having been caught wallowing with the gambler, naked beneath one of the wagons. She and Odessa had fallen from grace before leaving Amarillo, and now, she reflected, they were no better than a pair of whores. She wondered if Duval would try to rescue them, or if he would leave them to a fate he doubtless believed they deserved.

"It'll be risky, Faro, trailin' Utes with just three men," Dallas Weaver said, as the first gray light of dawn crept into the eastern sky.

"No more risky than leavin' just three of you to defend the wagons," said Faro.

"Two," Dallas said. "We don't know where Durham is. Maybe the Utes got him, too."

"I doubt it," said Faro. "When I hit a streak of bad luck, it's *all* bad. I reckon he'll wait for me to ride out, and then he'll come slitherin' in."

"I'll bend a Winchester muzzle over his head," Dallas said.

"Resist the temptation until a better time," said Faro.

"If you're attacked, you'll need him for defense. Collins, Shanghai, and me could be so far outnumbered, we'll need the rest of you before we can even attempt a rescue."

"I hope not," Collins said. "It'll mean leaving the wagons unguarded."

"It's a choice we may be forced to make," said Faro. "Let's ride."

They rode in an ever-widening circle around the area where the wagons were, and the tracks—when they found them—were faint.

"Four horses," Shanghai said. "They come with intentions of grabbin' somebody."

"They don't aim to make it easy for us," said Faro. "When they can, they're keepin' to ground that's hard as granite. Best we can hope for is some woods, with overturned leaf mold."

"I suppose there's still a chance for an ambush," Collins said.

"There's always a chance for that," said Faro, "but it's less likely if there are a large band of Indians, and they're well dug in. We may be able to do no more than locate their camp, waiting until dark to attempt a rescue."

"But we may not *have* until dark," Shanghai said. "Unless they're taking captives for ransom, or to be sold as slaves, they may begin the torture sometime today."

"Perhaps, if all else fails, I can pay the ransom," said Collins.

"I doubt it," Faro replied. "They'd strip us clean as

a Christmas goose, and then I'd not be surprised if we ended up fighting for our lives."

"If their camp ain't a great distance, they're leadin' us there in a roundabout way," said Shanghai. "We've rode at least a dozen miles."

"If they're thinkin' ambush," Faro said, "now's the time to counter it. I'll continue east, followin' this trail. Shanghai, ride south a mile or two, and Collins, you ride north a mile or two. Then both of you swing back east, paralleling me."

"That's risky as hell," said Shanghai. "If they've doubled back, and one of us misses their trail, you're dead."

"It's a chance somebody has to take," Faro said. "I'm counting strong on you both."

The three separated, and Faro rode on alone, following the dim but legible trail. There was no sign of an ambush, and Faro grew more confident. The Utes knew the strength of the teamsters, and the lack of an ambush pointed toward a well-defended Indian camp. It was still early and there was no wind. Somewhere ahead, a dog barked, and Faro reined up. His outriding companions had heard the dog, and they soon rode back to join him.

"You were obviously right," said Collins. "Their numbers are great, and they're telling us they're not afraid of us."

"That means we'll have to outmaneuver them," Faro said. "There's no wind, but if it rises, it'll come out of the west or northwest, so we'd better leave the horses here and go the rest of the way on foot."

*   *   *

The Indians led their horses with their captives into a canyon that widened enough to accommodate a stream that tumbled down a wall of rock at the blind end. The camp was strung out along the canyon walls, making attack difficult, except from the rims. There were no lodges, and women cooked over open fires. The Indians reined up, and all activity ceased as the inhabitants—men and women alike—gathered around to view the captives. Mamie and Odessa were shoved off the horses, landing on their backsides on the ground. Some of the squaws pointed to the naked Mamie, shouting and laughing. Others took hold of Odessa, stripping her, flinging the rags of her clothing into a fire.

"Damn you," Odessa bawled. "Damn all of you."

The squaws wasted no time. From slender trees that lined the stream, they broke off limbs for use as switches. They then surrounded the hapless captives and began switching them unmercifully. Only when their bodies were crisscrossed with bloody streaks, and when they had cried until they could cry no more, did the punishment cease. They both lay belly-down, heaving and whimpering with pain. The Indians then seemed to lose interest, for there was the smell of roasting meat. Dogs whined for a morsel, but were kicked out of the way. One of the braves shouted something, and two of his companions slid down from the rim. Obviously, they believed their camp secure enough for them to take the time from their sentry duty to eat.

"Two of the varmints on the rim," said Shanghai, "but there may be more."

"Not likely during the day," Faro said. "My God, there must be sixty or seventy of them, including the squaws."

Only when they moved closer were they able to see the inert bodies of Mamie and Odessa McCutcheon.

"They look dead," Collins said.

"No," said Faro. "They've been switched until they're afraid to move. That means the Utes aim to torture and eventually kill them."

"My God," Shanghai said, "we can't fight them, not even with Winchesters. There's too many. Some of 'em would get us, sure as hell."

"Even if we rode back for the rest of our outfit," said Faro, "we wouldn't have a prayer against so many of them. Besides, we don't have that much time. With torture on their minds, they'll get on with it. Probably after they eat. Whatever's to be done, we'll have to do it ourselves, and quickly. Collins, did you put some of those capped and fused sticks of dynamite in your saddlebag?"

"Yes," said Collins. "A dozen sticks."

"Then let's make tracks back to our horses," Faro said. "We're about to even up the odds a mite."

Chapter 6

In a single motion, Tarno Spangler and Dallas Weaver drew the Colts in response to a noise in the underbrush. Then Hal Durham appeared, wearing only his ruined socks.

"Uh-uh," Durham said. "You can't shoot me. You may need my help fighting Utes."

"Shootin' you would be too quick," said Tarno. "I got in mind carvin' off a choice part of your carcass. It'll play hell with your love life, but won't hinder you from shootin' Indians. Get him, Dallas."

As though it had been rehearsed, Dallas tackled Durham, bringing the gambler down on his bare backside in the brush. Tarno had his Bowie shoved under his waistband, and as he approached Durham, he drew the formidable weapon.

"No," Durham screamed, "no."

Dallas sat on Durham's legs, and while he couldn't rise, he had doubled his fists and was flailing about with his arms. Tarno seized him by the hair of his head and slammed him against the ground. He then knelt, one knee on each of the gambler's arms.

"Hell, you ain't man enough to deserve hair on your

chest," said Tarno. "I reckon I'll start there and work my way down."

Durham began trembling when he felt the blade of the Bowie against his bare skin. It was razor-sharp, and it glided down the gambler's chest, shaving clean. The deadly blade had reached Durham's belly, when Dallas spoke.

"Tarno, this is a thing that's almighty in need of bein' done, but remember last time you done this? Faro and Shanghai wasn't there, and they give you hell because they missed it. If they miss it again, your hide won't hold shucks."

"Damn it," Tarno said regretfully, "you're right. I reckon I'll have to put it off until they get back. Besides, this is somethin' Mamie and Odessa ought to see."

Striving mightily to contain their laughter, they turned the gambler loose. Unmindful of briars and thorns, Durham scrambled away on hands and knees until he could stagger to his feet and run.

"That'll give the varmint somethin' to think about," Dallas said. "Do you reckon you could go through with that, for real?"

"I got some Comanche blood in me," said Tarno. "What do you think?"

"I think I'll keep my britches on when you're around," Dallas said.

Faro said nothing until they reached the horses, and when he spoke, it was to Shanghai Taylor.

"Shanghai, I'm goin' to lure that bunch of Indians down-canyon after me. It'll be up to you and Collins to rescue Mamie and Odessa. Tie a couple of lariats together and hoist them up over the rim."

"A splendid plan," said Collins, "unless the Indians don't go after you."

"In that case," Faro said, "you'll have to back off, leaving Mamie and Odessa to face whatever the Utes have in mind. But I'm counting on the confidence of the Utes in their superior numbers. I'll ride downcanyon, barely within range, and cut loose with my Winchester. One of you—whoever remains on the rim, with the horses—will take six of these sticks of dynamite. If all the braves don't come after me, or if they return too soon, use the dynamite. I'll let them get close enough, and throw some of it myself. Collins, I want you to go down the ropes into the canyon. In the free end of the lariat, make a loop that will go under the arms of the women. Shanghai, using the horses, will lift them over the rim."

"Rope against their bare skin will be painful," said Collins.

"Not near as painful as bein' tortured to death by Utes," Faro said. "Be damn careful when you go into that canyon. I can lure the braves away, but I can't help you with the squaws. Most of them carry a skinning knife, sufficient to gut you or slit your throat. I'm countin' on you, Shanghai, for some help from the rim. Some of those braves may wise up to what we're doin', and turn back. I'm countin' on you to discourage them with your Winchester."

"You got it," Shanghai said. "Come on, Collins."

Leading his horse until he was almost out of Winchester range, Faro headed down the canyon rim.

While Shanghai and Collins must remain far enough back from the rim so as not to be seen, Faro could see them from his lower elevation, far down the canyon. With a leather thong he bound the oilskin-wrapped bundle of dynamite to his saddle horn, and from an oil-skin pouch he removed half a dozen matches. These he clenched in his teeth for the time of need. It was still early enough until there was no wind, and Faro looped the reins about a sapling so the horse wouldn't spook. On the rim, Shanghai spoke.

"We may not have much time, Collins. Soon as them braves light out down-canyon, get over that rim as quick as you can. This end of the rope will be looped around my saddle horn, so I'll be free for some Winchester work from up here. Get ready. Faro will cut loose *pronto*."

Shanghai had barely spoken the words when Faro cut loose with the Winchester. The first three shots dropped two Indians and had the desired effect. The rest of the braves ran for their horses, and galloping them close to the canyon walls, went after Faro. Collins was down the doubled rope in an instant, just in time to face a screeching squaw with a knife in her hand. Collins caught the upraised arm and flung her head-first into the stone wall of the canyon.

"Levi," Odessa cried, "thank God."

She seemed about to throw her arms around him, but Collins wouldn't have it.

"Raise your arms, damn it," Collins snapped.

She did, and Collins slipped the noose over her head and under her arms. Shanghai was ready, and she gasped as the rope went taut and she was lifted off the ground. Collins had to fend off two more knife-wielding squaws before Odessa was safely to the rim. The rope was dropped a second time, and without a word, Mamie raised her arms. Quickly, Collins dropped the loop into position, and Mamie was pulled to safety.

"Damn," Faro said, as the charging Utes kept close to the canyon wall from which he was firing. After dropping the first two, he hadn't accounted for any of the others, for he lacked a target. Quickly, he withdrew a stick of dynamite, thumbed a match into flame, and lighted the fuse. While he was unable to throw the dynamite among them, he did the next best thing. He threw it as far as he could, dropping it on the canyon rim. The explosion had the desired effect, loosing massive amounts of rock and dirt. There were the shouts of Indians and the scream of horses, and before the echo of the first blast had died away, Faro threw a second stick of dynamite. The Indians who had survived turned their horses and galloped up-canyon, shouting as they saw Levi Collins being lifted from the canyon's floor. Barely missing him, arrows thunked into the canyon wall. While Faro was well out of range, Shanghai Taylor had perfect targets. He shot three Indians off their horses, forcing the others to back off.

"That's enough, Shanghai," said Faro under his breath. "Ride, damn it, ride."

Seizing Odessa, Collins all but threw her astraddle his horse.

"Damn it," Odessa snapped, "must you be so rough? I've had enough of that."

"Shut up," said Collins in a dangerously calm voice.

Mamie said nothing as Shanghai Taylor helped her astraddle his horse. He mounted and led out, Collins following.

"I suppose it would have been expecting too much for you to have brought us some blankets," Odessa said. "Or do you not care if everybody sees us jaybird naked?"

"At this point," said Collins shortly, "I don't care a damn if everybody in California, New Mexico, and all points in between see you just as you are right now. I doubt that Durham will be shocked, for he's seen it all before."

Nothing more was said, and despite possible pursuit, they were forced to stop and rest the lathered horses. It was there that Faro joined them.

"You done it just right, *amigo,*" Shanghai said.

"You and Collins handled your part of it pretty slick," said Faro. "The three of us might have been killed, and we didn't get a scratch."

"I don't suppose it matters to you that Odessa and me are bloodied and hurting," Mamie said.

"Not really," said Faro. "You could have been bloodied and dead if we hadn't risk our necks comin' after you."

Faro studied them critically. They were a mess, and, knowing it, had the grace to blush. Faro laughed.

"Go ahead and get your eyes full," Mamie said. "When we get back to camp, perhaps we'll climb up on a wagon box, so the others can have a good look."

"Not a bad idea," said Shanghai. "Why limit yourselves to a tin-horn gambler? Any one of us is a better man than Durham. Just let us know when to meet you under the wagon."

While the McCutcheons deserved it, they didn't like it. Faro and Collins roared with laughter. Quickly, Faro became serious.

"We'd better ride. We hurt those Indians, but there's still more of them than of us. If they catch up to us, I doubt we can escape them."

With two of the horses carrying double, it was an obvious truth. But they reached the wagons without difficulty. When Mamie and Odessa were lifted off the horses, Dallas Weaver and Tarno Spangler looked on with interest.

"Go ahead and look," said Odessa, raising her hands above her head. "The others have had their chance, and we wouldn't want the rest of you to be left out."

"We're obliged, ma'am," Tarno said, with as straight a face as he could manage.

"*Sí,*" Dallas agreed.

Solemnly the pair circled the women, studying them from various angles. It all became so ridiculous, Mamie laughed.

"I reckon the two of you had better spend some time at the creek," Faro said, "but not a step farther."

"Perhaps you'd better send someone to watch us, so we don't stray," said Odessa.

"After last night," Faro said, "I reckon I had. Tarno, you and Dallas go with them to the creek and see that they don't do anything foolish."

"*Sí,*" said Tarno. "Even if they do somethin' foolish, we'll see that the Indians don't get 'em."

"By the way," Faro said, "did Durham ever show?"

"For a few minutes," said Dallas. "Tarno had his Bowie and was about to whittle off a part of the gambler's carcass he didn't figure he could do without. Last time we seen him, he was headed into the brush."

"If the Indians get him, it's his funeral," Shanghai said. "I ain't riskin' my hide again today, especially for him."

"I feel the same way," said Collins.

But Durham had found his clothing and dressed himself. He appeared just as the McCutcheons returned, naked, from the creek. He watched with interest, his face revealing nothing.

"We've lost half a day," Faro said. "We move out in half an hour. Odessa, are you able to return to the wagon?"

"Yes," said Odessa sourly, "and I'm going just like I am, without a stitch."

"I couldn't care less," Faro said, "but there may be splinters on that wagon box."

They all laughed—even Mamie—and when Odessa mounted the wagon box, she was dressed. Again the wagons rolled west, while Faro scouted ahead.

The twin explosions along the back trail were heard by Perro Cara and his outfit.

"Dynamite," Slade observed.

"Yeah," said Kritzer, "but why? Could this gold strike be somewhere *behind* us?"

"I don't think so," Slade said. "That second blast sounded like an echo of the first, so it couldn't have anything to do with the gold strike."

"Here comes Dog Face," said Hindes. "Explain it to him."

"You heard them explosions," Dog Face said. "You got any answers?"

"No," said Slade, "but I doubt it has anything to do with the gold strike."

"Then you don't think the claim's somewhere behind us."

"No," Slade said. "Word I had was them wagons is travelin' five hundred miles, back into these mountains, and they ain't gone near that far. You're friendly with this bunch of Indians. Why don't you send a couple of them along the back trail to read sign?"

"I already have," said Dog Face. "I just wanted your thinkin'."

"By God, he don't trust us," Hindes said when the renegade leader had gone.

"No," said Peeler. "He just tried to trick you into sayin' somethin' he could use agin us. We better watch for a chance, and when it comes, run for it."

"Hell, he don't trust Sangre and Hueso," Slade said. "Why should he trust us? Until them wagons reach the gold strike, we're safer here than anywhere else."

"I'm with Slade," said Withers. "If we break with this outfit now, we'll have all them after us, along with God knows how many other Utes, as well as them *hombres* with the wagons."

"I'll stay for the time bein'," Hindes said, "but the first time that one-eyed varmint looks slant-ways at me, with his gun in his hand, I'm gone."

"Your choice," said Slade. "If you're smart, you'll stick until we can all make a run for it together."

They waited, bickering among themselves, until the Indians sent to investigate the explosions returned. Again Dog Face approached, and when he spoke, he seemed a bit more genial.

"You was right, Slade. The explosions had nothin' to do with the claim. Them Utes grabbed a couple of captives, and the teamsters went after 'em. Found their camp in a canyon, and dynamited a wall. Pretty slick."

"Just don't forget they got dynamite," said Slade. "A man that knows how to use the stuff can lick an army."

"I'm considerin' that," Dog Face said. "Before we clash with them, we may have to take the dynamite away from them."

"That I'll have to see," said Slade.

"Oh, you will," Dog Face said. "You'll be right in the midst of it."

He turned away, leaving Slade wondering what he meant. Hindes looked at Slade with humor in his eyes, but had the good sense not to speak.

"We'll be crossing four streams," said Faro, when he returned to the wagons. "Could all be tributaries from the same river."

"They are," Collins said. "They flow into the San Juan. Once we cross the fourth, we will have traveled about one-third of our journey. Two-thirds of the way in, we'll cross the Colorado."

"One other thing," said Faro. "I found tracks of two unshod horses headed northeast. Could be scouts from that bunch ahead of us, checking out the explosions."

"That's bad news," Dallas Weaver said. "If they're

bein' led by a white renegade, he'll know about dynamite, and there goes our edge."

"Maybe not," said Faro. "They don't know how much we have, or how handy we are in the use of it. Any fool can blow up a canyon wall. I have other plans."

"They may attack us in force, planning to take the wagons and the dynamite from us," Collins said. "That would kill any plans you have for the dynamite."

"I doubt the Utes have any interest in anything but the wagons and their contents," Faro said, "and for that reason—if we're dealing with a white renegade—I expect him to hold them off as long as he can. With their larger numbers, we can't afford to wait for them to come after us. We'll have to take the fight to them."

"You have the experience," said Collins, "so I'm not even going to ask how and when you intend to do that."

"Well, I am," Durham said. "The Utes walked off with Mamie and Odessa right under Duval's nose, so I don't have all that much confidence in his judgment."

"Durham," said Faro, "it was you who created the necessary diversion for that sorry situation last night. If you so much as mention it again, I'll beat your ears down to the tops of your boots. As for my judgment, you're stuck with it as long as you're part of this outfit. Makin' it as plain as I know how, you're welcome to get the hell out of here, anytime you feel so inclined."

Durham wasn't in the least disturbed, nor did he appear angry. He laughed, and then he spoke.

"I'll endure your bad judgment for a while, Duval, and when I go, it'll be my choice, not yours."

He then mounted his horse and rode back beyond the fifth wagon.

"Damn him," said Mamie, drawing her Colt, "I'll fix him."

"I don't think so," Shanghai said, seizing the weapon. "You fixed him last night."

"Back to your wagons," said Faro. "We're movin' out."

Mamie mounted her horse and Shanghai handed her the Colt. She colored, refusing to look him in the eye. Faro had again taken the reins, and Levi Collins rode ahead, as the five wagons again rumbled westward.

The Sevier River, Southwestern Utah.
August 20, 1870.

The trio of besieged miners awaiting the return of Levi Collins were forced to take stock of their precarious situation.

"Since we agreed to stay here and watch over the claim, things have changed," Isaac Puckett pointed out. "We wasn't plannin' on fightin' the Utes every blessed day and usin' up all our ammunition, and we wasn't expectin' it to take Levi so long."

"I agree," said Felix Blackburn. "These are things that Levi and none of us expected, so none of us are at fault, except for countin' too strong on things we couldn't be sure of. We don't know, for starters, if Levi ever made it to Santa Fe alive, or if he did, whether he was able to find teamsters to freight our stuff in."

"Yeah," Josh Snyder agreed, "and if he did, they may be fightin' Utes all the way. We can't set here until we're down to our last shells. We'll have to run for it."

"I think you're right," said Puckett. "Felix?"

"Much as I hate to give it up," Blackburn said, "I reckon we'd better go while we've still got some ammunition. We won't have to worry about the Utes takin' the claim, and if we do meet Levi, we'll have ammunition to fight our way back in. If Levi didn't make it, then we still got a small chance of gettin' out of here alive."

"What about the mules?" Snyder asked.

"We'll have to leave them," said Blackburn. "In either case, we won't need them. If we meet Levi with wagons, we'll be dependin' on them. If we don't, and I get out of here with my hair, I won't be comin' back, gold or no gold."

"Neither will I," his companions said in a single voice.

"So far, the Utes ain't bothered us at night," Blackburn said, "and that leads me to believe they ain't watchin' us that close. Soon as it's dark, we'll make our break, walkin' the horses as far as we can."

"I think we'd be better off travelin' at night and hidin' out durin' the day," said Josh Snyder.

"I don't agree with that," Blackburn replied. "This is the damndest canyon country I've ever seen. In the dark, you could ride off a rim and fall a hundred feet."

"True enough," said Puckett, "but can we afford to devote the nights to hidin' out? If we slip away tonight and get safely away, an hour after first light, them Utes will know we ain't here. Then they'll be after us like hell wouldn't have it."

"Then we'd better travel all night, takin' it easy on our horses," Snyder said. "Then when it's light enough to see, we ride as hard and fast as we can."

"That's how I see it," said Puckett, "and we'd better keep on doin' it until we get out of reach of these Utes, or until we meet Levi."

"I'm outvoted," Blackburn said. "Anyway, I reckon I wasn't considerin' the chance the Utes would come after us. There'll be a full moon for the next several nights, if the clouds will hold off. Today, let's hide our tools as best we can. We can't depend on our horses carryin' anything but us and the little grub that's left."

"If we all look busy, the varmints will suspect somethin'," said Snyder.

"Then we can't all look busy," Blackburn said. "You and Puckett, stayin' among rocks along this river, look for places to cache our tools. I'll fire just enough so's they can't get within sight of you to see what you're doin'."

"With only one of us shootin', they'll know somethin's up," said Puckett.

"Maybe," Blackburn said, "but it's a chance we'll have to take. It might just work in our favor, if they reckon we're low on ammunition. That would account for only one of us shootin' at them."

As soon as Puckett and Snyder made a run for the nearby river, arrows began zipping all around them. The barrage ceased when Blackburn fired rapidly into the brush from where the arrows had come. The banks of the Sevier were a jumble of stones that might have been scattered like pebbles by the hand of the Almighty. In places, it was a dozen feet down to the swiftly running water. Once Puckett and Snyder were over the edge, they could scarcely be seen, unless the observer was standing on the bank. Eventually the Utes would cross the river at some point and perhaps work their way near to the farthest bank, but by then, Puckett and Snyder should have accomplished their mission. Blackburn jacked more shells into his Winchester and prepared for the next barrage of Ute arrows.

"Collins," said Faro, "there's good water and graze here. I think it's time we laid over a day and had a serious look at that bunch somewhere ahead of us. We don't dare wait long enough for them to make the first move."

"I like the way you think, Duval," Collins replied. "If they strike first, with their far greater number, then we're goners."

"Then we'll ride at first light," said Faro, "and since we don't know where they are, or how well they're dug in, we may not be able to get close until after dark. That means we may be late returning. Dallas, while I'm gone, you're in charge. It would be a good time for that bunch of Utes somewhere on our back trail to slip in, with mischief on their minds. If you catch more than two under the same wagon at the same time, then you have my permission to punish them in any way you see fit."

The McCutcheons didn't have the courage to look him in the eye, but Hal Durham laughed.

"I'll help," Tarno Spangler said.

He had his Bowie in his right hand, running his left thumb along the razor-sharp blade. He grinned at Durham, and the gambler's laugh dribbled away and died.

The three miners waited until moonrise before attempting to escape. Leading their saddled horses, they made their way south, along the rocky banks of the Sevier. When they were well away from their former camp, they veered to the southeast, the shortest route by which they could return to Santa Fe. The way they expected Levi Collins and the wagons to come. If Levi was still alive, and there *were* any wagons. They stopped to rest as the first gray light of dawn crept into the eastern sky.

"God, my feet are killin' me," Josh Snyder said.

"So are mine," said Isaac Puckett. "I feel like I've come at least fifty miles."

"More like twenty," Felix Blackburn said, "but in a few minutes, it'll be light enough for us to mount up and ride. But we're still not far enough away that the Utes can't ride us down, if they're quick to learn we're gone."

"I can't believe we've come this far," Snyder said.

"Don't crow too loud," said Puckett. "Just when you begin praisin' lady luck, that's when the old gal kicks you off a canyon wall to the rocks below."

"Mount up," Blackburn said. "Even in this rough country, we can cover seventy miles before dark, as long as we rest the horses."

They rode on, thankful as the miles fell behind

them. After an hour at a slow gallop, they reined up to rest the horses.

"Oh, damn the luck," said Blackburn, his eyes on their back trail.

Snyder and Puckett followed his gaze and their hearts sank. On a ridge three hundred yards behind them were six mounted Indians.

"Fortune was with us as we rode to that other Ute camp," Levi Collins said. "What do you expect at this one?"

"A lot tighter security, for one thing," said Faro. "These Utes, likely throwing in with a white renegade, may be on the outs with the rest of the Utes. That means they'll keep a close watch, especially at night. This bunch, with a white man leading them, may not be dependent on bow and arrows. They could be armed with Winchesters, making it extremely dangerous for other Utes to attack them."

"So other Utes, armed with bow and arrows, would have to get in very close before they would have a chance," Collins said.

"Yes," said Faro, "and that generally means the defenders will have established a camp that's all but impossible to approach in daylight. Indians—when there are large numbers of them—tend to become overconfident, like those who captured Mamie and Odessa. But if we're dealing with a white renegade, after dark, he may ring the camp with enough men to hold off an army."

"How are we to find their camp without them first seeing us?" Collins asked.

"We'll follow their trail for a while," said Faro. "Once we're sure of the direction they are taking, we'll swing wide and approach them from a flank. There's no wind this early, but there should be later today. Tonight, for sure. We can't afford to ride past them, for that would have them downwind from us. We may have to travel a great distance afoot, so our horses don't nicker and give us away."

"I can understand the need for that," Collins said, "but if we're discovered . . ."

"Then we'll wish we'd gambled and taken the horses with us," said Faro.

Soon they reached the place where the Utes had obviously captured Slade and his men. They reined up, studying the tracks, and then warily followed them west.

Chapter 7

The day of rest afforded the teamsters while Faro and Collins scouted ahead wasn't all that restful. Despite their professed hatred of Hal Durham, Mamie and Odessa McCutcheon spent most of their time with the gambler, and he seemed to have charmed them all over again. Dallas Weaver kept an uneasy eye on them, and he wasn't surprised when, at noon, Odessa approached.

"Mamie and me aim to take a dip in the creek. That is, if you got no objection."

"None," Dallas said, "but let this be a warning. If you get yourselves carried off to an Indian camp again, I'm goin' to recommend you be left there."

"Durham's goin' with us," Odessa said.

"Then the same warning applies to him," said Dallas. "Tell him I said so."

She stalked off without a word, and the three of them headed down the creek where there was tree cover along the banks.

"If that don't rip the rag off the bush," Tarno Spangler said. "After all the varmint's done to 'em, they trot him along to watch, while they get naked and splash in the creek."

"I personally think Durham's a slick-dealing, snake-bellied, low-down bastard," said Dallas, "but I don't think he's done a thing to that pair of brass-plated females he wasn't invited to do. I can't speak for Faro, but far as I'm concerned, he can do anything to them he's of a mind to, includin' slittin' their throats."

"Amen," Shanghai Taylor said. "There's times when Faro's so damn forgivin' and tolerant, I believe he missed his callin'. He should of been a parson, in a boiled shirt, black britches, and claw-hammer coat."

But the troublesome trio returned unharmed. Mamie and Odessa didn't seem the least ashamed of their conduct, while Durham's smug expression rubbed the teamsters the wrong way.

"I know what Faro said," Tarno Spangler growled, "but come dark, we ought to force the three of 'em under the same wagon."

"Come dark, I don't care a damn what happens to them," said Dallas. "If Faro and Collins haven't returned, you, Shanghai, and me will have our work cut out for us. We'll have to stand watch. We can't count on Durham for but one thing, and that's no-account to anybody but the McCutcheons."

"I wonder if that's all of 'em?" Josh Snyder said, as he eyed the mounted Indians.

"My God, that's enough," said Isaac Puckett. "They're two to our one."

"This is their country, so we can't outride them," Felix Blackburn said. "They'll flank us and ride us down. If we can stay ahead of them until we reach cover, I'll fall back and maybe get a couple of them from ambush."

"But the others will surround you," said Snyder.

"I'm counting on that," Blackburn said. "With bow and arrows, they have to work in close. You and Isaac stay out of sight until they start movin' in. Then you cut loose with your Winchesters. It's our only chance."

"We can see six of them," said Puckett. "That don't mean there ain't more."

"A chance we have to take," Blackburn replied. "They're waitin' for us to make our move. Let's ride."

The three kicked their horses into a fast gallop, and with a chorus of whoops, the Utes took up the chase. The pursued galloped through a small stand of trees, and while temporarily hidden, Blackburn took his Winchester and rolled out of the saddle. Puckett caught the reins of his horse without the animal breaking stride. Blackburn dropped down behind a stone upthrust and readied his Winchester. When the hard-driving Utes appeared, he dropped the first two. The remaining four split up, two riding to his right, and two riding to his left. They would attempt to flank him, knowing that Blackburn had no cover except from a frontal attack. Almost immediately, there was the bark of a distant rifle, as Blackburn's companions bought in. Following a second shot, there was silence. The next sound Blackburn heard was the thump of horse's hooves, as his companions returned.

"We picked off two more of 'em," Puckett said, "and it looks like there was only six of 'em. The other two lit a shuck back the way they come."

"Worked like a charm," said Snyder.

"This time," Blackburn replied. "They miscalculated, expecting us to run for it. If we had, they'd have flanked us, taken cover, and rode us down. While we've freed ourselves of this bunch, God knows how many more are between here and Santa Fe."

"I still ain't sure we're free of this bunch," said Puckett, "way they hounded us back at the claim. Now, after we gunned down four of 'em, the others may be mad enough to foller us to Santa Fe."

"That's why we're goin' to ride as fast and as far as we can, while it's light," Blackburn said. "Tonight, even if we must travel afoot, we'll keep moving. We can't count on meetin' Levi, with wagon loads of grub and ammunition. We may have to go the distance with the little that we have."

"I have the feeling we've followed this trail about as far as we can afford to," Faro said, reining up his horse.

"I was beginning to get nervous, myself," said Collins, reining up beside him.

"I think we'll ride north a couple of miles," Faro said, "and then west from there. We should be able to see or hear some sign of the camp. With so many men and horses, there should be something to warn us."

They rode north and then west, walking their horses. Wind had risen, and a sometimes breeze from the west brought the sign Faro had been seeking.

"Smoke," said Collins.

"This is where we leave the horses," Faro said. "This bein' canyon country, I look for 'em to be pretty well dug in. One thing we can turn to our advantage, if they're in some canyon. There's a chance we can work our way in close enough to take their measure from the canyon rim, without being seen."

"If not today, then certainly tonight," said Collins.

"Like I said," Faro replied, "these renegade-led Utes are likely to be more cautious at night. There'll be more braves on watch, and while we'll have the darkness for cover, there may be twice as many sentries."

"I yield to your experience," said Collins. "If we're discovered—even if we escape—we'll have lost our advantage."

"Exactly," Faro said. "We're here for two purposes. First, we want to know just how many outlaws and Utes are in this bunch. Second, we must know the lay of the land, so we can plan our attack."

"I am learning there are certain advantages on the lawless frontier," said Collins. "We are preparing to attack these Utes, led by men we perceive as outlaws, while they've done nothing to us. While I believe our suspicions are justified, in a civilized society, we would be crucified."

"I can agree with most of what you've said," Faro replied, "but there's an old saying that all is fair in love or war. There has never been a society so civilized that it didn't at one time or another engage in war, for prestige or profit. This, my friend, is war, just as surely as was the recent conflict between North and South. I can't prove these men we're stalking are thieves and killers, but common sense tells me that if we don't go after them, they'll be comin' after us. I'm countin' on the same gut feelin' that kept me alive through four long years of shoot-or-be-shot."

"You could write a book, Duval," said Collins. "You are an educated man."

"Self-educated," Faro said. "I was born into a share-cropper family, and all we had to read was the Bible and an almanac. The Bible was considerably better readin'. I learned to write by copying lines of scripture from it."

Faro and Collins had continued on foot for more than a mile before the trees thinned out, giving way to open land laced with arroyos of varying magnitudes.

"There," Faro said softly, pointing.

Momentarily the wind had died, and a tendril of gray smoke was barely visible against the blue of the sky.

"Distances out here are deceiving," said Collins. "They may be very close."

"Generally, where there's this many canyons, at least one of them will have water," Faro said. "Let's look for water. If we can find it, and it's fallin' into a canyon, it may be the one we're lookin' for."

Eventually they found a fast-running stream, and they could hear it—like distant wind—as it rushed over a stone abutment and fell into the canyon below.

"No promises," said Faro softly, "but this may be it. The falling of the water will be helpful in coverin' our approach, and it's likely the camp will be near the head of the canyon."

There was a considerable pool of water at the foot of the fall, so the camp itself was far enough down-canyon to afford a good view. Except for a time-worn gap through which the water flowed over the rim, there was no access to the canyon below. Finding hand- and toeholds in the stone parapet, Faro and Collins climbed high enough to see over the edge and into the canyon. From their position they could see half a dozen Indians strung out along the east and west rims. Their grips in the stone were precarious, and it was soon necessary for Faro and Collins to climb down.

"Obvious enough why they don't post a sentry up here," Collins panted, once they were safely down. "Men would have to go over this thing on a rope, one at a time, and I don't see a blasted thing to which to anchor the rope."

"We won't be goin' into this canyon on a rope," Faro said. "Not from any position. All together, there must be near a hundred men down there. That bunch whose tracks we were following couldn't have been more than a quarter of the total. There wasn't an Indian in the lot armed with bow and arrows. Meetin' this outfit in anything less than an ambush would be the finish of us. Of the seven white men, did you notice anything unusual?"

"Four of them were keeping pretty much to themselves," Collins said. "I presume they are the men who were trailing us, who were captured by the renegades."

"I don't think we can refer to them as captured," said Faro, "because they all still had their weapons. For whatever reason, they've been accepted into the gang."

"They must have convinced these renegades they can be helpful," Collins said.

"That could account for them still being alive," said

Faro. "If one of them took a hunk of that gold ore from your coat pocket, it's likely in the hands of the renegades now."

"I'm afraid you're right," Collins agreed. "There's too much logic to be denied. Their presence here most surely is because of us. That piece of ore assures them there's gold, but they don't know where it is."

"That's the straight of it," said Faro. "Nothing else makes sense."

"Now that we've learned this much," Collins said, "what are we going to do?"

"I don't believe we're in any immediate danger from them," said Faro, "because we're still far from the claim."

"An excellent point," Collins said, "provided *they* know that. But how are they to be aware of it?"

"I seem to recall there being questions to our destination before we left Santa Fe," said Faro. "Are you sure one of us didn't refer to this as a five-hundred-mile journey?"

"Now that you mention it," Collins replied, "I can't say that I didn't speak of the distance, myself. It was a way to avoid talk of the claim."

"It's possible, then, that we can travel another three hundred miles before we have to face up to this bunch of renegades. Trouble is, if we wait too long, they'll come after us, and we'll be fighting them at a time and place of their choosing," Faro said. "And we can't afford that."

"So we must plan an attack soon," said Collins.

"Yes," Faro said, "and I think that's the last thing they'll be expecting. They've taken our measure and know we're few in number. Should any of this bunch do any scouting, they'll find our tracks and know we've been watching them. If we're to attack them, we must make our move while we still have the element of surprise on our side. Let's get back to the horses."

"You'll be including the others in this plan, then," said Collins.

Shanghai, Tarno, and Dallas," Faro said. "I don't look for much help from anybody else. Do you?"

Collins sighed. "No, I suppose not."

In the absence of Faro and Collins, things were not going well in the wagon camp. While Shanghai, Tarno, and Dallas had kept to themselves, they couldn't avoid hearing the sometimes violent arguments involving the McCutcheons and the ne'er-do-well gambler.

"Should I go on to California," Durham said, "I refuse to take more than one of you with me. One woman, one man."

"You ain't observed that rule up to now," said Odessa in an ugly tone.

"A man can mend his ways," Durham said smugly.

"A man can," said Odessa. "That eliminates you."

"I won't allow you to anger me," Durham said. "I'm only takin' one of you with me."

"Which one?" Odessa demanded.

"I haven't made up my mind," said Durham. "Let's just say the one of you proving herself the most deserving. Impress me."

"I gave you the thousand dollars for the mules and wagon," Odessa said.

"You did, damn it," Mamie shouted, "and half that money was mine."

"Now, ladies," said Durham soothingly, "haven't I given unselfishly of myself to each of you? How far must a man go to earn a meager thousand dollars?"

"You sneaking bastard," Odessa bawled, "you got things all turned around. It's you that should be payin' *us,* not us payin' *you.*"

"Oh, come now," said Durham, tilting his hat back on his head, "I only took what was offered. I never presumed either of you the kind to expect money for a gift."

"By God," Shanghai Taylor said, "he beats all. Whatever he's got, if I could bottle an' sell it, I'd never have to whack another mule's behind, as long as I live."

"Yeeehaaa," Tarno shouted, "they're fightin' again."

Seizing one another, Mamie and Odessa had fallen to the ground. Odessa grabbed a fistful of Mamie's shirt, ripping off all the buttons. Not to be outdone, Mamie wrought similar destruction with Odessa's shirtfront. They cast aside the shirts, leaving each of them bare to the waist.

Shanghai laughed. "They'll be jaybird naked again 'fore this is over. You ain't gonna stop it, are you, Dallas?"

"Not even if they kill each other," Dallas said.

From somewhere within his coat, Durham produced a cigar and proceeded to light it. He then watched with considerable satisfaction as the McCutcheons fought over him.

"Five dollars says Mamie loses her Levi's first," Shanghai said.

"No bet," said Tarno. "That Odessa's a she-wolf. Look at them claw marks there on Mamie's back."

It was as though Odessa had heard the potential wager, for she seized the waistband of Mamie's Levi's, ripping off the buttons. Mamie quickly retaliated in a similar manner, and the pair kicked themselves free of their Levi's.

"I got it figured out," Dallas said. "That pair of whores likes to wrassle naked before an audience. They're just usin' Durham for an excuse."

"You may be right," said Tarno. "Whatever they was in Texas, they sure missed their calling."

"Hey, Durham," Shanghai shouted, "when you get to California, you can always start a whorehouse. All you'll need is the house."

Durham made the mistake of laughing, and the two struggling women suddenly ceased fighting and clawing each other. Durham saw what was coming, but he didn't move fast enough. Mamie and Odessa sprang at him like wounded cougars, pounding him with their fists. The gambler doubled up as Mamie drove a knee into his groin, and before he could recover from that, Odessa performed a similar feat. Durham rolled over on his belly and refused to move even as the vengeful duo pounded his head, neck, and shoulders.

"So," Odessa snarled, "you think we belong in a whorehouse."

"No," came the muffled voice of the gambler, "you're not civilized enough for that. This is the last straw. I've changed my mind about going to California, and if I planned to, I'd not take either of you. You have all the finesse of a pair of dogs. Both of you can go to hell."

Odessa seized a heavy stone with the intention of crushing Durham's skull, but she dropped it when Mamie shoved her. Caked from head to toe with dirt, sweat and blood, the unpredictable pair started toward the creek. Durham lay where he was, unable or unwilling to get up.

"I swear," said Shanghai, "I've seen more naked female here in these mountains than I've seen in all my time in Saint Louis and Independence."

"You can likely take Durham's place with them two," Tarno said. "I reckon he's about used up."

"I've never been so woman-hungry I'd take another *hombre's* leavings," said Shanghai. "Especially not Durham's."

The trio from the claim on the Sevier River had just begun their second night in their bid for freedom. Again they walked, for the country was broken, laced with drop-offs that could mean the death of man and horse.

"I wish we knew which way them Indians went when they left that spring back yonder," Josh Snyder said.

"It was near dark when we got there," said Isaac Puckett. "They headed out north."

"Yeah," Felix Blackburn said, "but I know what Josh is thinking. They often do that to confuse the *hombres* they're after. We'll have to take it slow and careful. Far as we are from our claim on the Sevier, we got to consider the possibility that some of the varmints have managed to get ahead of us. They'd know they're ahead of us, because there wasn't any recent tracks."

"They've never attacked us at night," said Josh. "While we got to watch our step tonight, we got to be especially watchful at dawn."

"We must of come more than a hundred miles," Isaac said. "If we can hold out for another night and another day, we should be halfway to Santa Fe."

"From what I've heard of these Utes," said Felix, "in the days when they took white captives to be sold as slaves, they often raided Santa Fe. With our luck, they'll dog us to within sight of the town."

"We can't afford to give up on Levi," Josh said. "If he's comin' back at all, he's got to be on the way."

They went on, walking and leading their horses, often forced to take long detours to avoid dangerous drop-offs. An hour before dawn, they rested.

"I think it's time we rode half a dozen miles south," said Felix. "If there's an ambush somewhere ahead, we'd best ride around it, if we can."

"Yeah," Isaac said, "and once they discover what we've done, they'll be after us with intentions of riding us down."

"I'm counting on that," said Felix. "We'll keep an eye on our back trail, and at the first sign of pursuit, we'll lay an ambush of our own, like we done before."

They rode south until Blackburn judged they had ridden far enough. They then continued eastward, finding the terrain a little less broken.

"We should of done this sooner," Isaac said. "It ain't so rough, and we can make lots better time."

"Don't get too excited," said Felix. "Just when you think this country's levelin' out, it laughs in your face and confronts you with a deep canyon."

It might have been a prophecy, for when they topped a ridge and looked down, there was the canyon. While they might have led their horses down the canyon wall, the floor was wide—a quarter mile or more—and it was a litter of insurmountable hummocks of stone. Attempting to cross would be time-consuming, for at any point they might have to retrace their steps. The three stared at the yawning abyss, and Isaac Puckett spoke.

"My God, if the Utes showed up while we was fightin' our way across that, we'd just as well take our Colts an' shoot ourselves. They'd be within arrow range, and there's all kinds of cover along the rims."

"We may have to ride for miles to get across," Felix Blackburn said. "Those Indians may have been holdin' back until we reached this very place. All they'd have to do is come after us from the north and west, and then ride us down."

"I don't like your predictions," said Josh Snyder. "You spoke of this damn canyon, and it showed up."

Blackburn laughed, but it escalated into a startled yelp, for there was an ever-growing cloud of dust to the west.

"God Almighty," Puckett said, "here they come."

The trio kicked their horses into a fast gallop, racing eastward along the jagged rim of the massive canyon, seeking a place to cross. Behind them, the dust cloud separated as some of the pursuers swung away to the north, closing that avenue of escape. The desperate trio must continue punishing their lathered horses, or risk a slow, hazardous crossing of the formidable canyon. Blackburn slowed his heaving horse, looked back, and then spoke the inevitable words.

"If we kill our horses, they'll get us anyhow. Into the canyon."

The three of them were out of their saddles in an instant, and tired as the horses were, they fought the reins as they were led near the canyon rim. Blackburn got his horse over the edge first. They slid and fell two-thirds of the way down before the frightened horse regained its balance. Blackburn had struck his head on a stone, and when they got to the canyon floor, he lay there holding the reins. He arose just in time, for his companions and their mounts came tumbling and sliding down.

"Come on," said Blackburn, shaking his head. "We have to get as far into these rocks as we can."

Even as he spoke, the Utes were dismounting, shouting their excitement. To the horror of the three men below, they could see at least a dozen Indians, and they had no way of knowing there weren't more. Arrows whipped all around them until they were able to reach a huge stone hummock.

"Unlimber your Winchesters," Blackburn panted. "This is the best cover we'll have, and if we don't even the odds some, we're goners."

The Utes, believing their prey was intent only on escape, raced boldly along the rim, seeking targets. For just an instant, the desperate trio stepped from cover and fired. Three of the attackers died, and the rest retreated from the canyon rim, shouting angrily. Again within the safety of their cover, the three had no time to gloat, for some of the Utes had mounted and were galloping along the canyon rim.

"We didn't run into this canyon coming from Santa Fe," Snyder said. "That means it peters out somewhere, and these damn Indians know it."

"You can count on it," said Blackburn. "They aim to get on the other rim before we can get across. We'll be within range of their arrows from either side."

"Only if they get there before we do," Puckett growled. "Let's go."

But enough Utes had been left behind to counter just such a move. No sooner had they left cover than an arrow thunked into Puckett's left shoulder, just above his shoulder blade. With a groan, he sagged against his horse.

"Go on," Snyder shouted, "I'll lead your horse."

But an arrow grazed the animal's flank, and it reared. A second arrow ripped through the throat of the unfortunate beast, and it fell. It lay there kicking, its thrashing about becoming less and less as its life bled into the stony canyon floor. Puckett groaned, as much for the loss of the horse as from the arrow. He stumbled along, Snyder helping with a firm grip on the wounded man's gun belt.

"Come on," Blackburn shouted. "We're goin' to make it."

But they didn't. The half a dozen Utes who had ridden away had been able to cross the canyon, and now galloped along the opposite rim. They reined up, shouting and nocking arrows to their bow strings. But their joy was short-lived, for somewhere behind them came a thunder of gunfire. The six tumbled over the rim, dead before they reached the canyon floor.

"Thank God," Isaac Puckett shouted. "We're in the company of white men, and we're safe."

He was only half right.

By the time Faro and Collins returned to the wagons, Durham had disappeared, while the McCutcheons—having washed off mud and blood—had donned fresh clothing.

"Where's Durham and the McCutcheons?" Faro asked.

"I don't know," said Dallas, "and I don't give a damn."

"They've been at it again, then," Faro said.

"They have," said Dallas. "I'll spare you the sorry details."

"God bless you," Faro said.

"You're not going to include them in what we've learned?" Collins asked.

"I can't depend on them not to raise hell every time I turn my back," said Faro, "so the very last thing I'd do is trust any one of the three in a situation that might get us all shot dead."

"God bless you," Dallas said.

"Amen," said Shanghai and Tarno, in a single voice.

"Shall I tell you what Collins and me learned," Faro said, "or should I pass the collection plate first?"

"Talk," said Dallas. "I'm ready for somethin' serious to happen today, be it good or bad."

"What we have to tell you is some good and some

bad," Faro said. "I don't reckon you'll have any trouble figurin' which is which."

Faro spoke for fifteen minutes, allowing Collins to fill in some details. Shanghai, Tarno, and Dallas listened in silence. When the grim discourse had ended, Faro's three companions remained silent, awaiting his plan. Faro spoke.

"We're up against impossible numbers, and our only chance is to hit them before they come after us. So the question is not *should* we attack, but *when*. We may be safe for the next three hundred miles, but we can't be sure of that. I can't tell you why I believe it—call it an uneasy hunch—but I believe we should hit them tonight. Do any of you object to that?"

There were no objections, and it was a wiser decision than any of them knew. Because of events unknown to them, they were but a few hours away from a devastating attack by the renegade, Perro Cara, and his band of bloodthirsty Utes. . . .

Chapter 8

"Come on," Felix Blackburn shouted. "Let's greet the gents that saved our bacon."

With Josh Snyder helping the wounded Isaac Puckett along, they fought their way through the jumble of rock to the opposite side of the canyon. But when they looked toward the rim, they couldn't believe their eyes, for there was a line of mounted Indians, and each of them had a Winchester under his arm! Blackburn was first to recover from the shock and was raising his own Winchester, when a cold voice stopped him.

"I wouldn't do that, pilgrim."

Blackburn lowered the weapon, and a skeleton-thin rider made his way through the line of mounted Indians to the canyon's rim.

"Who are you?" Blackburn demanded.

"Hueso. Don't mind the Utes. They won't bother you, long as you don't make sudden, unfriendly moves."

He nodded to the Indians and five of them uncoiled lariats. A loop was dropped over the heads of the three men and the two horses. The men were quickly brought up to the canyon rim, but it was with considerable difficulty the horses were assisted in climbing up the steep wall.

"We're obliged," Blackburn said. "Our *amigo,* here, is in need of havin' this arrow removed and his wound doctored."

"Mount up," said Hueso. "The wounded one can double with me."

Before mounting his own horse, Blackburn helped the wounded Isaac up behind the thin man. When he led out, riding eastward, six of the dozen Indians fell back behind the newly rescued white men. There was no conversation, and when they rode into the canyon, Puckett, Blackburn, and Snyder stared in dismay. In addition to the formidable number of Indians, there were seven white men, all of them armed. Josh Snyder looked as though he was about to do something desperate, and Blackburn shook his head. They rode almost to the head of the canyon, where a fire had burned down to the coals. A pair of the ugliest men the trio of miners had ever seen were hunkered there, drinking from tin cups. There was a blackened coffeepot on the coals, sending forth an aroma of fresh coffee. The ugly duo got to their feet, and the one missing an ear spoke.

"What you got there, Hueso?"

"These gents got on the bad side of some Utes," Hueso said. "One of 'em has an arrow drove through an' needin' his wound tended. I reckoned you might find 'em interestin' to palaver with."

"I reckon," said the ugly one. "I'm Perro Cara. That's Dog Face, in English. Who are you gents?"

"Felix Blackburn, Isaac Puckett, and Josh Snyder," Blackburn said, answering for the three of them. "That's

Puckett with the arrow. We'd appreciate some doctorin'
for him."

"Quintado," Dog Face shouted.

A buckskin-clad Indian approached the fire.

"Médico," said Dog Face, pointing to Puckett.

The Indian nodded. From among cooking utensils, he
took an iron pot and filled it with water from the stream.
Removing the coffeepot, he placed the iron pot on the
coals and surrounded it with resinous pine.

"We're all out of whiskey," Dog Face said, his eyes on
Puckett. "That arrow will have to be drove on through,
and it'll hurt like seven kinds of hell. Quintado's got
herbs that'll heal the wound."

"Do what needs doin'," Puckett gritted.

He cried out in pain as the Indian drove the barb on
through, and afterward, seemed unconscious. Except for
Quintado, the rest of the Indians paid no attention, but
Slade and his companions were very interested. Hindes
spoke.

"Who are they, and what are they doin' here?"

"If I had to guess," said Slade. "I'd say they been
watchin' over that gold claim that's somewhere west of
here. Sounds like the Utes run 'em off."

"My God," Kritzer said, "that means this renegade
bunch just got their hands on the *hombres* that can lead
'em to that gold claim."

"Yeah," said Withers, "and when Dog Face figgers it
out, how long will it take him to decide he don't need
us?"

Hindes laughed. "About as long as it takes to pull a
trigger five times."

"We got to bust out of here," said Peeler frantically.

"I won't question the need for that," Slade said. "It's the *how* that's botherin' me. For the last few minutes, that bunch of Utes has been watchin' us. Hell, even *they* know somethin' is changed."

Slade was more right than even he realized, for Dog Face wasted no time. As soon as Isaac Puckett's wound had been treated and he was sleeping, the renegade leader turned to Josh Snyder and Felix Blackburn.

"What are you gents doin' this far in the mountains, in Ute country?"

"Don't you think that's kind of our business?" Blackburn replied.

"It was," said Dog Face, "but it's mine, now. If my outfit hadn't showed up, all of you would be graveyard dead. Your lives oughta be worth somethin', don't you think?"

"We're in your debt," Blackburn said, "but I think we have the right *not* to reveal our personal business."

"I generally collect my debts," said Dog Face. As though by magic, a Colt appeared in his big hand. "Sangre, take their guns."

Sangre did as bidden, and there was nothing Blackburn and Snyder could do. When they were unarmed, Dog Face slid the Colt under his waistband. Then he spoke.

"I'm askin' you one more time. What are you doin' in these mountains that's worth the risk of your hair and your lives?"

"We've been prospecting," said Blackburn grudgingly.

"Have any luck?" Dog Face demanded.

"If we had," said Snyder angrily, "do you think we'd be running away?"

"Matter of fact, I do," Dog Face said. "Unless a man's a damn fool, a mountain of gold ain't worth havin' his carcass shot full of Ute arrows."

"I said we've been prospecting," said Blackburn. "I never mentioned gold."

"Havin' them Utes after your hair, I reckon it slipped your mind," Dog Face said, "but maybe I can refresh your memory."

The piece of gold-laced ore he had taken from Slade he tossed to Blackburn.

"You son of a bitch," Josh Snyder bawled, "you killed Levi Collins!"

Dog Face laughed. "Not yet, but now we can afford to. He's back yonder a ways, him and some mule jockeys, with five loaded wagons. We been waitin' on them, but now we got you three. These Utes is gettin' anxious about them wagon loads of goodies. I reckon we can go after 'em tomorrow at first light."

"Damn you," Blackburn snarled, "we're not leadin' you anywhere."

"You'll regret those words, Mr. Blackburn," said Dog Face. "You're speaking as a man that ain't familiar with Ute torture. Half an hour at the hands of these Indians, and you'll betray your own mother."

Sangre and Hueso laughed. Seeking reassurance, Josh Snyder looked at Felix Blackburn, but in his friend's eyes there was only naked fear. While Slade and his companions hadn't been close enough to hear the conversation, they had seen Dog Face pull a gun and disarm the new arrivals.

"He's showin' 'em that piece of ore he took from you, Slade," said Hindes. "Damn the luck, an' damn you, for givin' it to him."

"That's all that's kept us alive," Slade snarled. "If you had somethin' better in mind, then why the hell didn't you come through, when it could of done some good?"

"We're about to get the bad news, all in a single dose," said Withers. "Here comes the dog, himself."

"Good news, Slade," Dog Face said. "These three gents Hueso brung in just happen to know where that gold claim is, so we ain't got to wait and foller them wagons. Tomorrow, at first light, we'll take them wagon loads of grub and goods. Like I promised, you and your boys is gonna be right in the midst of it. I want the five of you to ride in first, and get their attention. Tell 'em anything you want, so's they're off guard, and we'll hit 'em from ever' direction."

"And we'll be the first to die," Slade said bitterly.

"Well, hell," said Dog Face, "when a man takes to outlawin', there'll always be some risk."

He laughed and then walked away, as though unaware of the temptation Slade and his companions were facing. As though on signal, he whirled, drew his Colt, and shot the gun out of Slade's hand as it cleared the holster. Again he laughed, slipped the Colt back under his waistband, and then he spoke.

"I could've killed you, Slade, but I didn't want you to miss the fun in the mornin'."

He made no move to take the weapons from Slade's four companions, for the shot had alerted the rest of the camp.

"Damn you, Slade," said Hindes. "Now they won't take their eyes off of us."

Slade said nothing. There was no feeling in his right hand, and his Colt lay a mangled ruin at his feet.

"If we got to ride ahead of this attack," Peeler said, "we can break loose, ride like hell, and warn the bunch with the wagons. Maybe we can throw in with them against this outfit."

"Peeler," said Kritzer, "you ain't been payin' attention. Dog Face and his bunch aims to surround them wagons. They ain't got a prayer, and neither have we. We're done for."

Slade still said nothing, and they could see the defeat in his eyes. They settled down to brood about their situation, which seemed more impossible by the minute. Blackburn and Snyder had seen Dog Face draw his Colt and fire, and their wonder grew. Except for the sleeping Isaac, the two were alone, and it was Blackburn who spoke.

"If there's any way, we must escape and warn Levi and the teamsters. If they're all wiped out, we'll be kept alive just long enough to lead this bunch back to the claim."

"You think this one-eyed varmint ain't expectin' us to try and run for it?" Snyder said. "He only needs one of us alive to lead him to the claim."

"Isaac's in no condition to run," said Blackburn. "We don't have much time, but we'll have to wait until tonight, and see what happens. I can't believe Levi and the teamsters ain't had Ute trouble already. Maybe this attack won't come unexpected."

* * *

Durham and the McCutcheons, having heard Faro and Collins ride in, had returned in time to hear Faro's argument favoring an attack.

"Durham, I want you to stay here and entertain the McCutcheons," Faro said. "It seems to be a full-time job."

"I suppose we'll be using dynamite in this attack," said Collins.

"We'll have to," Faro said. "It's the only advantage we have."

"After our attack, we got to stop 'em from comin' after us," said Shanghai. "It won't be easy, even with dynamite, there's so many of them."

"I don't see how we can kill them all," Faro said, "and we shouldn't have to. Usually, the purpose of a camp such as theirs is to gain protection of the canyon walls. Wouldn't you say that's the case here, Collins?"

"Definitely," said Collins. "They're dug in near the head of the canyon, where the rims are highest."

"I'm hoping we can dynamite the canyon walls," Faro said. "We can't hold them at bay for long, but maybe long enough to thin out their ranks with our Winchesters."

"A remarkable plan," said Collins, "but you say the sentries are likely to be doubled after dark."

"They are," Faro said. "It'll be up to Shanghai, Tarno, Dallas, and me to move in and silence them. I think before we do anything else, we'll take another look at the situation from the head of the canyon. We should be able to get some idea as to where the lookouts are."

"We'll need more dynamite, then," said Collins.

"Yes," Faro said. "Break out another two cases, with caps and fuse."

"Do you aim to move the wagons any closer than this?" Tarno asked.

"No," said Faro. "We won't find a better position of defense, for there's no cover for them to approach us."

"We should be camped in an arroyo, where we have some protection," Durham said. "There's no cover here."

"Durham," said Faro, "you'd better stick to the few things you seem to understand."

"Yeah," Dallas said in disgust. "When the fightin' starts, crawl back under your rock."

"What about Mamie and me?" said Odessa. "We can shoot."

"If we're attacked, and you can find time from your other activities," Faro said, "feel free to join in."

Collins brought two cases of dynamite, and broke open the wooden boxes.

"I'll cap and fuse it," said Collins, "while you separate it into bundles of the strength you want. What fuse lengths do you want?"

"I'll want two bundles of a dozen sticks each," Faro said, "both with a two-minute fuse. All the rest with fuses of not more than ten seconds."

"My God," said Dallas, "if two dozen sticks of that stuff don't bring down the canyon walls, we might as well give it up for a lost cause."

"It'll flatten the walls and anybody close by," Faro said. "The concussion ought to take out maybe half those Utes, and I'm countin' on it scarin' hell out of the others. It'll be up to us to go after the renegade leaders with our Winchesters. Without them to lead the attack, I'm hoping the Utes won't go after the wagons. Unless Utes are different from most other Indians, enough dead can convince them their medicine's gone sour."

As the sun slipped toward the western horizon, Utes—three to each wall—began to ascend to the canyon rims for sentry duty. At three intervals along the canyon rims, ropes had been secured, the loose ends reaching almost to the canyon floor. The sentries simply climbed the ropes to their positions on the rims.

"Without them bastards on the rims," Hindes said, "we could shinny up them ropes and be out of here."

"I reckon your horse is gonna shinny up that rope ahead of you," said Slade. "Otherwise, you'd be afoot."

"But I'd be alive," Hindes said. "That's all that concerns me now."

"Hindes," said Kritzer, "I knowed if you talked long enough, you'd say somethin' that made sense."

Near the opposite canyon wall, Felix Blackburn and Josh Snyder sat with the wounded Isaac Puckett, who still slept. The two miners had watched the six Ute lookouts ascend the canyon walls.

"Maybe a way out," Snyder said, "but we could never take Isaac."

"Forget it," said Blackburn. "With Ute lookouts on the rim, we couldn't make it, with or without Isaac. It'll take something more."

"A miracle, maybe," Snyder replied.

Thirty miles eastward, a miracle was in the making. Levi Collins, Faro Duval, and the teamsters saddled their horses. Mamie, Odessa, and Durham watched, saying nothing.

"Of necessity," Faro said, "we're leaving these wagons undefended, except for the three of you. While I can't ask anything of you, I *can* remind you of something. The Utes we're goin' after is only a small part of the total. There's a considerable party of them behind us somewhere, likely mad as hell. This would be a prime time for them to attack, and after what we did to them last time, they won't be in any mood to take captives."

Faro said no more, and when he led out, the others followed. Without a word, Mamie took her Winchester from the saddle boot, while Odessa retrieved hers from the wagon box. Durham took his own weapon from his saddle boot, and the trio settled down to wait and watch.

"Collins and me will try and have a look from the head of the canyon, first," Faro said. "We'll only get one chance at this, and we'll have to make it good."

Moonrise was only a few minutes away, and a light wind was out of the northwest. When Faro judged they were near the place where he and Collins had left their horses earlier, he reined up. The others reined up near him.

"Shanghai, Tarno, and Dallas, I want you to remain here with the dynamite," said Faro. "From the head of the canyon, Collins and me will try to get some idea as to where the Utes are on the rims. We'll have to take them out before we can even think of planting the dynamite."

Faro and Collins drifted into the shadows and were gone.

"This all seems too simple," Dallas said softly.

"Yeah," said Shanghai. "Kind of like the war. When we all throwed in with General Lee, we was lookin' to be home by Christmas."

"Five long years of hell," Tarno said, "and I never saw home or family again. Christmas is just another day to try and forget."

On that somber note, conversation died, and the three waited in silence.

Again, Faro and Collins were able to approach the head of the canyon, and by climbing near the notch where the water cascaded over the edge, they could see into the canyon below. As before, most of the men were congregated near the deep end, seeking the protection of the overhang of the canyon rims.

"Those ropes up the canyon walls should point us to the sentries," Faro said. "Three ropes up each wall."

"My God," said Collins. "My God."

"What is it?" Faro asked.

"See that man on the blanket, and the two sitting beside him?" said Collins.

"Yes," Faro said. "They weren't here earlier today."

"The man on the blanket is Isaac Puckett, and the others are Josh Snyder and Felix Blackburn," said Collins. "My partners from the claim."

"Damn," Faro said. "That complicates things."

"It does," said Collins. "They're too far down-canyon. If we dynamite the walls, they will die in the explosion."

"Then we'll have to get them out of there first," Faro said. "But before we can do even that, we'll have to dispose of the sentries. Let's get back to Shanghai, Tarno, and Dallas."

Quickly, Faro related the changed circumstances to his three companions.

"We can wait until moonset," said Shanghai. "Is there a fire?"

"Yes," Faro said, "but burnt down to coals. It won't provide much light."

"Then after we eliminate the lookouts," said Shanghai, "we can hoist them three up the canyon wall on ropes."

"We can also get shot to doll rags," Tarno said, "if we're caught, and then it'll be too late to set off them two big charges of dynamite. They'll come boilin' out of that canyon like mad hornets."

"Maybe not," said Faro. "When we've eliminated the sentries, we'll set the big charges of dynamite midway down the canyon. Shanghai, you'll stand ready to light one of the fuses, and I'll be prepared to light the other. Tarno and Dallas, you'll help Collins with the rescue. Collins, you'll have to get the attention of those men, and they'll all have to be hauled out of there at the same time. Keep your horses out of sight on the rim, and be ready to drop three ropes. The minute you have those men on the rim, get them on your horses and ride, because that's when Shanghai and me will light the fuses. You'll have two minutes before she blows."

"My God," Collins said, "I wish it hadn't come to this."

"But it has," said Faro, "and with your partners to lead them to the claim, this bunch of renegades wouldn't have wasted any time attacking us. It's all the more important now that we cripple them."

"My God, yes," Dallas said. "If we hadn't followed

Faro's hunch and come after them tonight, we wouldn't have known they'd taken your partners captive. We'd have gone on thinkin' we had plenty of time, because they needed to follow us to the mine. They'd have taken us by surprise, and with a larger force, gunned us down to the last man."

"We'll wait for the moon to set, then," said Faro. "Who wants to go after the Utes on the rim?"

"You need only two men," Tarno said, "and Shanghai's near as good with a Bowie as I am. Them Utes is in for a dose of almighty bad medicine."

"You got it," said Faro.

"I'll take the three on the west rim, then," Tarno said. "Suit you, Shanghai?"

"Sí," said Shanghai. "Let's move into position. The minute the moon sets, we'll start to stalk them varmints."

Like shadows, they were gone.

"My God," Collins said, "they're taking their lives in their hands, yet they go about it as though it's all in a day's work."

"On the frontier, it is," said Dallas.

"Yes," Faro said. "A man does what must be done, and all too often, death is one of the painful side effects."

Ever so slowly, the moon descended, finally disappearing. The darkness seemed all the more intense, and in a remarkably short time, Shanghai and Tarno returned.

"Six less Utes," said Tarno.

"Shanghai," Faro said, "take this bundle of dynamite along the west rim to about the place where the third sentry was. I'm takin' the other bundle to a position along the east rim. Collins, Tarno, and Dallas, I want the three of you on that rim directly above those three *hombres* we must bring out of there. Once you make your move, don't waste a second. Ready?"

"Ready," said the three in a single voice.

"Then allow Shanghai and me ten minutes to place the dynamite," Faro said. "Once you have them three men on the rim, do this. It's almighty dark, so light a match. Just for a second, and shield it with your hat, so only Shanghai and me can see it. That'll be our signal to light the fuses to the dynamite."

Collins, Tarno, and Dallas led their horses a round-about way. Coming in from the west, a light wind was to their backs, lessening the chances of one of their horses nickering and revealing their presence. A dozen yards from the rim, they halted, for there was one element of the rescue that hadn't been discussed.

"We have to get their attention," Dallas said.

"Droppin' the ropes will do that," said Tarno.

"Coming as a surprise," Collins said, "one of them could say something. Ready all the ropes, and I'll go down. We don't have the time for misunderstanding or confusion."

"Maybe you're right," said Dallas, "but make it quick. The movement of lettin' you down and haulin' you up could attract somebody's attention."

Dallas was more right than any of them realized, for Slade and his four companions were desperately seeking some means of escape.

"Somebody's comin' down the canyon wall!" Kritzer hissed excitedly.

"By God," said Slade, "they're comin' after them miners that Hueso brought in. This is our chance."

"They ain't gonna lift a finger to help us," Hindes said.

"I don't expect 'em to," said Slade. "To do what they're doin', they've had to get rid of them Utes along the rim. Them ropes they used to climb up and down is still there. It's a way out."

Nobody argued with that. Getting to their feet, they crept along the canyon wall to the first of the ropes dangling from the east rim. But the movement didn't go unnoticed from the west rim, where Tarno and Dallas had just lowered Levi Collins to the canyon floor.

"Damn it," said Dallas quietly, "them outlaws have figured out what we're up to, that we've done away with the Utes on the rim. They aim to climb out, usin' the ropes the Ute lookouts used. If we're seen, all hell will break loose, and the two dynamite charges won't be in time to save us or those *hombres* we came to rescue."

"It's all in Collins's hands," Tarno said. "We don't dare try to get his attention."

But Levi Collins had seen Slade and his men working their way toward the dangling ropes the sentries had used to ascend and descend the canyon walls. Blackburn and Snyder were on their feet, but wisely refrained from any greeting, when Collins reached the floor of the canyon.

"Dynamite charges are set on both rims," Collins said softly, "and we may be seen at anytime. There's friends on the rim to raise you up, and here's a rope for each of you."

"Isaac's hurt," said Blackburn. "Ute arrow."

"No help for that," Collins said. "Get the rope under his arms. Then you and Josh take the other two ropes. I'll stay here until you're safe, and cover you as best I can, if we're discovered."

"God bless you, Levi," said Blackburn.

Quickly, they looped one of the dangling ropes under the arms of the wounded Isaac Puckett. Collins tugged on the ropes and Puckett was raised to the rim. Blackburn and Snyder secured the remaining two lines under their arms and were being lifted out when one of the Utes near the head of the canyon discovered Slade and his companions using sentry ropes to scale the canyon wall. There was the sudden roar of a Winchester, and lead sang off the stone wall, just inches from Slade's head. Hindes and Peeler were still on the canyon floor, and Peeler seized the rope, right on Slade's heels.

"Hurry, damn it," Hindes cried, "or I ain't gonna make it."

Slade reached the top, scrambling over the rim, but Peeler was less fortunate. When a second Winchester roared, Peeler groaned and fell to the canyon floor. Desperately, Hindes fought the rope as slugs struck the canyon wall all around him. But the outlaws weren't the only targets. Their movement had alerted the renegades and the Utes, and before Snyder and Blackburn reached the safety of the rim, lead sang near them like angry bees. As they were pulled to safety, Levi Collins seized the third rope, but before he could get the loop under his arms, lead slammed into his back. He fell with a groan.

"My God," said Dallas, "Collins is hit."

"I'll have to go down after him," Tarno said.

"No," said Dallas. "He's a goner."

But Tarno, the half-Comanche, didn't listen. Taking a second rope, he went over the canyon rim. Lead repeatedly slammed into the canyon wall, and Dallas Weaver held his breath. Suddenly the rope down that Tarno had descended went slack . . .

Chapter 9

With all except one of Slade's bunch having escaped the canyon, the renegades began firing at the only remaining target. Slugs whined all about Tarno Spangler as he slid down the rope, and half a dozen feet from the bottom, lead ripped through the lariat. But Tarno landed on his feet, and seizing a second dangling rope, knelt and began working the loop over the head and shoulders of the wounded Levi Collins.

"You shouldn't have come," Collins grunted. "We'll never make it alive."

"We ain't dead yet," said Tarno, yanking the rope.

On the rim, Dallas breathed a sigh of relief when there was a tug on one of the other lariats. Tarno was alive! Dallas backstepped the horse as rapidly as he dared, aware that a Winchester on the opposite canyon rim had begun firing. Faro Duval was there, awaiting a signal to light the fuse, aware that his friends were in trouble. Dallas left the horse backstepping and went to the third lariat just in time to feel a frantic tug. Tarno was coming up! Dallas began backstepping the horse, leaving it just long enough to help the wounded Levi Collins over the rim.

"Hard hit?" Dallas asked.

"Shoulder," said Collins.

Dallas returned to the lariat that was drawing Tarno to the rim, praying that he would reach safety before one of the screaming slugs found him. But Faro's firing from the east rim had been deadly, and some of the return fire had been directed at his muzzle flashes.

"Were you hit?" Dallas asked anxiously, as he helped Tarno over the rim,

"Burned a couple times," said Tarno. "Light that match, while there's still time."

Using his hat to shield the match, Dallas popped it aflame. Immediately the firing from the east rim ceased. Tarno already had Collins on one of the horses, while Blackburn and Snyder had lifted Isaac Puckett to another.

"North, beyond the canyon, and then east," Dallas directed.

When Faro stopped firing from the east rim, he could hear shouted directions from the renegades below, as they attempted to organize pursuit. Quickly he lighted the fuse to the dynamite, pausing long enough to be sure it wouldn't sputter out. On the opposite rim, Shanghai had lighted his fuse, and satisfied that it wouldn't burn out, saddled his horse and rode north. Well beyond the head of the canyon, Shanghai and Faro came together.

"What about Tarno and Collins?" Dallas asked. "Have you seen them?"

"They're ahead of us," said Faro. "Collins was hit, and Tarno had to go down after him."

"We still could have pulled ours off mighty slick,"

Shanghai said, "if them damn outlaws hadn't made a run for the ropes the sentries had been usin'. I couldn't see much from my position on the rim. How many do you reckon escaped?"

"All except one, I think," said Faro.

They were far enough away to escape the effects of the blast, and they reined up, listening. The ground began to tremble before they heard the first thunder of the coming explosion.

"My God," Dallas said, "It's gonna be somethin'."

In the canyon, Dog Face cursed everything and everybody. Even with only the dim starlight, some of the Utes had caught up their horses and were galloping down the canyon toward the shallow end.

"Hell," said Sangre, "they ain't gonna find nobody in the dark."

Both charges of dynamite let go at almost the same instant. The rock and earth loosed by the blast had a rippling effect, like waves, and the initial explosion multiplied itself many times. Horses screamed and men were flung like leaves before a mighty wind. There was an echo that lingered, and then, but for the cries of the injured, silence.

As the distant thunder died away, Faro and Shanghai rode eastward, where they soon caught up to their companions, all of whom were riding double. Tarno and Collins rode one horse, Dallas and Snyder a second, with Blackburn and Puckett riding the third.

"I saw Collins go down," Faro said. "How bad?"

"Shoulder," said Collins. "After what Tarno did, you won't hear me complain."

"It was gettin' almighty busy down there, Tarno," Shanghai said.

"Busier than you'll ever believe," said Tarno. "There was a pair of slugs that almost had my name on 'em. I got burns on my hide to prove it."

"What about Puckett, the gent that was wounded?" Faro asked.

"Not in bad shape, for the shape I'm in," said a voice. "I'm Isaac Puckett, and I never seen anything like what you fellers done tonight."

"Neither have I," said another voice. "I'm Felix Blackburn. I reckon none of us ever expected to see Levi again, and when he showed up with *hombres* like you, it was nothing less than a miracle."

"I'm glad you gents feel that way," Collins said. "I promised the four of them half the claim to get them to come with me."

"A fourth of the claim," said Faro.

"No," Collins said, "half."

"Levi," said Blackburn, "after tonight, I'm not sure that's enough. I'd have gladly give it all to them, just to get out of that canyon alive."

"Damn right," Snyder said, speaking for the first time. "Them varmints had a piece of the ore you took, Levi. We reckoned they'd murdered you, and once they forced us to lead 'em to the claim, they'd have killed all of us."

"I think we'd better let the ownership of the claim ride for a while," said Faro. "That dynamite we set off will take care of some of those renegades, but I look for the rest of them to come after us."

"This man knows what he's talking about," Collins

said. "Isaac, Felix, and Josh, this is Faro Duval. He and his teamster friends, Tarno Spangler, Shanghai Taylor, and Dallas Weaver are responsible for what happened tonight."

"Don't sell yourself short, Collins," said Faro. "We all played a part, and you held up your end mighty well."

"Thank you," Collins said. "That means a lot, coming from you."

"With Levi and me wounded," said Puckett, "how are we going to defend ourselves from that bunch, when they come after us?"

"We're goin' to leave the wagons where they are for the time bein'," Faro said. "They'll be a while, pickin' up the pieces. By first light tomorrow, I aim to be at the head of that canyon. We need to know how many of the outfit survived, and how many may be comin' after us."

"It's possible that those Utes who survived the blast won't be all that interested in comin' after us," said Tarno. "I'm half-Comanche, myself, and while I'm not superstitious, most Indians are. Convince them their medicine's bad, and they'll back off."

"That's a proven fact," Faro agreed. "If enough of them died in that canyon, then I'll not be surprised if the rest of them haven't lit a shuck out of there by morning."

"That would be an added blessing," said Felix Blackburn. "We left our horses, saddles, and weapons down there. Maybe we can recover them."

"Maybe," Faro said. "We'll have to wait and see

what the circumstances are when we ride back there tomorrow."

"You ain't goin' alone," said Tarno. "I'm goin' with you."

"That means I'm stuck with that damn gambler and his pair of whores again," Dallas said.

"What?" Blackburn and Snyder asked, in a single voice.

"That's Hal Durham and a pair of females—Mamie and Odessa McCutcheon—from Texas," said Faro. "Once we reach camp and tend his wound, Collins can tell you all about them."

"Who were those men who climbed the sentry ropes and escaped?" Blackburn asked. "They were the ones who first got the attention of the renegades, and were the cause of them seeing Levi coming down the canyon wall to get us."

"We're pretty sure the five of them are outlaws who had been trailing us," said Faro. "One of them got his hands on a piece of the gold ore Levi showed us, and then they had the misfortune to get themselves captured by those renegades. I'm pretty sure four of them escaped, and I reckon somewhere along the way, we'll have to face up to them."

"What of those white renegades?" Dallas asked.

"There were three," said Blackburn. "Hueso and a dozen Utes gunned down another party of Utes that was after us. The other two—Perro Caro and Sangre— seemed to have more to say about the order of things, but Dog Face seemed to have the final say."

Once they could see the distant bulk of the wagons

in the starlight, Faro reined up and the others reined beside and behind him.

"Hello the camp," Faro said softly. "Faro Duval here."

"Durham," said a voice. "Come on."

Faro leading, they rode in and dismounted. To the surprise of them all, Durham and the McCutcheons were armed with their Winchesters.

"Dallas," Faro said, "dig a fire pit. With two wounded men, and Tarno having lead burns, we'll need hot water. Mamie, you and Odessa bring some blankets for Collins and his pard, Isaac Puckett."

To his eternal surprise, the McCutcheons did as bidden. Faro went to one of the five wagons and returned with a jug of whiskey. This he passed to Collins, who in turn, handed it to Puckett.

"Sorry you have to risk a fire because of Levi and me," said Puckett.

"With a fire pit," Faro said, "it's not that risky. The wind's out of the west, so if the smoke reaches some Utes, it'll be them to the east of us, and they already know we're here."

"Since we'll have a fire anyway," said Mamie, "what about food?"

"If it won't be too much trouble," Blackburn said. "Isaac, Josh, and me ain't had a bite of anything but jerked beef in days."

"We'll cook up somethin'," said Mamie.

"Put on enough coffee for all of us," Faro said.

After the rescued trio had been fed and everybody had coffee, Puckett and Collins were soon asleep, aided by pulls from the whiskey jug.

"Faro," Dallas said, "since you and Tarno aim to ride back to that renegade camp by first light, both of you grab your blankets and get what sleep you can. The rest of us will keep watch."

"Supply us some weapons and ammunition," said Blackburn, "and Josh and me will do our part."

"Yeah," Snyder said. "After what we been through, I don't never want to take any chances."

The night wore on, and an hour before first light, Faro and Tarno were up, saddling their horses.

"Like I said last night," said Faro, "since we have two wounded men, and we have no idea what those renegades will do, we'll keep camp here for a while. Tarno and me will eat when we return. Dallas, keep everybody armed and ready."

"*Sí*," Dallas said.

Faro and Tarno rode out, and there was no conversation. Dawn being near, the wind had died, and the stars seemed to be receding into that unknown universe where they spent their daylight hours. Sounding lonesome and far away, there came the quavering cry of a wolf.

"The varmints may be cleanin' up what's left after the explosions," Tarno said.

"If they are, it could be good news for us," said Faro. "Wolves won't come after the dead, if there's anybody else around. This bein' summer, game shouldn't be scarce."

They rode their horses to within a few hundred yards of the head of the canyon, reaching it just as the first gray fingers of dawn touched the eastern horizon. Unsure as to just what they could expect, they climbed the stone abutment until they could see above the time-worn gap through which the water flowed. Rock and dirt had blocked the canyon two-thirds of the way down, and water had begun backing up. There were the mangled bodies of more than thirty horses, and a dozen wolves were feasting on the carcasses.

"There's only one dead man down there," Tarno said, "and from where he lies, I'd say he's the outlaw that was shot tryin' to escape."

"Those three white renegades escaped the blast," said Faro. "I was afraid of that. Now we'll have them stalking us again."

"They won't have as many Utes with 'em," Tarno said. "They took their dead away, but every horse carcass has the look of an Indian pony. I'd bet there was a Ute died with every horse."

"You're likely right," said Faro. "We made some powerful medicine, and it's possible the Utes who survived the blast will shy away from us."

"I was expecting those walls to collapse and block the canyon," Tarno said, "and since they didn't, that stream will soon make itself another bed. It also should have provided us with some muddy footprints and hoofprints of those who escaped. You reckon it's safe for us to ride down to the shallow end of the canyon and look around?"

"I think we'll risk it," said Faro. "I have a feeling those surviving Utes left here in a hurry, and without them, the white renegades had no reason to stay. There's a chance we might find some live horses, and those three miners could use them."

*   *   *

Twenty miles west of the devastated canyon, Perro Cara and the remnants of his band had camped near a creek. Only fifteen Utes remained, and they had distanced themselves from the three white renegades.

"Damn savages," said Sangre. "They look at us like we was to blame for all that hell that busted loose last night."

"Somebody was," Hueso said. "We set there on our hunkers and let that bunch of mule whackers blast the canyon rims down on us. Not only that, they snatched away the three hombres that could of led us to that gold claim."

"Don't forget Slade and his bunch," said Dog Face sarcastically. "All but one of them escaped, and they'll be after the gold, too."

"I ain't forgettin' them," Hueso said, "and I ain't forgettin' it was you that blowed a pile of money— money that was part ours—armin' them Utes with Winchesters. Near fifty of the varmints has rode off and left us, takin' the guns with 'em. What do you aim to do about that?"

"Gut-shoot you, by God, if you say another word," said Dog Face with a snarl.

"Oh, hell," Sangre said, "what's done is done. It wasn't a bad idea, havin' all them Utes sidin' us. How was we to know they'd get spooked and light out? Instead of chawin' on one another, we'd ought to be decidin' what we're gonna do now."

"Sangre's right," said Dog Face. "We got to figger a way to get our hands on that gold claim. We salvaged most of our supplies, and I'll talk to Quintado. If he can convince the rest of them Utes to stick with us, we'll manage."

"We still don't know where the gold claim is," Hueso said.

"So we're back to our original plan," said Dog Face. "We'll foller them wagons."

"They know we're after 'em, an they know why," Hueso said. "After what they done last night, you think they ain't gonna be ready for us?"

"I ain't expectin' it to be easy," said Dog Face. "Damn it, anytime you don't like the way the stick floats, then mount up and ride."

Hueso laughed. "I'll stick around. But I'm warnin' you, *amigo.* I don't aim to squat ever' time you holler froggy, and I don't aim to swaller ever' damn-fool idea that wanders through your head."

The two men glared at each other, and Sangre's little pig eyes glittered. There might not be a three-way split, after all. . . .

Intent only on escape, Slade, Hindes, Withers, and Kritzer vanished into the night, and so were far enough from the canyon that they weren't affected by the explosion. They hunkered in the shadows a mile to the west, catching their breath.

"Damn," Hindes said, "no horse, no gun, no grub."

"It ain't been that long," said Kritzer, "that you'd of been satisfied just to get out of there with your hide in one piece. Peeler wasn't so lucky."

"Question is," Withers said, "what are we gonna do now?"

"I can't speak for nobody else," said Slade, "but I ain't givin' up on that gold claim."

Hindes laughed. "Slade, you'd try to sneak through the pearly gates after you'd done had your ticket punched for hell."

It rubbed Slade the wrong way. His left foot shot out and his boot heel caught Hindes under the chin, slamming the back of his head into the trunk of a tree. Hindes slumped forward and didn't move. Kritzer took Hindes's wrist and then reached for the big artery in his neck.

"Is he all right?" Withers asked anxiously.

"Not where I come from," said Kritzer. "He's dead. You busted his neck, Slade."

"I had enough of his mouthin' off," Slade growled.

"It was just his way," said Withers. "I'm wonderin' how long before you come down on Kritzer and me."

"Long as you and Kritzer don't push me," Slade said, "we'll get along."

"I didn't think Hindes was pushin' you," said Withers. "There's a mean streak in you, Slade, that I ain't never liked, and the more I see of you, the less I like it. I'm pullin' out, goin' back to Santa Fe."

Slade laughed. "Withers, you're a damn fool."

"I have been," Withers said, "but no more."

Withers got to his feet, and to Slade's surprise, so did Kritzer.

"If Withers is a damn fool," said Kritzer, "then so am I. I'm leavin' with him."

Slade stood up, and unbelieving, watched them vanish into the darkness.

"You'll never make it," Slade shouted. "You hear me, you'll never make it."

But there was only silence, and for a long moment, Slade stood looking down at the body of the dead Hindes. Finally he began walking, and the fingers of a west wind were cool as they touched his sweating face. . . .

When Faro and Tarno reached the shallow end of the canyon, it wasn't difficult to see what had happened following the blast. Tracks of three shod horses and those of fifteen unshod animals led westward. Many more tracks of unshod horses led due south.

"Not many Utes went with the white renegades," Tarno said. "Less than twenty. I'd say the rest have split the blanket."

"That's good news for us," said Faro, "but it looks like they may have taken any extra horses with them. I don't think we'll pursue that bunch that rode south."

"I won't argue with you on that," Tarno said. "After last night, they'd gut-shoot a white man, just on general principles."

"We'll ride on back to the wagons," said Faro. "Lacking horses, Collins's *amigos* will be ridin' a wagon box."

"None of us will be goin' anywhere for another three or four days," Tarno said. "That is, if you aim to allow Puckett and Collins some time to heal."

"No reason why we shouldn't," said Faro. "Most of the urgency in us getting these wagons to the claim was the three miners Collins had left behind, and their need for food and ammunition. We've taken care of that part of the problem, and in so doing, we have three more men to stand with us against the Utes and out-laws."

When they reached the wagons, their breakfast and hot coffee was waiting. After they had eaten, Faro and Tarno reported what they had seen at the canyon and their speculation as to what had become of the rene-gades and Utes.

"We're not rid of the varmints, then," Dallas said.

"No," said Tarno. "While most of the Utes seem to have left the white renegades, we still may have to fight them. The same holds true of the renegades. While they're reduced in number, I don't look for them to leave us alone. I think scouting ahead is going to be even more important from here on. We'll remain here until Puckett and Collins are well enough to travel. How are they, this morning?"

"Puckett's doin' well, considerin'," Dallas said, "but Collins has a raging fever. We've been dosin' him with whiskey. Blackburn and Snyder's been takin' care of them."

"I reckon there's been no other trouble, if you know what I mean," said Faro.

"I know what you mean," Dallas said, "and no, there's been no more trouble out of them. Two wounded men seems to have had a sobering effect."

"God knows, we needed one," said Faro.

The day passed uneventfully, but along toward sun-down, Tarno spotted a pair of distant figures stumbling in from the west.

"Who in tarnation are *they*?" Shanghai Taylor won-dered.

"There were five other white men held captive in that canyon besides us," Blackburn said. "That could be two of them."

The two came on, and when they neared the wagons, Faro challenged them.

"Who are you, and what are you doing here?"

"Kritzer and Withers," said one. The other seemed too weary to respond. "We've been held prisoner by renegades and Indians. Last night, we managed to escape."

"Come on," Faro said. "We'll have supper in a while."

"We're obliged," said Kritzer. "We ain't had a scrap of grub since yesterday mornin', and not much, then."

Hal Durham had come forth to witness the arrival of the two, and he quickly turned away, but not before Faro had seen recognition in his eyes. Durham didn't appear during supper, and when the meal was finished, Faro questioned the new arrivals.

"Usually, I don't ask a man his business, but you gents are without horses, guns, or grub, and these mountains are full of Utes. Where are you bound?"

"Santa Fe, I reckon," said Withers.

"Yeah," Kritzer agreed. "Where else could we go?"

"It's a good two hundred miles," said Faro. "I reckon I don't have to tell you how slim your chances are."

The two said nothing, their eyes on the tin cups of coffee in their hands.

"I'm not one to leave a man without a gun, horse, and grub," Faro continued, "but we already have three men without horses or guns. Grub won't save you from the Utes."

"We ain't expectin' nothin'," said Withers. "We was half starved, you fed us, and we're obliged for that."

"We have two wounded men," Faro said, "and we'll be here two or three more days. You're welcome to at least stay and eat."

"We're obliged," said Kritzer.

Not until the newcomers had fallen into an exhausted sleep did Tarno and his outfit have a chance to talk.

"I'm almost certain they're two of the five men held captive by the renegades," Blackburn said.

"I think so, too," said Snyder, "but what became of the others?"

"At least one died tryin' to escape the canyon," Tarno said. "Some of the others may have been hit. Or maybe this pair only wants to get back to Santa Fe."

"I don't doubt they were held captive," said Faro, "but they're not telling it all. They were part of a five-man outfit stalking us, until they had the misfortune to be captured by the renegades and Utes."

"We can't trust 'em," Dallas said. "When does a man stop bein' an outlaw?"

"I don't know," said Faro, "but for reasons of my own, I'd like to keep them around for a while."

"So would I," Tarno said. "Durham shied away from 'em mighty quick."

"Where is he and the McCutcheons?" Faro asked. "I haven't seen any of them since before supper."

"They've been mighty quiet," said Dallas. "I've been countin' my blessin's."

"This is still Levi Collins's responsibility," Faro said, "and I'll want to talk to him about this Withers and Kritzer. Maybe we'll just take them with us, if only to see how Durham handles it."

"My God," said Shanghai, "that's like havin' the foxes watchin' the henhouse."

"Not quite," Faro said. "If Withers and Kritzer are who we think they are—and they can hardly be anyone else—then they already *know* where we're bound, and why. There is a small chance they're leveling with us, and I've always been one to give a man benefit of the doubt. At least, until he convinces me I'm a sucker."

"You told this pair we're short on guns," Shanghai said. "Collins bought a dozen new Winchesters, and enough shells to stand off every Ute in these mountains."

"You know that, and I know that," said Faro. "Let's leave it that way, until we have a better understanding of this situation."

That ended their discussion, for much depended on what Levi Collins had to say.

A pair of Utes caught Slade well before he reached the renegade camp, and with a Winchester at his back, marched him before Dog Face.

"Well, damn," Dog Face said, "if it ain't Slade. I reckoned we'd seen the last of you. Where's the rest of your boys?"

"Run out on me," said Slade, "and I'm near starved. I could use some grub."

"Well, now," Dog Face said, "you done some runnin' of your own. Why should I feed you, when we ain't all that well off, grub-wise?"

"Because I aim to be part of your outfit," said Slade desperately. "None of us has got a handle on that gold claim anymore, unless we follow the wagons. They know about you, and they're armed to the teeth. You're gonna need all the help you can get."

"I can't argue with that," Dog Face said. "Sangre, Hueso, what do you think?"

"I think you oughta gut-shoot the bastard right now," said Hueso.

"Damn right," Sangre agreed. "You can't trust him."

Dog Face laughed. "Hell, I can't trust nobody, in-cludin' you two. They don't like you, Slade, and that's a feather in your hat. Before, you had your own outfit, but now there's only you. By God, I'll take a chance on you, but you don't answer to nobody but me. You got that?"

"I got it," said Slade.

"There's stew on the fire," Dog Face said. "Help yourself."

Grateful, Slade turned away, but the hate in the eyes of Sangre and Hueso sent chills up his spine, and he longed for a gun. . . .

Chapter 10

Southwestern Colorado. August 28, 1870.

By dawn, Levi Collins was awake, his fever having broken during the night.

"We need to talk," Faro said, "if you're feelin' up to it."

"I think, after I've had some cold water, hot coffee, and some food, I'll be ready for anything," said Collins.

"Mostly," Faro said, "there is something you need to know about. I'll talk while you eat, and then you can tell me what you think."

"Anything that has to do with this expedition, I'll trust your judgment," said Collins.

"I'm obliged for your confidence," Faro said, "but this is a strange situation that came up late yesterday. Frankly, I've decided how I believe we should handle it, but you deserve to know my reasoning."

While Collins ate, Faro talked. When Collins finished the last of his coffee, he spoke.

"So you believe Hal Durham, the gambler, knows these men who showed up late yesterday. That would put Durham squarely in cahoots with those outlaws who were following us."

"It would," said Faro.

"Then there's the McCutcheons," Collins said. "Are they also involved with these outlaws, or is their relationship with Durham strictly personal?"

"They have nothing to do with the outlaws," said Faro. "I think they're victims of an uncommonly rotten judgment, and their involvement with Durham began in Amarillo, like they say. Troublesome as they are, they've kept Durham from accomplishing what he must have been sent here to do."

"You think it was Durham who slugged me and took the ore, then," Collins said.

"Yes," said Faro. "Nothing else makes sense. I was sure of it yesterday, when Kritzer and Withers showed up. Durham has a pretty solid poker face, but it slipped for just a second. He knows these *hombres*, and they know him."

"Go ahead and deal with this situation as you see fit," Collins said. "In fact, if you're reasonably certain Kritzer and Withers are no longer seeking to take the claim from us, I'd be willing to hire them for the duration of this journey. We can always use a couple more guns, when the Utes come after us."

"That would certainly be a means of keeping them around, and in contact with Hal Durham," said Faro. "If we're right about Durham, he'll make some move toward Withers and Kritzer, and if they respond with any interest, we'll know where they stand."

"Tell Kritzer and Withers I'm offering them each two hundred dollars to deliver these wagon loads of goods," Collins said. "I will provide them with food, weapons, and shells. I shall expect them to assist in any way they can, especially in our defense against the Utes. We have no horses for them, of course."

"That's a more than generous offer," said Faro. "They'd be fools not to accept."

Faro presented the offer Collins had made, and the two readily accepted.

"We're obliged," Kritzer said.

"My God, yes," said Withers. "I'd side you just for grub, a gun, and ammunition."

When Durham made an appearance, he pointedly ignored the two men, further adding to Faro's suspicion that he knew them.

"He knows them, all right," Dallas Weaver said, when he had a chance to talk to Faro in private. "You didn't ask them why they was bein' held captive by the renegades?"

"No," said Faro. "It's possible they're playin' straight with us, and I want to use them to unmask Durham. If he's the Judas I think he is, then I want him where I can get my hands on him. He'll know, by Kritzer and Withers showin' up here, that the outlaw bid for the claim didn't pan out. He looks like the kind who will attempt to enlist the help of Kritzer and Withers, with the intention of takin' the claim for himself."

"You don't think Kritzer and Withers will throw in with him, then," Dallas said.

"No," said Faro, "but Collins is goin' along with my hunch, and I want him to see the proof, if I'm right."

"I hope you're right," Dallas said. "That'll be two more guns against the Utes. Ten of us, not includin' Durham and the McCutcheons."

As he could, Faro spoke privately to Shanghai Taylor, Tarno Spangler, Isaac Puckett, Felix Blackburn, and Josh Snyder about his intentions of taking in Kritzer and Withers. He said nothing, however, to the McCutcheons and Durham.

"We have extra Winchesters," he told the wounded Puckett. "When you're able, you'll be given one, and the ammunition."

Faro then made his way back to Kritzer and Withers.

"I was wrong about one thing," Faro said. "In talking to Levi Collins, I'm told he has several extra Winchesters in one of the wagons. Each of you will be allowed use of one, with ammunition supplied."

"Thank God," said Kritzer. "All I want is a chance to get out of Ute country alive."

"I want somethin' more than that," Withers said. "Before I go, I'd like to get them three white renegades in my sights."

Faro said no more. Durham was watching, and if Faro's suspicions held up, then the next move would belong to the gambler.

"Slade," Dog Face said, "I got an assignment for you. I want you to ride back and have a look at them wagons. I wanta know what that bunch is doin'. We can't afford for 'em to catch us nappin' again."

"I'll need a horse and a gun," said Slade.

"You'll have both," Dog Face said. "In fact, I'll do better than that. I got a spyglass you can use, an' bring ever'thing up close. Just don't use it when you're facin' the sun."

Slade rode out an hour after first light. Sangre, Hueso, and Dog Face watched him go. Dog Face laughed, aware of the hatred that bubbled within his companions.

"You'll be sorry," Hueso predicted.

"Yeah," said Sangre. "Either of us could of went."

"Don't be a pair of damn fools," Dog Face said. "I'm testin' him. If a man's bound to let me down, then I'll let him do it in a small way. In some way that don't get me kilt."

Slade rode eastward, elated that he was being allowed to prove himself. While he did not for a minute believe he would share in the gold claim, there was virtually nothing he could do on his own. He would ingratiate himself to the renegade leader and bide his time. There would be time enough to contemplate a double-cross, if and when they actually got their hands on the elusive gold claim.

When Slade reached the canyon where the explosions had taken place, he rode north. Even in daylight, the teamsters would be ready for trouble, and he dared not approach them from the west. He finally had to settle for a tree-clothed ridge three-quarters of a mile away, and was thankful for the spyglass Dog Face had provided. He was careful to remain within the shade of a tree, so that the sun didn't reflect off the glass.

"Well, by God," he grunted to himself. "There's Withers and Kritzer, and they got themselves Winchesters. Maybe old Slade's chances is better than they seemed."

He spent half an hour with the glass, and to his dismay, he found Durham was still part of the outfit. While he didn't know how Durham had survived, or how Kritzer and Withers had worked their way in, his devious mind devoured the information and spat out the obvious conclusion. Obvious to him, anyway. The three of them would eventually team up, making their own bid for the gold claim.

"Damn them," he said grimly, "they'll root old Slade out, will they?"

Slade had seen enough. He mounted up and rode back to the renegade camp. When he dismounted, there were frowns on the faces of Sangre and Hueso. Dog Face laughed. The remaining Utes watched Slade curiously.

"Well?" said Dog Face impatiently.

"They ain't moved from where they was," Slade said. "Don't look like they plan to anytime soon."

"How many men they got?"

"I'd say ten, includin' the three they took off your hands," said Slade. "They got men on watch with Winchesters, in the daytime."

Slade carefully avoided mentioning that two of the men were Withers and Kritzer, and he didn't mention Durham at all. Sangre and Hueso had listened in silence. Hueso spoke.

"I can't see that we've learned a hell of a lot we didn't already know. We knew this outfit has at least a pair of wounded *hombres*, so they ain't goin' anywhere for a while. We knew they hauled three *hombres* out of the canyon, so that's three more than they had, and it don't take a heap of brains to see the need for keepin' watch in the daytime, when you're in Ute country."

"Well, you just go on figgerin' all this out in your head," said Dog Face. "Me, I just wanted a firsthand look, and Slade took care of that. More important, he done what I asked him, without mouthin' off. Maybe the pair of you can learn from him."

The two turned away without a reply, and the look that Dog Face cast at their backs spoke volumes. It wouldn't be difficult to drive a wedge between them and the renegade leader, Slade decided, as he set about devising a means by which he might accomplish it to his advantage.

Southwestern Colorado. September 2, 1870.

"If you aim to stay with the wagon," Faro told Odessa, "one of the men will need to ride your horse. You'll also have somebody ridin' the wagon box with you."

"I can stand it if they can," said Odessa.

"Josh," Faro said, "you or Felix can ride Odessa's horse. The other rides with Odessa on the wagon box."

"Felix is handsomer and easier to talk to than me," Snyder said. "I'll take the horse."

Odessa said nothing, but Faro thought she looked at Blackburn with more than a little interest.

"Isaac," said Faro, "you'll ride the box with Dallas. Withers, you can ride with Shanghai, and Kritzer with Tarno. I generally take the lead wagon, with Levi Collins takin' over for me, while I'm scouting ahead. Any questions before we move out?"

There were none, and the wagons rumbled westward. There was a frosty bite to the wind, and far to the west, a band of dirty gray clouds hugged the horizon. Collins had been riding ahead, and rode back to meet them when they stopped to rest the teams.

"I hate to say it," Collins said, "but those are snow

clouds. If it doesn't reach us before dark, it'll be here sometime tonight. It may snow for several hours or several days. Out here, you never know, so it's best to prepare for several days."

"We've enjoyed weather like that on the Kansas plains," said Faro. "At least, out here there's some cover. I reckon we'd better start lookin' for a place to hole up."

"It's not a bit too soon," Collins said.

"Take the wagon, then," said Faro, "and I'll ride ahead and see what I can find."

As the wagons again took the trail, Faro rode out. He veered a bit to the south, for the country in that direction looked rougher, lending itself to the possibility of a canyon in which they might wait out the storm. He had ridden not more than ten miles when he saw a line of trees ahead that he found lined a canyon rim. He rode to the east rim, and while there was protection from the elements and a stream along the floor, there was no graze.

"Damn," said Faro softly, "there goes the grain."

But the next canyon might also be lacking in graze, and it might be many miles ahead. He looked to the west, and not only did the gathering clouds appear darker than before, they seemed much closer. A man couldn't afford to gamble in snow country. Wheeling his horse, Faro rode back to meet the wagons. This would be their haven from the storm, if they could get there in time. Reaching the wagons, Faro rode back along the line with word of the sanctuary ahead. As far as the wagons were concerned, snow was the greatest hazard, for when it became deep enough, it concealed broken terrain and drop-offs that could snap an axle or shatter a wheel. Faro allowed Levi Collins to continue with the wagon. They needed to veer slightly to the southwest to reach the lower end of the canyon, and knowing the way, Faro rode ahead. The storm clouds swept in more rapidly than any of them had expected, and a rising wind whipped showers of snow into their faces. Mules tried to balk and had to be driven onward. The fine snow showers soon gave way to big flakes that quickly made their presence felt, for the ground was white as far as the eye could see. Reaching the shallow end of the canyon, Faro waited, directing the wagons in. Collins took the lead wagon to the head of the canyon and the others followed.

"Unharness the teams," Faro ordered. "Then those of us with horses will snake in some firewood."

Shanghai, Tarno, and Dallas, familiar with what must be done, followed Faro back to the lower end of the canyon. They sought windblown trees, and it was a land that offered plenty of them. With axes from the wagons, they trimmed off enough branches to avoid the trunks' becoming entangled as they were dragged back to the canyon. The snow fell thicker all about them, and they had difficulty finding the canyon mouth.

"One more time," Faro said, as they loosed the lariats.

Kritzer, Withers, Blackburn, and Snyder took axes provided by Levi Collins and began chopping the logs into manageable lengths. Faro, Shanghai, Tarno, and Dallas soon returned with more wood.

"We'll have to make do with this for a while," said Faro. "Snow's gettin' deep, and it's almighty cold."

"The snow may last only two or three hours," Collins said, "or it may snow the rest of the day and all night. I suppose there's nothing predictable about this country except its unpredictability."

"I never heard it put that way," said Dallas Weaver. "Most of the snowstorms we've had to live with caught up with us on the Kansas plains. Only thing there was less of than shelter was wood."

"Yeah," Tarno said. "In snow time, we near 'bout had to take an extra wagon loaded with firewood."

The McCutcheons soon had two roaring fires next to the canyon's west rim, and even with some snow blowing in, it was a protected camp.

"We'll have to keep the fires going," Faro said, "with whoever's on watch tending them. If it snows long enough and deep enough, we may be killing wolves to keep them from our horses and mules."

The snow continued for the rest of the day, with no indication as to when it might cease. Collins wasn't optimistic.

"I think we're in for a bad one," he said.

"Thank God we pulled out when we had the chance," said Felix Blackburn. "We'd have been out of ammunition and grub long before now."

"Yes," Collins agreed. "Even without the other problems we've had, the snow would have kept us from getting to you in time."

"There are enough of us for two five-man watches," said Faro. "We'll change watches at midnight, and here's the lineup. Collins, Blackburn, Tarno, Dallas, and Withers, you'll take the first watch. Shanghai, Puckett, Snyder, and Kritzer, you'll be joining me for the second watch. Any questions?"

"Yes," Durham said. "Am I not worthy of taking my turn?"

"Only if you can keep your mind on the business at hand," said Faro. "Can you?"

"I'll try," the gambler said, without the slightest embarrassment.

"Then you'll take the first watch," Faro said, "answering to Levi Collins. But at the first damn hint of trouble, with you at the root of it, you'll answer to me. Take my word, there'll be more than a spanking awaiting you."

"I reckon you don't want Odessa and me on either watch," Mamie McCutcheon said.

"Frankly, no," said Faro, "and you damn well know why, so we won't get into that. I want to remind you—all of you, in fact—that you're not to be up and moving about, if you're not on watch. Otherwise, you're subject to being shot or carried away by hostile Utes. In either case, you're in big trouble, because I'm not a patient man when carelessness is involved. Have I made myself clear?"

"Yassuh, massa," Odessa McCutcheon said.

Mamie started to laugh, but it died away when everybody else remained silent. Even Durham wasn't amused. Angrily, Odessa drifted away, Mamie following.

"This is a cold damn camp," Hueso complained.

"Sure as hell is," said Sangre. "We should of moved on west an' found us a canyon."

"I ain't wantin' to get too far ahead of them wagons," Dog Face said. "I told you that. How do you feel, Slade?"

"Like you do," said Slade wisely. "It won't snow forever."

"Good old Slade," Hueso said. "Always ready for some apple polishing."

"I favor a man that can give me a straight answer without brayin' like a mule-headed *asno*," said Dog Face. "Slade, when the snow lets up, I'll want you to ride back and bring me another report on them wagons."

"*Sí*," Slade said. "They're holed up somewhere."

Sangre and Hueso glared venomously at Slade, who managed to avoid any obvious sign of smugness. Dog Face laughed, enjoying the animosity he had created. He was playing both ends against the middle, knowing that any one of the three might shoot him in the back if the spoils were sufficient and the opportunity presented itself.

Because of the storm, darkness came early to the canyon where the teamsters had taken refuge. It was near midnight before Hal Durham had a chance to speak to Withers.

"I need to know where you and Kritzer stand," Durham said softly.

"You'll have to talk to Kritzer," said Withers. "Me, I stand with the *hombres* that's givin' me a chance to get out of Ute country alive."

"That's a damn lie, and you know it," Durham hissed angrily. "You got your eye on that gold claim, you and Kritzer, and you ain't rootin' me out. Either you work with me and we'll split, or I'll ruin you with Collins and Duval."

"Go ahead, damn you," said Withers. "You can't drag Kritzer and me into it without admittin' you was workin' with Slade and the rest of us."

"I'll find a way," Durham said. "You better talk to Kritzer, before you do anything foolish."

"If I talk to Kritzer," said Withers, "it won't be in your favor. Now leave me the hell alone."

While Levi Collins wasn't able to hear the conversation, he was aware that it was taking place. When the watch changed at midnight, he mentioned it to Faro.

"Interesting," Faro said. "If Withers and Kritzer are who we *think* they are, that's all it'll take to convince me that Durham's a Judas of the first water."

"There's a chance that Durham believes they're here for the same reason he is, then," said Collins. "That should create some conflict."

"It should work to our advantage," Faro replied. "If Withers and Kritzer become too friendly with Durham, then we'll know the three of them are up to no good. Call it a gut hunch, but I don't believe Withers and Kritzer will turn on us. Theirs was a life-and-death situation, here in Ute country, before we took 'em in."

"The snow's about done," said Collins. "We're lucky. It could have become a two- or three-day blizzard."

"We'll still be here until the sun melts it and sucks up the moisture," Faro said. "I'd say two days, at least."

"The weather changes quickly in this high country,"

said Collins. "While it's bitter cold tonight, we may be sweating by tomorrow afternoon."

But the weather was even more eerie than Collins had predicted, for during the night the snow changed to rain, and by dawn there was mud.

"We'll be here at least another day," Faro said. "Maybe longer. One thing we can do to better our situation while we wait. We can lead the horses and mules out to graze, and save our grain."

"An excellent idea," said Collins. "I'll take charge of that, if you like."

"Go ahead," Faro replied. "Just don't go too far, and don't forget the possibility of Indians. Take four men with you."

"I'll go," said Withers.

"So will I," Kritzer said.

"Let me go," said Durham. "I want to get out of this canyon for a while."

"I reckon I'll go along, too," Dallas said, his eyes on Durham.

It seemed strange, after the howling snowstorm, to feel the morning sun warm on their backs. Collins and his men got the horses and mules headed toward the shallow end of the canyon, and Faro watched them go.

"That damn gambler's got somethin' up his sleeve besides extra aces," said Tarno. "I hope you had some good reason for lettin' the varmint go along."

"I did," Faro said. "He went after Withers last night, but Kritzer's on second watch. I want Durham to spend a little time with Kritzer."

Without going too far afield, Collins found suitable graze for the horses and mules. There was little to do except wait, and Dallas remained with Collins. Seeking not to appear too obvious, Durham took his time getting to Kritzer. Withers made it a point to avoid both of them.

"That Durham's a nervy bastard," Dallas said.

"You know what he's up to, then," said Collins.

"Pretty much," Dallas said, "but I think he's barkin' up the wrong tree. I got faith in Faro's hunches."

"So have I," said Collins. "I've heard it said if you give a man enough rope, he'll hang himself."

Durham found Kritzer as unreceptive as Withers had been.

"I suppose Withers talked to you," Durham said.

"Yeah," said Kritzer, "and I ain't got a damn thing to say that he ain't already said."

"Maybe you'd better think about it," Durham said angrily. "I can talk to Collins or Duval and get both of you booted out."

"Not without gettin' yourself booted out along with us," said Kritzer triumphantly. "I done told Withers, and now I'll tell you. Duval treated us white, better than we deserved, and I'll risk gettin' booted out just to see you get yours. Withers and me aim to tell Duval and Collins what we once was, just so's we can tell what kind of Judas you are. The kind you've been since the day you throwed in with this outfit."

"You're bluffing," Durham scoffed.

"Try us, you slick-dealing bastard."

"A word from either of you," said Durham, "and you're dead men. I swear it."

"We took your measure, and I don't think so," Kritzer said. "We don't aim to turn our backs on you."

"Damn it," said Durham desperately, "I'm trying to help you."

"You lyin' varmint," Kritzer said. "You wouldn't hoist your own mammy out of a pit of rattlers, unless she paid you for the rope."

Kritzer turned and walked away, leaving Durham clenching his fists and gritting his teeth in frustration.

Dallas laughed. "Durham ain't been told what he wanted to hear."

"Whatever Withers and Kritzer have been in the past," Collins said, "I believe we have just seen Faro Duval's judgment justified. I believe we'll know for sure before this day has ended."

The showdown came just after supper, before the first watch began.

"Mr. Collins and Mr. Duval," said Withers, "Kritzer and me has got somethin' we feel the need to say."

"They've trumped up lies against me!" Durham bawled.

Clearly, he intended to shoot one or both men, as he snaked the Colt from beneath his coat. But Tarno Spangler had been quicker on the draw, and slammed the muzzle of his Colt against the back of Durham's head. He collapsed like an empty sack. The Mc-Cutcheon sisters knelt beside him, receiving looks of disgust for their concern.

"Withers," said Faro, "you and Kritzer go ahead. I believe the truth of what you are about to tell us has just been proven."

Withers and Kritzer told the truth of it from the time Slade had first learned of the wagons and the danger-ous trek into the mountains, until they had parted company with Slade after their narrow escape from the renegades.

"It's about the way we had it figured," Faro said. "You don't know what happened to Slade?"

"No," said Kritzer, "but he won't never give up. Not till he's dead."

"It's helpful, knowin' he's out there," Dallas said. "It's the close-up rattler you don't know about that's able to get to you."

"We ain't told you much you didn't already know," said Withers, "so I guess we ain't helped our cause."

"You've done exactly the right thing," Faro said. "If you had intended finishing what Slade started—with or without Durham—you couldn't have afforded to reveal him for the thieving varmint he is."

"I have a question for either of you," Dallas said. "If Durham hadn't forced your hand by pullin' a gun, would you have told us about him, Slade, and yourselves?"

"Likely not," Withers said. "A man don't fancy lookin' a fool, even when he is."

"While we might not of said anything," said Kritzer, "we didn't aim to turn agin you. While we ain't always been honest, our word's good, and we got some pride. Durham was aimin' to force us to throw in with him, to keep him from spillin' the beans about us bein' part of Slade's gang. We was without horses, grub, or guns, and you took us in. Even if our talk got us run off, along with Durham, we wouldn't do you wrong."

"That kind of honesty won't go unrewarded," said Collins. "You have my word."

Durham sat up, rubbing his head.

"He's alive, damn it," Shanghai said. "What are we goin' to do with him?"

"He's going with us," said Faro, "and we'll keep our end of the bargain, but there'll be one big difference. We know why he's here, and he won't be armed. Shanghai, take the Winchester from his saddle boot, and Tarno, take his Colt."

"I got it," Tarno said.

"You can't leave me unarmed," said Durham. "The Indians . . ."

"Durham," Faro said, "it's not the Indians you should be concerned with. One wrong move from you, and you'll wish the Utes had hold of you, instead of me. When we reach the end of this trail—unless I have to kill you between now and then—you'll be allowed to take your weapons and go. Until then, any man in this outfit can gut-shoot you with my blessing, if you get out of line."

"Well," said Durham, getting to his feet and dusting off his coat, "I suppose you'll be relieving me from the first watch."

"Wrong," Faro said. "You'll remain there so we can watch *you*."

Chapter 11

As Slade was about to depart Dog Face's camp, five more Utes rode in. They looked at Slade suspiciously as they dismounted. Dog Face nodded to them as though he had fully expected them to return.

"Ungrateful varmints," Hueso said, "and you take 'em back without a word."

"Why not?" said Dog Face. "You was whinin' because they rode off, takin' their Winchesters. Well, five of 'em are back. What do you expect me to do, take a switch to 'em?"

Sangre thought that hilariously funny, and erupted into a fit of laughter. The Utes all looked at him as though he'd lost his mind.

"You damn fool," Hueso said in disgust, "the only reason they ain't done scalped you is 'cause you look like it's already been done."

"Shut your mouth," said Sangre. "You just got a mad on 'cause Slade's rode out to look around. Dog Face, why don't you take a switch to *him*?"

"Both of you shut the hell up," Dog Face snarled.

Slade rode east, avoiding the low places where the mud was deepest. As yet there was no wind, and he looked for a tendril of smoke that might guide him to whatever sanctuary the teamsters had taken against the storm. He expected to find them in camp, for there was little chance of moving the heavy wagons through mud. Pausing on a ridge, he drew the spyglass from his saddlebag and searched the country ahead of him. He didn't doubt his quarry had holed up in a canyon if they had been fortunate enough to have found one, and he really didn't expect to see anything helpful through the glass. But he was at a high enough elevation that there was mostly brush for the next several miles, and suddenly he was seeing grazing horses and mules through the glass. There were men with them, and he was facing the sun.

"Damn," he said, hastily lowering the glass.

But one of the men who had taken the animals to graze was Tarno Spangler, and the sharp eyes of the half-Comanche had seen the sun reflecting off the spyglass. He watched for it again, but saw it no more. Still it was significant enough that he told Faro of it.

"That renegade outfit," Faro said, "and we'll give as good as we get. When we take the trail again, I'll find out where they are."

"Short of following us," said Collins, "they have no way of knowing our destination."

"Maybe they just intend to follow us," Faro said, "but we can't be sure of that. We can't be sure they don't aim to attack, capture some of us, and apply some Ute torture."

"It's the kind of thing the Comanches would do," said Tarno, "and it's always worked surprisingly well."

"You ain't seen fit to come right out and tell us,"

Odessa said, "but from what I've heard, it appears you aim to risk all our scalps for a gold claim somewhere back in these mountains."

"God forbid that you and Mamie should feel slighted," said Faro. "It's true. There is a gold claim, but I don't recall you bein' hog-tied and dragged into this. You chose to come with us because we're using your teams and wagon, and you know who roped us into that. Anytime you get to feelin' your scalps are worth more than the teams and wagon, we won't object if you just saddle up and ride on."

Mamie laughed. "You're a caution, Duval. Whatever gave you the idea we wasn't goin' to stick with you to the bitter end?"

"You been honest with us, Duval," Odessa said, "so I reckon we can be honest with you. Mamie and me has been wonderin' if, somewhere beneath that iron hide of yours, they ain't some flesh and blood. Before we split the blanket with this outfit, one or both of us aim to get you under a wagon and find out."

None of their previous antics had surprised Faro Duval, but this time they had gone too far. Their brazen challenge got to him, and his face flamed with embarrassment. While the rest of the outfit kept straight faces, Hal Durham howled with laughter. But it lasted only until Faro got to him. But the gambler ducked, and Faro's fist only clipped him on the side of his head, sending him sprawling.

"You're a big man, Duval, pushin' your way around," Durham snarled, "but I won't always be without a gun."

"When that day comes," said Faro, "I'll be careful

not to turn my back. Actually, I aim to do my best to avoid killing you, because you and this pair of foolish, desperate females deserve one another."

"Damn you, Duval," Odessa shouted, "you watch who you're callin' foolish and desperate."

"Don't push me," said Faro, "or I'll use a different set of words. I'm through trying to treat the pair of you as ladies, when you've been behaving like pigs. From now on, I'll shove your heads in the slop."

None of his companions had ever seen Faro Duval so angry. When he stalked away, nobody followed. When suppertime drew near, the McCutcheons seemed to have forgotten their offer to do the cooking. Levi Collins approached Felix Blackburn.

"You're the best cook among us, Felix. Can we depend on you?"

"Yes," Blackburn said. "I'll do it."

Nothing was said to the McCutcheons. Blackburn got a fire going, and wasted no time impressing them all with his ability. He turned out Dutch-oven biscuits that had the men all gathered near the supper fire, waiting. The McCutcheons remained aloof, their noses in the air.

"I hope they stay miffed from now on," said Shanghai. "They wasn't bad, but Felix is great."

"He is," Josh Snyder said, "but we never got much benefit of it, when there was just the four of us. It took all of us, with Winchesters, just to keep the Utes at a distance."

"Well, it's gonna be a mite different, this time," said Tarno. "I don't fight Indians worth a damn on jerked beef and branch water."

Durham and the McCutcheons avoided the supper fire as long as they could, and when they finally approached, they were subdued. After filling their tin plates and tin cups, they retreated in silence.

"They all got a burr under their tails," Dallas said.

"I hope it stays there," said Tarno. "I've never seen Faro so killin' mad."

Faro Duval had pretty well kept to himself after his confrontation with Durham and the McCutcheons, and nobody bothered him.

"Leave him be," Shanghai said. "It ain't often he builds up such a head of steam, and I reckon it bothers him because they got to him."

When the sun eventually dried up enough of the mud, everybody was ready for the trail. For two days, Faro had said little, and nobody said or did anything to try his short-fused patience. Faro rode out, scouting ahead, and by riding wide, toward the north, he soon found the tracks of Slade's horse. While the mud had dried, the trail was clear, and he followed it. Since it was still early, there was no wind, but there was a distinct gray smudge of smoke against the blue of the sky.

"Maybe ten miles, horse," Faro said. "Let's try and get close enough to see how many men are in this camp."

Faro rode far enough north of the telltale smoke until he found decent tree cover. He then rode west until he was within a mile or two of the smoke. Leaving his horse and taking his Winchester, he proceeded on foot. There was scant cover as he descended to the lower elevation, and soon he was on hands and knees, creeping from one clump of brush to the next. Finally he could progress no farther without being seen, and had to content himself with his position. He could see the smoldering fire and four white men hunkered around it, but where were the Utes? A whisper of sound behind him was all the warning he had. The Ute sprang like a cougar, a deadly knife in his upraised fist, and Faro had no choice but to shoot. The roar of the Winchester sounded like a cannon in the stillness of the early morning. Knowing where there was one Indian there were likely to be others, Faro had little choice. He ran for his horse, but they were there ahead of him. Six of them with Winchesters at the ready. Faro allowed his Winchester to slip to the ground and lifted his hands. With the muzzle of his rifle, one of the Indians pointed to Faro's gun belt, and there was nothing he could do except unbuckle it. One of the Indians seized the gun belt and with another leading his horse, they marched Faro toward the renegade camp. The Ute Faro had shot was only wounded in the shoulder, and he had his recovered knife in his other hand. He looked at Faro hungrily, saying some venomous words in his own tongue, but one of his companions restrained him. As the group approached the fire, the four whites got to their feet. One of the Utes spoke rapidly, pointing first to Faro and then to the Indian who had been wounded. Dog Face responded just as quickly, and the seven Utes moved reluctantly away. The renegade fixed his one good eye on Faro and spoke.

"You ain't made no friends, pilgrim. Beaver Tail wants your scalp, and likely some other parts of your carcass."

"I'm not here to make friends with you or your pet

Indians," Faro said. "I'm scouting ahead for a party I'm sure you know about, and I have as much right here as you do."

Dog Face laughed. "Well, by God, ain't you got sand. It ain't a bad idea, makin' you some *amigos* amongst the Utes, if you aim to ride these trails. Next time you come sneakin' around my camp, I'll let these heathen cut your gizzard out, along with any other parts they fancy. Slade, return his weapons."

Unbelieving, Faro buckled his gun belt around his middle and took his Winchester, but his eyes were on the assembled Utes.

"Mount up and ride," Dog Face ordered.

Faro mounted and rode north, chills creeping up his spine. At any moment he expected to hear the roar of a Winchester and feel the slug slam into his back, but he was soon out of range. Finally he relaxed, wiping his sweating face on the sleeve of his shirt.

"That was a damn fool move," Hueso said, as Faro rode away.

"Yeah," said Sangre. "You should of let the Utes draw an' quarter the bastard."

"The dumbest Ute in the bunch has got more brains than the two of you combined," Dog Face replied. "We ain't killin' nobody until I say so. That bunch is suspicious, but they got nothin' agin us, and until they lead us to that gold claim, they're worth more to us alive than dead."

"I think so, too," said Slade, his eyes on Sangre and Hueso.

"You *would*," Hueso said.

Dog Face laughed, and his two disgruntled companions didn't like the way things were shaping up. The Utes had taken care of the wounded Beaver Tail, and they now eyed the four white men without friendliness.

As Faro rode back to meet the wagons, he was thoroughly angry with himself. There had been no excuse for his having gotten so close to the renegade camp without considering the whereabouts of the Utes he knew were there. He was alive, thanks only to a whim of the renegade leader, and the only thing he had learned was that Slade was obviously one of the renegades. Certainly not worth the risk of his life, he thought in disgust, and he was tempted not to mention the incident to the rest of his outfit. But in the stillness, they likely had heard the shot. In the lead wagon, Collins saw him coming and called a halt to rest the horses. They all gathered to hear his report, and it took but a moment for him to understand why.

"We heard a shot," Dallas Weaver said, "and we was all set to grab our guns and come a-runnin'. But there wasn't any more shots, and we reckoned you either had things under control, or it was too late. Looks like you come out all right."

"Yes," said Faro, "but in a humiliating kind of way."

He held nothing back, telling them of being forced to shoot the Indian, of his capture, and of his release by the renegades.

"I didn't learn a damn thing," he admitted, "except that Slade is part of the renegade outfit."

"To the contrary," said Collins, "I'd say you learned

a lot. Now we know they want us alive until we lead them to the claim."

"Yeah," Kritzer said, "and we know there's nothin' Slade won't do. Elsewise, he sure as hell wouldn't of throwed in with that scruffy bunch."

"After today," said Tarno, "I'd say we better not get too close. Indians ain't the forgivin' kind, and that bunch of Utes will be watchin' for you. Get within Winchester range and they'll kill you."

"I agree," Collins said. "Let's not take needless risks when there's little to be gained. I think it'll take every man of us with a gun in his hands before we reach the end of this trail."

"You're right," said Faro. "I walked into that like a real short horn, and only with a pile of luck and more than my share of the grace of God am I alive."

Durham laughed. "Duval gets his tail feathers clipped by a few Indians and he's done got religion. There'll be prayer meetin' on Sunday morning, with dinner on the ground."

"Shut up, Durham," Shanghai growled.

Mamie and Odessa McCutcheon wanted to laugh, but thought better of it. The rest of the men seemed a little uncomfortable, but Faro ignored the grinning gambler. The wagons again took the trail west. The sun was barely noon-high when Durham kicked his horse into a gallop past the wagons.

"There's Indians on the back trail," he shouted. "Since you took my guns, I hope you won't mind if I don't join in the fight."

In an instant, the men were off the wagon boxes, Winchesters in their hands. Collins leaped from the saddle and came on the run. The Utes had attacked the last two wagons, and as they swept past, Odessa McCutcheon and Felix Blackburn shot two of them off their horses. But the Indians were well within range and their arrows began taking a toll. One of the deadly barbs ripped through Dallas Weaver's left shoulder and another tore into Josh Snyder's right thigh. Mamie McCutcheon fell with a cry, wounded in her right side, just above her gun belt. But it had been a costly charge, and the Utes rode away, leaving nine dead behind.

"Isaac, take over the reins for Dallas," Faro said. "Josh, can you stay on the horse, or do you want a place in one of the wagons?"

"I'll stay with the horse," said Snyder.

"Felix," Faro said, "you can join me in the first wagon, while Collins takes his horse. Some of you help Mamie up on the box with Odessa. We'll stop at the nearest water and tend the wounds."

Having gotten well ahead of the wagons, Durham hadn't received a scratch. He now rode back, just as Faro Duval stepped down from the first wagon.

"Here," said Faro, handing the gambler his Colt and Winchester. "Next time you pull iron on anybody in this outfit, you'd better shoot me first, because if you don't, I'll kill you."

Durham accepted the weapons without comment. The wagons rumbled on, taking more than two hours to reach water. While the teams were being unharnessed, Felix Blackburn got a fire going and put on a pot of water to boil. Now familiar with the procedure, Levi Collins took three quarts of whiskey from one of the wagons. The first he gave to Dallas Weaver, the second to Josh Snyder, and the third to Mamie McCutcheon.

"Mr. Collins," Mamie said, "who's goin' to take this arrow out of me?"

"I don't know," said Collins. "Why?"

"I want Duval to do it," Mamie said.

"I'll tell him," said Collins. "Drink the whiskey."

"I'll want some help," Faro said, when Collins informed him of Mamie's request. "I'll not lay a hand on either of these females without a witness."

"I can't say I blame you," said Collins. "I've never seen such conduct. They've gone out of their way to humiliate you. I'll ride shotgun for you while you remove Mamie's arrow, if you like."

"I'd be obliged," Faro said.

Faro spent three nerve-racking hours removing the arrows. Finished, his shirt was soaked with sweat and he was more than a little sick to his stomach.

"You'd better stretch out in the shade for a while," said Felix Blackburn. "There's hot coffee when you're ready."

"I'm obliged," Faro said.

"We'll remain here for the night," said Levi Collins. "I think we've all had enough for this day."

Faro slept the sleep of the exhausted, and when he awoke the sun was down and Felix had supper ready.

"How are the wounded?" Faro asked.

"As well as can be expected," said Collins. "They're sleeping off the whiskey. Durham and Odessa, too."

"Durham and Odessa?"

"Yes," Collins said. "Odessa offered to stay with

Mamie, and I left her a full quart of whiskey. Durham joined her and they killed the bottle."

"When Mamie needs more whiskey," said Faro, "see that she gets it. But not a drop more."

"I'd already made that decision," Collins said. "I was a damn fool."

Faro laughed. "It was your turn."

With Dallas Weaver and Josh Snyder wounded, each watch was a man shy.

"I'll look in on the wounded during the first watch," Collins said, "if you'll check on them during the second."

"*Bueno,*" said Faro. "I think we might as well plan on laying over an extra day."

"Perhaps two," Collins said, "and then only with the wounded riding the wagons. But we can't spare too many days. We don't know how long the good weather's going to hold. There could be more snow anytime, and it could be with us a lot longer."

Collins's prediction proved accurate, and after a two-day delay, when they again took the trail, those all-too-familiar gray clouds hovered on the horizon.

"It's time to look for shelter," said Faro. "I'll be back soon as I can."

"Don't shoot any more Indians, Duval," Durham said. "They seem a little touchy."

Faro set his jaw, kept his silence, and rode out.

"By God," said Tarno Spangler, "Faro's got more patience than I have. I'd have done shot that varmint dead."

"I never trusted or liked Durham from the time Slade tied in with him," said Kritzer, riding with Tarno on the wagon box. "Somebody's gonna kill that gambler, just on general principles, and I hope I'm around to see it."

Faro sought a canyon with water, and if possible, some graze, but found nothing that seemed suitable. He finally settled for a spring with a run-off in a brush-and tree-lined hollow. Even then the wagons had to travel almost fifteen miles before the storm struck. He met the wagons, and Collins reined them all up to rest the mules.

"It's a good fifteen miles," Faro said, "and no canyon. Just a spring in a hollow, with some tree and brush cover. We'll have to depend on our extra canvas and the wagons to protect us from wind and snow. We don't have any time to spare."

The clouds swept in, and by early afternoon, the warm sun was a memory. The wind was out of the northwest, and had an icy bite to it. But the wagons were within sight of the tree-lined hollow when the first windblown sleet rattled off the wagon canvas.

"Line the wagons up lengthwise, as close as you can get them," Faro ordered. "We'll want them strung out along the hollow, beyond the run-off. Unharness the teams. Then I'll want Shanghai, Tarno, and Dallas to help me erect the snow and wind breaks. The rest of you—Levi, Isaac, Felix, and Josh—take the available horses and begin snaking in some fallen trees for firewood. Get as many as you can. Without canyon walls, we'll need more and bigger fires, just to be comfortable."

Faro, Shanghai, Tarno, and Dallas broke out the protective canvas they carried. There was none for the fifth wagon, so they set to work on the remaining four. With U-bolts at each end, they anchored a sturdy hickory pole to the first and last wagon bows as high up as they could reach. The pole had brass hooks at twelve-inch intervals that matched the brass eyelets in the long side of the canvas barrier. A similar pole with brass hooks was then placed flat on the ground and U-bolted to a front and rear wagon wheel. When a long protective canvas barrier was secured at top and bottom, the bulk of the heavy wagon securing it, the four men moved on to the next wagon. When four such barriers had been put in place, they set about erecting the overhead canvas. To the same pole that was bolted to the wagon bows front and back, they quickly hooked brass eyelets in the canvas that ran the length of the wagon. At the end of each wagon, a dozen feet distant, they drove into the ground an iron spike five feet in length. At the upper end of the spike was an iron ring, and within each wagon was an iron rod, each end of which fitted the iron ring. At proper intervals along the iron rod were hooks for securing the long end of the canvas. Durham and the McCutcheons had watched the shelters taking shape, not offering to help, and when they were near finished, Mamie spoke.

"You got too much slope on the outside, where it comes away from the wagon. If the iron posts you drove into the ground was longer, the overhead canvas could be flat, with more headroom."

"It could also accumulate enough snow to bring it down on your head, likely taking the wagon bows and canvas with it," Dallas said.

"Yeah," said Tarno, with ill-concealed disgust,

"we've done this a time or two before, and we're startin' to get the hang of it."

Collins and his companions had dragged in their first load of wood and had gone after more. Faro turned to Durham and spoke.

"I know it's asking a hell of a lot, but could you get an ax and begin chopping that wood into decent lengths?"

To Faro's surprise, Durham said nothing. He took an ax from one of the wagons and attacked one of the tree trunks. Without being asked, the McCutcheons took kindling from beneath a wagon's possum belly and got a fire going under one of the canvas shelters by the time Collins and his companions returned with more snaked-in firewood.

"We'll have to ride a ways to find more wood," Collins said.

"One more run, then," said Faro. "Shanghai, Tarno, Dallas, and me will take a turn."

"The rest of us will get some axes, then, and whittle this down to firewood length," Collins said.

"You know," said Felix Blackburn, as they went for the axes, "these shelters attached to the lee side of the wagons may be exactly what we'll need when we begin working the claim. Once we change the course of that river into Devil's Canyon, there won't be a lick of shelter. It's all on the side that'll be dynamited away."

"I think we'd better avoid speaking of diverting the river into Devil's Canyon," Collins said. "At least, until we must reveal the need."

"You ain't told Duval and his *compañeros* that part of it, then," said Snyder.

"No," Collins admitted. "I saw no need to, until we reach the claim."

"Until they're in too deep to back out," said Puckett.

"Backing out is the last thing I'd expect of them," Collins said. "After all this *is* a rich claim. They certainly haven't been misled, and that's what matters."

The storm roared all night and was still going strong at dawn. The horses and mules had no shelter except the trees and brush that lined the hollow. The animals came near the wagons to receive their rations of grain, and then turning their backs to the storm, drifted away.

"It's gonna be hell, keepin' the wolves away from them," Dallas said, "if the varmints come prowlin' around."

"We'll have to group them as near the wagons as we can," said Faro. "Be listenin' for the first cry of a wolf."

But the first sound they heard above the howling of the wind was the distant nicker of a horse.

"Maybe one of ours," Collins said.

"If it ain't one of ours, it means somebody's out there," said Tarno. "Maybe trouble."

"Maybe not," Faro said. "Listen for the horse to nicker again."

The horse did nicker a second time, more plaintive than before.

"Nobody's tryin' to silence him," said Shanghai. "Likely his rider ain't able."

"He's got to be to the west of us," Faro said. "The

wind's from that direction. Tarno, will you go with me?"

"I reckon," said Tarno, "if it's a stray horse, we can use him. If he has—or had—a rider, the poor bastard will need buryin', when the ground thaws."

"One of us can go with you, if you want," Collins said.

"No," said Faro. "Throw some more logs on the fire."

Faro and Tarno tied woolen scarves over their ears, thonged down their hats, donned sheepskin-lined coats and gloves, and stepped out into the storm. In places the snow had already drifted deep, and they had to fight their way through it. Faro looked back, and the new-fallen snow had already begun to cover their tracks. They couldn't go much farther without the risk of becoming lost. Just when Faro was about to give up and turn back, the horse nickered again. The animal saw them through the swirling snow and reared. There was no saddle. Faro had brought a lead rope, and looped it around the animal's neck. Only then did he see a human hand reaching—as though in mute appeal for help—from a snowbank. Tarno had seen it, too, and he seized the hand. He sought a pulse, found none, and shook his head. But Faro Duval didn't give up. Taking the Indian's other arm, he lifted him out of the snow, and with Tarno's help, got him belly-down across the horse. Then they began the slow, seemingly hopeless task of getting him to their camp. The horse often stumbled, apparently from weakness and the cold. Finally, through swirling snow, they saw the dim outline of one of the wagons. Shanghai and Dallas saw them coming and came to meet them. Leading the horse as near the shelter as they could, they lifted off the Indian and placed him on a blanket near the fire.

"Some of you grab a blanket and rub some life back into that horse," Faro said, "and then give him a measure of grain."

"Here's some whiskey," said Collins. "If he's still alive, it'll bring him around."

"I found a pulse," Tarno said, "but it's almighty weak."

"You should have left the heathen out there," said Durham contemptuously. "He'd have been one less we'll have to shoot."

"This Indian's no danger to anybody," Faro said. "He has only a knife."

It was true. The Bowie, attached to a rawhide thong, dangled down the Indian's back, beneath his buckskin shirt.

"Get his moccasins off, so's we can rub some life back into his feet," said Shanghai.

Faro removed the frozen moccasins, and what they saw sobered them all. The Indian's left foot was horribly mutilated. It appeared to have once been broken at the ankle and had twisted inward.

"My God," Dallas said, "the poor varmint's crippled, and under that buckskin, he's all bones. He was half starved before the storm got him."

Chapter 12

Collins and Snyder got a quantity of whiskey down the half-frozen Indian, while Faro, Shanghai, and Dallas worked with his hands and feet. Tarno had a blanket and was rubbing down the horse.

"His horse ain't been eatin' no better than he has," Tarno said. "He's so weak he can barely stand."

"There's no room for the horse near the fire under the shelter," said Isaac Puckett, "so why don't we start up a fire outside that he can get to?"

"Go ahead," Collins said. "We seem to have plenty of wood."

Despite the wind-driven snow, they soon had a roaring fire going, and the horse did not have to be led to it. Moreover, some of the other horses and mules came to it, enjoying the warmth.

"Uh-oh," said Tarno, "we've started somethin'. Now we got another fire to watch."

"Nothing wrong with that," Faro said. "This snow shows no signs of blowing itself out, and we may end up shooting wolves to protect our livestock. The fire will be a help."

"The Indian's pulse is stronger," said Shanghai.

"When he's slept off the whiskey and gets a bite of grub, he'll be all right."

"Huh," Durham scoffed, "what the hell good is a crippled Indian? For that matter, what good is an Indian with two good feet?"

"He ain't near as crippled as *you* are, Durham," said Tarno. "Just in a different way."

"He may not be a Ute," Shanghai said. "He may have been banished from his tribe. Some tribes do that, when their people become old and infirm, or disabled."

"How cruel," said Mamie McCutcheon. "The old and the crippled are less able to take care of themselves. This poor fellow's just skin and bones."

Durham laughed. "He's a man, Mamie, and the part that'll interest you is probably in good order. Why don't you adopt him?"

The gambler was standing directly behind Mamie, and it was the wrong thing to have said. In a swift move that endeared her to them all, she turned and planted her right fist in Durham's face. When he stumbled backward and sat down in one of the fires, nobody lifted a hand. Instead, there was laughter and shouting as Durham sprang to his feet with the seat of his trousers and the tail of his coat afire. Throwing himself into a snowbank, he wallowed around until the fire was out. He lay there wiping his smashed, bleeding nose on the sleeve of his coat, glaring at them all in undisguised hatred.

"By God," said Withers in awe, "the ride from Santa Fe was worth that."

"It was," Kritzer agreed. "Ma'am, you've just earned my undying admiration."

"Thank you," said Mamie modestly. "Maybe I ain't always what I should be, but I'll never mistreat the old, the crippled, or the hungry, Indian or not."

"Amen," Felix Blackburn said. "What ye do unto the least of mine, ye have done unto me."

The most unlearned among them recognized the scripture, and Durham wisely kept his mouth shut. He got to his feet and went to the farthest wagon, where his saddlebags were. There he began rummaging for clothing to replace that which had been damaged.

"Tarnation," Shanghai said, "only way I know it's another day is that my gut's howlin' for breakfast. It's snowin' just as hard as ever."

"Yes," said Faro, "and I look for us to have a wolf problem before the end of the day, even if the snow lets up."

"The Indian's awake," Puckett said.

"Tarno," said Faro, "you're half-Comanche. See if you can understand him, and maybe get him to understand you."

"The Spanish once owned this country," Tarno said. "If he knows any Spanish, we can talk."

"*Nombre?*" said Tarno, kneeling beside the Indian.

"*Oso Espiritu,*" the Indian replied.

The Indian spoke Spanish fluently. Faro and some of the others understood some of the conversation, and it ended only when Felix Blackburn brought a tin cup of coffee and a tin plate of food. The Indian accepted the offering gratefully. Tarno then began to tell them in some detail what he had learned.

"He's a Paiute," said Tarno, "and Paiute country is

somewhere far to the west. He's been driven from his tribe to die. His foot was mangled in a fight with a grizzly, and the bear escaped. A superstitious medicine man convinced the tribe that our Indian's soul had been stolen by the bear, so they named him *Bear Spirit* and cast him out."

"My God," Dallas said, "what are we gonna do with him? He can't wander through these mountains alone, with a twisted foot and only a knife."

"If he don't starve," said Shanghai, "the Utes will kill him. It's surprising they haven't already."

"I don't know what's to become of him," Collins said, "but he's human, and I won't see him left to starve or be murdered. He has a horse. He can go with us. Tell him that, Tarno."

"Good decision, Collins," said Faro.

Tarno conveyed the message to the Paiute, and he put down his tin plate. When he spoke, it was loud enough for them all to hear. "*Gracias. Muchas gracias.*"

Felix Blackburn refilled the tin cup with coffee and the tin plate with more food, and the hungry Indian accepted it gratefully. Despite the continuing storm, everybody seemed cheered by the decision to help the homeless Paiute. Durham looked upon them all with disfavor, but nobody seemed to care what he thought. The storm raged on, and before the end of the day, there was bone-chilling evidence that Faro's prediction was about to come to pass. Somewhere to the west, borne on the wind, came the mournful cry of a wolf, and on the heels of it, like an eerie echo, there was a distant answer.

"They're coming," Faro said. "Throw some more logs on that outside fire. I'm going to start another, and we'll try to keep our livestock between them."

"Lord, yes," said Tarno. "It'll be hard as hell to see 'em in this blowing snow. We'll need the light from the fire, so they can't get right on top of us."

Quickly the second fire was started, with enough space between the two for the gathering of the horses and mules. The animals needed no urging, for the crackling flames were saving beacons in an ominous world of swirling white. With the line of wagons and their protective canvas at their backs, and with armed men at both flanks, the attacking wolves had to come at them head-on.

"They've stopped howling," Collins said hopefully.

"When you don't hear the varmints, you'll soon be seein' 'em," said Dallas.

The first attacking wolves took the last approach any of them had expected. There was the sound of ripping canvas as two of the brutes sprang to the top of one of the wagons. Three Winchesters roared, sending the dead wolves over and away from the wagon. But it seemed almost like a diversion, for more than a dozen wolves charged the camp head-on. Horses and mules spooked, and in crowding closer, spoiled the aim of many of the defenders. A horse reared, a hoof striking Faro's shoulder with such force that he was slammed against the side of the wagon. Dazed as he was, he wasn't ready for the wolf. It sprang, driving slashing front claws into Faro's shoulders. Arms numb, he tried to reach his Colt, but could not. Lowering his head to protect his throat, he went limp. He had to get on the ground so that one of his comrades could shoot the beast. The scene was total chaos as horses and mules screamed, wolves snarled, and the roar of Winchesters became a continuous roar of thunder.

As Faro went down, expecting at any moment to feel the wolf's fangs tear into his throat, a miracle took place. The recently rescued Paiute had been under the wagon, and he came out with a cry as chilling as that of the wolves themselves. With his left arm the Indian got a choke hold around the wolf's massive neck. In his right hand was his Bowie knife, and he began driving it repeatedly into any part of the wolf he could reach. Seeming to forget Faro, the wolf turned his head, snapping and snarling at this new threat. Faro rolled away, getting his hands on his Winchester. The firing had all but ceased. The entire front of Faro's shirt was bloody as he staggered to his feet.

"My God!" Shanghai shouted.

"Help the Indian," Faro said.

But even as he spoke, there was only an ominous silence from beneath the wagon, and his fears quickly became reality.

"The Paiute's dead," said Tarno. "That big bastard of a wolf got to his throat. Looks like he killed the varmint with the last of his strength before he died."

"Damned strange," Dallas said. "We lost only one horse, and it belonged to the Paiute."

"He was just a homeless Indian and an outlaw," said Faro, "but as a man he stood nine feet tall. But for him, I'd be dead. Who else was hurt?"

"Felix and Withers," said Collins, "but they'll heal. Some of the horses and mules need doctoring, too."

"Some of you tend to Felix and Withers, some of you to the livestock, and the rest keep watch in case the wolves return," Faro said.

"Out of that shirt, or what's left of it. You've been clawed worse than Felix or Withers," said Mamie McCutcheon.

Faro needed help getting the shirt off. His clawed arm and shoulders already had begun to stiffen.

"For the time being," Collins said, "I think we'll wrap the Indian in some blankets."

"Do that," said Faro.

Blackburn and Withers had already been stretched out on blankets. Mamie and Odessa McCutcheon had water boiling on two of the fires, and Levi Collins had brought the medicine chest, along with several bottles of whiskey.

"Go ahead and join them," Mamie said, spreading a third blanket.

Faro did so, watching Kritzer, Snyder, Dallas, Tarno, and Shanghai rope the dead wolves and drag them away into the darkness. The horses and mules still huddled close to the fires, terrified at the wolf scent and the smell of blood.

"How many of the gray devils?" Faro asked.

"Eighteen dead, including the one the Indian knifed," said Collins. "My God, that took courage."

"Maybe more than you realize," Faro replied. "He could have stayed under the wagon until one of you shot the wolf."

"But any one of us would have been too late to save you," said Collins.

"Yes," Faro said, "It was his life or mine, and he

made the choice. It's enough to humble a man. He'd known me only a few hours."

"No matter," Felix Blackburn said. "A simple act of kindness taking only a few minutes can make an impression that lasts a lifetime."

"It just did," said Withers, who had been listening.

"Strange as it may sound," Collins said, "I believe this crippled Paiute saw the fight with the wolf as a means of redeeming himself, to prove his courage."

"It's about the only thing that makes any sense," said Faro. "Losing an impossible fight with a grizzly cost him the use of a foot and the respect of his tribe. That's enough to destroy an Indian, and when life drags a man down low enough, he's likely to start thinking of death with honor. I lost a friend on the battlefield at Gettysburg. He had taken a bad one in the spine and had been paralyzed from the waist down. He wouldn't allow himself to be moved, except to leave him with his back to a tree. When the rest of us were driven back, he kept firing until the enemy rushed his position."

"God," said Odessa McCutcheon, "it must have been terrible, leaving him there."

"It was," Faro said. "He was my brother."

"The water's boiling, Odessa," said Mamie. "Come help me."

By the time the men who had dragged away the dead wolves returned, the roar of the storm had subsided. The snow was only an occasional windblown dusting, and incredibly, a few stars twinkled timidly in the western sky.

"This couldn't come at a better time," said Dallas.

"There's snow drifts deep enough to swallow a man on a horse."

"Yeah," Shanghai agreed, "and it gets some complicated when you got a skittish horse on one end of the rope and a pair of dead wolves on the other."

"Did you see any more wolves?" Collins asked.

"No sign of any," said Tarno. "I reckon we accounted for enough of the varmints to make an impression on the others. How bad are the wounded?"

"Faro's wounds are the worst," Collins said. "Could be a week before we can move him."

"Three days," said a groggy Faro Duval.

"Won't matter if it takes a week," said Dallas. "When this snow melts, there'll be mud like you've never seen."

"That's something we can't change," Collins said. "We'll consider the wounded first and then the terrain ahead. Has anybody seen Durham?"

As though in answer to the inquiry there came a prolonged, rattling snore from beneath one of the wagons.

"Damn," said Kritzer in disgust. "The lobos should of got him instead of the Indian."

"My sentiments exactly," Tarno said. "Maybe next time it can be arranged."

"Come daylight," said Collins, "we'll roust him and put him to chopping wood. Unless the sun comes out and it gets warm in a hurry, we'll be snaking in more logs. That is, if we can find them."

"Finding them won't be a problem," Isaac Puckett said, "but getting to them will be."

"He's right about that," said Shanghai. "We'd best

get an early start, 'cause we'll have to break trail for the horses. It'll be an all-day job.''

"You men know what to do," Collins replied. "Get started after breakfast. I'll break out some axes so Durham and me can begin chopping wood."

Collins noted with a sigh of relief that as soon as the McCutcheons had doctored and bandaged the wounded men, they had then turned their attention to preparing breakfast. They were needed, especially with Felix Blackburn among the wounded. He had noticed Mamie taking an interest in Felix, while he seemed interested but wary. He half hoped Felix would respond, drawing Mamie's attention away from the no-account gambler. Now if there was just somebody to occupy Odessa's time.

While the renegade camp hadn't been visited by marauding wolves, it hadn't fared well during the storm. There had been no windbreaks except the few leafless trees. The Utes—now twenty-five in number—had taken refuge in a thicket where they kept their own fires and cooked their own meals. The bitter cold had kept Sangre, Hueso, and Slade scrambling for enough wood to feed their own fires for warmth. Sangre and Hueso had complained constantly. Slade had kept his silence.

"Look at them damn Utes," Hueso growled. "There they set, with plenty of firewood, eatin' our grub."

"Yeah," said Sangre. "And they're starin' at us like we was calves trapped in a bog hole."

Dog Face laughed. "You varmints do beat all. You hate them Utes, and then you ain't got the brains to understand why they're just itchin' to cut your gizzards out. You want more firewood, saddle your horse an' drag some up."

"I ain't seen you draggin' none up," Hueso snapped.

"You won't neither," said Dog Face. "It's me that's keepin' you alive in Ute country. Let somethin' happen to me and you won't be needin' firewood. It'll be plenty warm in hell."

"It's plenty warm in California," Sangre said.

"Go on," said Dog Face, "if you're comfortable with a rope around your scrawny neck."

Slade laughed, enjoying the expressions of hate and frustration on the faces of these troublesome renegades.

"What'n hell are you laughin' at?" Sangre roared.

"You and the turkey buzzard," said Slade. "The pair of you are funnier than a team of dancing bears."

Dog Face laughed. Sangre lunged at Slade, but Slade was expecting that. He stepped aside and slammed a murderous right into Sangre's beefy face. The big man went head over heels into a snowdrift. Spitting blood and curses, he came up clawing for his Colt, only to find Slade had him covered.

"Back off, Slade," Dog Face said. "This ain't no time for them Utes to see us fightin' amongst ourselves. I dunno how much longer I can keep 'em on a tight rein, if them cussed wagons don't come on."

"I could ride back and check on 'em," said Slade.

"Too soon," Dog Face replied. "Them wagons won't be movin' till the snow melts and some of the mud dries up. Besides, I may have need of you here."

The threat wasn't lost on Sangre and Hueso, for not

once during their stormy alliance with Dog Face had the renegade spoken of needing them. Their hatred of Slade fed on itself and continued to grow.

"How long have I slept?" asked Faro.

"Near eighteen hours," said Odessa McCutcheon. "How do you feel?"

"Like I been chewed up and spit out," Faro said. "I need maybe a gallon of water to rid myself of the whiskey taste."

"We saved you some supper," said Mamie.

"Bring that, too," Faro said.

There was snoring, and looking around, he found Blackburn and Withers sleeping peacefully. In the light from the fire, sweat glistened on their faces, evidence their fevers had broken. Seeing Faro was awake, Collins knelt beside him.

"We had sun for most of the day," said Collins. "If we're as fortunate tomorrow, the snow will be gone."

"And there'll be an equal amount of mud to replace it," Faro said.

"Unfortunately, yes," said Collins, "but those of you who were wounded can use a couple more days to heal, and since we can't move the wagons anyway, it's not costing us any time."

Mamie brought Faro his supper and while he was eating, Dallas joined him.

"While we're layin' over," Dallas said, "we ought to grease the wheel hubs and axles of all the wagons. Shanghai, Tarno, and me can do it tomorrow."

"Do it," Faro said. "And we'll be that much ahead."

"The ground should be thawed enough to bury the Indian, too."

"*Bueno,*" Faro said. "He's more than earned the right to a decent burial."

Three days later, the wagons again rumbled west. Faro sat on the high box of the lead wagon, allowing Collins to scout ahead. The weather had turned unseasonably warm, and thanks to melted snow at higher elevations, Collins had no trouble finding abundant water with some decent graze. Sundown was less than an hour away when the camp came to attention. A rider approached from the west.

"Rein up," Collins ordered, "and identify yourself."

"Luke Tindall," the rider shouted.

"Dismount and come on," said Collins.

Tindall dismounted, and as he drew near, the most striking thing about him was the lawman's star pinned to his shirt. He carried two Colts and the *buscadera* rig rode low on his hips, seeming too large. While he had an admirable manner about him, Faro didn't like him, for something didn't ring true. He addressed himself to Collins, ignoring the rest of them.

"Horse is lame," Tindall said. "I was hopin' for a swap. Any chance?"

"Sorry, no," said Collins. "There's another camp west of here. Did you stop there?"

"Naw," Tindall replied. "Two or three whites and the rest was Indians. I got o use for a white man that hunkers down with heathen."

"Tindall," said Faro, "you're a good four hundred miles from Santa Fe, and even farther from any settlements to the west. What possible business could a law-man have in these mountains where there's mostly hostile Indians?"

"Friend," Tindall said coldly, "you tend to get a mite personal. I don't see the need for you knowin' my business."

"Well, I do," said Levi Collins. "We don't know that you won't return after dark and try to take one of our horses."

It was an insult—obvious and intentional—that no man on the frontier could overlook. Tindall eased his hands close to the butts of his Colts.

"Don't even think of it, pilgrim," Tarno said.

"Damn it," Tindall growled, dropping his hands to his side. "What kind of lawman do you think I am?"

"That's exactly what we're trying to find out," said Collins.

"All right," Tindall growled, "if you got to know, I'm trailin' a bank robber name of Harlan Taylor. Stuck up a bank in the Bay Area an' escaped with more'n twenty-five thousand."

"How do you know Taylor came this way?" Collins asked.

"I trailed him till I had to hole up from the storm," said Tindall. "He's wanted all over California, so he couldn't stay there."

"An uncommon long ways to trail a man," Faro said. "You want him that bad?"

"Bad enough to chase him clean to Santa Fe," said Tindall. "Since you can't spare me a fresh horse, am I welcome to stay the night? My cayuse might be better, come mornin'."

"You're welcome to stay," Collins replied.

After supper, Tindall sat with his back to a wagon wheel, shuffling a deck of cards. Except for Hal Durham, he was ignored, but he was quick to notice Durham's interest.

"Care for a few hands?" Tindall asked.

"Maybe," said Durham, "but I never play for fun. You got money?"

"Enough," Tindall said.

Spreading a blanket for money and cards, they settled down near one of the fires. The rest of the camp—even the McCutcheons—shied away.

"That *hombre*'s unlike any lawman I've ever seen," said Faro.

"If you mean the gambling, that's the least offensive thing about him," Dallas said. "Wild Bill never gets so busy bein' a lawman that he'd turn his back on a poker game."

"Wild Bill don't wear a gun belt that's too big for him, with another man's initials cut into the leather," said Faro.

"Faro's right," said Tarno. "You got to look close, but there's an H.T. cut into the back of that gun belt. Flesh that out some, and get Harlan Taylor, not Luke Tindall."

"My God," Collins said. "We've taken in a thief and a murderer."

"That's how it stacks up to me," said Faro, "but there's a matter of proof. Or the lack of it."

"He ain't let them saddlebags out of his sight since he showed up," Shanghai observed.

"Still no evidence," said Faro.

"If your suspicions are correct," Collins said, "then he shouldn't go unpunished. What are we to do?"

"Nothing," said Faro, "unless he tips his hand in some way."

But Durham and Tindall had been playing less than an hour when trouble erupted. Durham had won consistently. Suddenly Tindall got to his feet and backed away.

"You been cheatin'," Tindall said.

Durham laughed. "We're using your cards."

"No matter," said Tindall. "I'm declarin' this game finished and takin' back my money."

"The game is finished," Durham said, "but the money stays."

Dallas and Tarno had their hands near their Colts, but Faro shook his head. Durham had gotten himself in a bad situation, and now he must play out his hand. And he did. Tindall drew and fired first, but Durham was swift as a striking rattler. He threw himself to the side, and belly-down, shot Tindall twice. Tindall stumbled backward, fell and lay still. Durham still held the Colt in his fist, a killing fury in his eyes.

"Put away the gun, Durham," Faro said.

"He drew first," said the gambler defensively.

"I'm not denying that," Faro said. "It's all that's saving your worthless neck from a rope."

All eyes turned to the blanket where the money and cards lay. There was less than a hundred dollars, and oblivious to them all, Durham was gathering it up.

"Shanghai," said Faro, "you and Tarno wrap Tindall in a blanket. We'll bury him in the morning."

"I suppose there's no reason why we can't have a

look in Tindall's saddlebags," Collins said. "It might confirm our suspicions."

"No reason," said Faro. "Go ahead."

"No," Durham shouted. "I'm claiming the saddlebags and whatever's in them."

"I don't think so," said Faro coldly. "Killing a man doesn't entitle you to everything he has. Especially when it may not be his. Fetch the saddlebags, Collins."

The saddlebags were opened and the contents dumped on a blanket. There were bundles of paper currency in large bills. Some of them were still wrapped in paper bands bearing the name of a California bank.

"There must be twenty-five thousand and more," Collins said.

"Splittin' it even, that's more than two thousand apiece," said Durham. "I'm entitled to my cut."

"You're entitled to nothing," Faro replied. "This money belongs to a California bank, and I aim to see they get it back, once we return to Santa Fe."

Durham said no more. Taking a pair of his blankets, he rolled in them and was soon asleep.

Chapter 13

Tindall was buried at first light, before breakfast.

"We didn't bury him anywhere near the Paiute," Shanghai said, when he, Blackburn, Tarno, and Withers had finished the grisly task.

"*Bueno*," said Faro. "The Indian was worth a hundred of him."

Before the wagons again rolled west, Faro spent a few minutes with Levi Collins, discussing their position.

"We're less than a hundred miles from the Colorado River," Collins said.

"Do you know where it's shallow enough to cross the wagons?"

"There are plenty of shallows," said Collins, "but where the Colorado passes through Utah, there are deep gorges where no wagon could ever cross."

"We may be forced to travel miles out of our way, then," Faro said.

"I'm afraid so," said Collins. "The way we're headed, we'll reach the river at or near the place where we first forded it with pack mules."

"Then we'll make camp there and ride the river in

both directions until we find a place to cross the wagons. If worst comes to worst, we might have to take picks and shovels and create our own crossing," Faro said.

"Perhaps," said Collins, "but don't count on it. There are long stretches where the Colorado flows through deep canyons with stone rims clear to the water."

"We'll cross it," Faro said.

"The wagons are movin' again," Slade reported.

"*Bueno,*" said Dog Face. "I think we'll stay where we are and let them get ahead of us."

"They better not be goin' beyond the Colorado," Hueso said. "They'll never get them wagons across."

"Ain't nothin' there but one deep gorge after another," Sangre added.

"Well, Slade," said Dog Face, "ain't you got your opinion?"

"Yeah," Slade replied. "Too many *hombres* have a weakness, and they expect to find the same weakness in others. Underestimating his opponents can get a man killed. If them wagons need to cross the Colorado, they'll cross it."

The insult was directed at Sangre and Hueso, and they were very much aware of it. Dog Face laughed, and the uneasy alliance continued.

The Colorado River. September 30, 1870.

Slowly but surely, Felix Blackburn's interest in Mamie McCutcheon grew. When Blackburn was on watch, Mamie didn't sleep much.

"What do you want out of life, Mamie?" Felix asked one night.

"I don't feel I have the right to expect much," said Mamie.

"Why not?"

"You mean you haven't heard how Odessa and me made fools of ourselves over a certain tinhorn gambler?" Mamie replied.

"Some of it," said Felix frankly. "Why don't you tell me the rest?"

"You're sure you want to hear it?"

"Yes," Felix said.

For most of an hour she talked while Blackburn listened. When she had finished, there was a long moment of silence. Mamie held her breath, fearing his response.

"Let he who is without sin cast the first stone," said Felix.

"You quote scripture like a preacher," Mamie said.

"I spent two years in a Louisiana prison," said Felix. "I spent it reading the Bible. I figured I had some catching up to do. So, you see, somewhere along the way, we've all played the fool, doing things we can't be proud of."

"It's kind of you to say that," Mamie said. "I can't imagine you in prison. Do I have the right to ask what you did?"

"Yes," said Felix. "I killed a man over a saloon whore. Her name was Mary Lou, and she wasn't quite seventeen. She promised that if she had the money, she'd straighten up and return to her family in Georgia. I gave her two hundred dollars and she quit the saloon. But a week later, I found her in a different saloon.

When she took a man upstairs, I followed. I kicked the door in, and the man she was with pulled a gun. I shot him and she bashed me in the head with a brass lamp. When I woke up, the law was there and the dead man didn't have a gun. Nothing I could say made any difference."

"Framed," Mamie said.

"Yes," said Felix.

"But your intentions were good," Mamie said.

Felix laughed. "I heard the broad road to perdition is paved with them."

"But you seem to be a better, stronger man," said Mamie.

"Thanks," Felix replied. "I like to think so. I've heard that no experience is all bad when you learn from it."

Felix sat with his back to a wagon wheel, his rifle beside him. Wordlessly, Mamie moved over next to him, taking one of his hands in hers. . . .

"There she is," said Collins, "the Colorado."

"Tarnation," Dallas said. "That's some river."

"Tomorrow," said Faro, "we'll ride it in both directions. We'll find a place to cross if we have to build a bridge."

"That'll take time, building a bridge," Shanghai said.

"Perhaps not as long as going miles out of our way up or down the river," said Collins.

Durham listened to their plans, and his devious mind began creating one of his own, for he had seen the saddlebags of stolen money in Faro Duval's lead wagon. Duval would most surely be one of the men riding the river. Durham needed only a few short minutes, with a diversion of some kind. . . .

"Collins will ride upstream while I ride downstream," Faro told them after breakfast.

"Rest of you stay with the wagons and keep your rifles handy. We haven't had any Indian trouble for a while."

Faro and Collins rode out, and less than an hour later, the Indians attacked from the south and the east. Unlike before, they didn't come to kill. Instead, they spooked all the mules, stampeding them north.

"Ride them down," Dallas Weaver shouted.

It was an unnecessary command, as every one of them knew they dared not lose the mules. Madly they pursued the Utes along the north bank of the Colorado. While firing from horseback was difficult, they managed to kill two of the invaders. The others, fearful of being ridden down in a crossfire, forgot about the mules and rode for their lives.

"Let 'em go," shouted Tarno.

Clearly they had to give up the chase, for they had saved their teams, while leaving their wagons undefended. Only Odessa McCutcheon was there, for her horse had not been saddled. It was the chance Hal Durham had waited for, and he ran to Faro Duval's lead wagon, seizing the saddlebags. He dropped off the wagon box, only to be confronted by Odessa.

"Get out of my way," Durham snorted.

"No," said Odessa.

But as she lifted her Winchester, Durham flung her back against the wagon, where her head struck an iron rim. Before she could rise, Durham leaped on his horse and galloped west. Hiding in the brush, he avoided the men returning with the mules. Faro and Collins were last to return to the wagons.

"The Utes come after the mules," Shanghai said. "We got only two of 'em, but we saved the mules. There was nobody hurt but Odessa."

"Durham took that bank money and lit out," said Odessa.

"About what we expected of him," Levi Collins said.

Faro said nothing, but the looks he exchanged with Collins suggested that they might have planned for just such an event.

"Why the sudden interest in the mules?" Odessa wondered.

"Game's in short supply," said Faro. "The Indians eat mules."

"God," Mamie said, "I can't imagine that."

"Depends on how hard up you are for grub," said Josh Snyder. "I've had mule a time or two."

"You never told us about that," Isaac Puckett said.

"I ain't exactly proud of it," said Snyder. "Me and a couple more damn fools stayed too long in the north country. Got snowed in neck-deep, back in the Absarokas. Grub-wise, we was down to the soles of our boots and our pack mule. So decided to eat the mule. We had mule on Sunday, mule on Monday, and mule again on Tuesday."

"Then what happened?" Mamie asked.

"We throwed up on Wednesday," said Snyder. "There was a break in the weather and we shot us a buck deer. Tough old critter, but compared to mule, he was prime."

Hal Durham slowed his horse to a walk, knowing he must spare the animal. He just couldn't believe there was no pursuit. The enormity of what he had done shook him. He was alone in Ute country, and somewhere there was Slade and the pack of renegades he'd thrown in with. Somehow he must convince them he intended going on to California without them knowing of the money. So intently was he pondering the situation, he rode into the Indians. Nine of them had reined up their horses and waited, their Winchesters ready. They said nothing, backstepping their horses so that he could ride on. Three of them fell in behind, while three rode on either side of him. Durham swallowed hard, for he knew where they were going. When they reached the renegade camp, Durham reined up. The three renegades were the ugliest men Durham had ever seen. It was Slade who spoke.

"Get down. You got some talkin' to do."

"I got nothin' to say," Durham replied.

"You're alone in Ute country," said Slade. "Why?"

"I got tired of the high-handed ways of the teamsters," Durham replied. "I'm goin' to California."

"Without grub, I reckon," said Slade. "It's near seven hundred miles."

"I was hopin' you could sell me some supplies," Durham said.

Dog Face laughed. "You just left five wagon loads of supplies, and you're tryin' to buy from us. Why?"

"I can answer that," Slade said. "He's done something to get on the bad side of that bunch with the wagons, and they run him off."

"That's a lie," said Durham. "They're bound for a gold claim somewhere, and I couldn't figure a way to deal myself in, so I left. What was the use in me goin' on with them?"

"That part about the gold claim is true," Slade said, "but why would you give up their protection from the Utes and ride off without grub?"

"I see what you're gettin' at," said Dog Face. "Sangre, you and Hueso search him. Slade, check out his saddlebags."

"No!" Durham shouted.

But Sangre held a Colt on him while Hueso made the search. Durham said no more, swallowing hard as Slade went for the saddlebags.

"Nothin' on him but a couple hunnert, a deck of cards, and a pistol," said Hueso in disgust.

"Saddlebags, then," Dog Face said.

"Everything in those saddlebags is mine," said Durham.

"Hell," Slade said. "There's nothin' here but wads of wrappin' paper from a store in Santa Fe."

"That can't be," said Durham. "There was twenty-five thousand . . ."

"You lie," Sangre hissed, cocking the Colt.

"Hold it," said Slade. "He's a tin horn that would raise a pair against a straight flush. He ain't sharp enough to come up with somethin' like this, if it wasn't the truth."

"Slade's right," Dog Face said. "*Hombre*, tell us about that twenty-five thousand you thought was in them saddlebags, and it had better be good."

Durham had no choice, and they listened in rapt attention as he talked.

"Damn it," Slade said. "They switched saddlebags on you. You should have expected that."

Dog Face was laughing while Sangre and Hueso scowled. Hueso spoke.

"Why can't I shoot him? He ain't of no use to us."

"He might be," said Slade. "I ain't sure that bunch with the wagons won't take him in, if he's desperate enough."

"No," Durham said, "there's nothin' in it for me. They'd expect me to sell them out."

"And you would, to save your hide," said Dog Face.

"They'll shoot me," Durham protested. "If they do take me in, what's in it for me?"

"You go on livin'," said Dog Face, "And if you don't sell us out, there'll be somthin' in it for you. Just don't say nothin' about bein' here. Now ride."

Durham mounted and rode back the way he had come. But only until he was clear of the outlaws' camp. He then rode south for ten miles before again riding west. He would take his chances with the Utes.

"What do you think of our chances of crossing the Colorado?" Collins asked.

"Not good, from what I've seen of it," said Faro. "But the Indian attack cut short our inspection. What do you think?"

"I think we could travel a hundred miles up or down stream without finding a place to cross these wagons," Collins said.

"Then we'll have to cut some trees for stringers and

build a pole bridge. We have axes, hammers, and spikes," said Faro.

"That makes sense," Collins replied. "When we're ready to return to Santa Fe, we'll need it again."

"It'll have to be plenty strong," said Felix. "That ore will be heavier than what we're hauling now."

They began by felling three firs with forty-foot trunks. Two of them were strung across the gorge, twelve feet apart, with the third one in between for support. Stakes were driven deep to anchor the stringers on both banks of the river.

"Now comes the hard part," Faro said, as they began their second day of labor. "We'll need enough logs, fourteen feet long, to build a corduroy road."

While some of them began felling and trimming the needed trees, others took their axes and flattened the logs at each end and in the middle, where they would be placed side by side and spiked to the stringers. By the end of the second day the bridge was finished.

"We'll cross at dawn," said Faro.

"I'm impressed," Levi Collins said during breakfast. "I always believed teamsters just drove wagons, fighting Indians and outlaws when they had to. This bridge is a touch of genius."

"We're considerably more than just teamsters," Dallas Weaver said. "It's the long shots that pay."

"Yeah," said Shanghai. "Here in the West, it's gettin' the job done that counts."

"The hard part may still be ahead of us," said Faro. "Mules are skittish. We'll have to blindfold and lead them across, keeping their heads up. Let them look down and they'll balk, for sure."

"That's gospel," Dallas said. "Never let a mule see anything except what he thinks is solid ground under his feet, and if it ain't solid ground, don't let him see nothin'."

After breakfast, after the teams had been harnessed, Faro brought out a leather bag in which there were strips of thin embroidered leather.

"*Tapojos,* the Mexicans call them," said Faro. "In Texas, they're called blinkers."

With blinkers covering the eyes of the teams, the first wagon crossed the bridge without difficulty. The rest of the wagons quickly followed, and when all had crossed, Faro had a word with Collins.

"You've been this way before. Is there enough water ahead of us?"

"Yes," Collins said. "As I recall, we should be able to veer south maybe half a dozen miles and we'll be following a river for a ways. When it forks, we can then follow the south fork to within a day's drive of our claim on the Sevier."*

"I'll take over the lead wagon, then," said Faro, "and we'll follow you. Don't get too far ahead. Those Utes that came after the mules may follow us."

"I'll be on the lookout for them," Collins replied.

But the danger of attack was far greater along the back trail, and with that in mind, Faro spoke to Withers and Kritzer.

"Saddle a pair of the horses and ride behind the last

*The Green River, which flows into the Colorado in southeastern Utah.

wagon. If you see anything along our back trail, sound off. Those Utes may follow us."

"We'll watch for them," Kritzer promised.

Hal Durham had ridden west only a few miles when he reined up to rest his horse. He had crossed a river, but had no idea how far he might be from the next water. He had no intention of returning to Faro Duval's caravan. Therefore, he had to avoid Slade and the renegades with whom he had allied himself. The more Durham thought about it, the less inclined he was to attempt to reach California. He was certain the river he had just crossed flowed into the Colorado, but prior to that, it meandered toward the northeast. Following it, he would eventually reach a settlement, perhaps in eastern Colorado. There he could buy supplies to see him through to Denver. With that in mind, Durham turned back to the river he had crossed, and following it, rode north.

Along the Green River, in eastern Utah.
October 2, 1870.

Durham's small supply of food was quickly exhausted, along with grain for his horse, and he had ridden for two days surviving only on dogged determination. It was with some relief that he heard dogs barking somewhere ahead. By the time he could see the string of cabins along the river, the dogs had discovered him. Half a dozen hounds came yipping to greet him, spooking his horse. There were eight cabins in all, and well before Durham got close, men were there to greet him. There were eight of them, not a friendly face in the lot, and each was armed with a long gun.

"That's far enough," one of them shouted. "You ain't welcome here."

"I'm just passing through," said Durham desperately, "and I need food. I can pay."

"Come on," the hostile one replied, "but don't do anything foolish."

Durham rode closer, and when he reined up, they gathered around. But every man had his rifle at the ready, and they waited for Durham to speak.

"My name is Durham, and I'm on my way to Colorado. I need food for myself and grain for my horse."

"Where you from?" one of the men demanded.

"Santa Fe," said Durham.

"You do things the hard way, pilgrim," his antagonist said. "You don't go from Santa Fe to Colorado through Utah. What are you doin' here?"

"I was with some wagons heading west," said Durham, "and we had a falling out. I had to quit them, and I thought I might reach Denver."

"That ain't near good enough, is it, Luke?"

"Naw," Luke said. "You must of had a powerful reason for fallin' out with them folks, in the midst of Ute country. Tell us the truth, an' maybe we'll help you."

"All right," said Durham. "There's five wagons loaded with supplies, and one of them was mine. They're on their way to a gold strike. There's ten men, and they cheated me out of my share, so I had no reason to go on."

"Well, now," Luke said, "that's mighty interesting. Tell us more about that gold strike, and just maybe we'll give you grub and grain for your horse. Don't you reckon, Ebeau?"

"Yeah," said Ebeau. "Where is this strike?"

"I got nothin' to lose," Durham said. "It's somewhere near the headwaters of the Sevier River, about seven hundred miles west of Santa Fe. That's all I know."

"That's close enough," said Ebeau. "Marklee, take him over yonder to the barn and fill a sack with grain. Rest of you, have your women contribute toward a sack of grub."

Within the hour, Durham rode northeast, only too glad to be on his way. There was food in his saddlebag, and behind his saddle, grain for his horse. Within him, there was grim satisfaction, for he had little doubt the hostile men he had encountered would quickly become claim jumpers.

"Good luck, Mr. Faro Duval and Mr. Levi Collins," said Durham aloud.

Dog Face had spent a long, troublesome day with the Utes who had remained with him, for their patience had grown thin. Their desire was for the five wagons and the goods they contained, rather than an elusive gold claim. To satisfy them, Dog Face had been forced to a decision not of his liking.

"Damn it," said Sangre, "it's too soon to ambush them wagons. We still don't know the way to the gold strike."

"By God, we're gonna have to find it without follerin' the wagons," Dog Face said, "or we'll end up with just the four of us. The Utes is goin' after them wagons without us."

"When?" Hueso asked.

"Seven suns," said Dog Face. "Seven days from today."

"Then we won't have enough time to foller the wagons," Sangre said. "How do you aim to find the gold strike?"

"I know this territory," said Dog Face, "and there ain't too many possibilities for gold west of here. Slade, think. Tell me ever' scrap you know about this strike."

"I don't know that much," Slade said. "From the little I learned from Durham, it's a good seven hundred miles west of Santa Fe, near the headwaters of some river."

"Ah," said Dog Face, "now we're gettin' somewhere. That seven hunnert miles eliminates the Colorado an' the Green. It ain't the Fremont, 'cause it flows into the Colorado, an' to git there, they'd of follered the Colorado south. They're headin' fer the south fork of the Green, I'd say, and there ain't nothin' west of there but the Sevier and the Great Basin of southern Nevada."

"You reckon the strike's somewhere along the Sevier River, then," Slade said.

"Nowhere else it could be," said Dog Face, "an' if they've been there, don't you reckon they left claim markers?"

"I see what you're gettin' at," Slade said. "They must have done some minin', too, or they wouldn't have ore samples."

"Right," said Dog Face. "There's time fer some of us to ride there, check out the claim, an' get back here before the Utes go after them wagons on their own."

"I'd go," Slade said, "but I don't know the country."

"You wouldn't be goin', if you knowed it like the back of your hand," said Sangre. "I purely don't trust you."

"Then I won't go," Slade said.

"You sure as hell won't," said Hueso. "I don't trust you neither."

"You varmints don't trust one another," Dog Face roared. "I'll go myself, by God. That is, unless you got your doubts about me."

"We ain't doubtin' you," said Sangre sullenly, "but I ain't sure we can control them Utes while you're gone."

Slade laughed, and after a moment, Dog Face joined in.

"What's so damn funny?" Hueso demanded.

"You two jokers," said Slade. "What kind of damn fools would expect one man to take over a gold strike, defendin' it against the bunch that's comin' to claim it, as well as God knows how many Utes that's determined to take his hair?"

"Well said, Slade," Dog Face said. "You greedy varmints ain't thinkin', but I reckon that ain't your fault. You ain't equipped for it. Since we're layin' the cards on the table, I got to say that I don't trust neither of you, together or separated, even if you knowed this territory, which you don't. So you got a choice, damn it. Slade goes or I go, and if I go, the pair of you has got them Utes to deal with."

"I ain't wet-nursin' a bunch of ornery Indians," said Hueso. "Not fer you, not even fer a gold claim."

"Me neither," Sangre said.

"Slade," said Dog Face, "ride when you're ready. Take grub fer a week."

Slade nodded, secretly pleased. The hostility between Dog Face and his pair of troublesome lieutenants was out in the open, and he was confident they could be eliminated once the gold strike had been located. Without a word, Slade saddled up and rode out, riding along the south fork of the Green.

The wagons had been drawn up along the river for the night.

"By tomorrow evening," said Collins, "we should reach the fork in the river. From there we'll take the south fork until it plays out. Then it's due west until we reach the bend of the Sevier."

"Seems like we ought to be out of Ute country by then," Shanghai said.

"Not necessarily," said Collins. "That's what we thought, but their country seems to be of their choosing."

"That's the truth," Felix Blackburn said. "We left the Sevier on the run, Utes after us every jump of the way. If those renegades hadn't shown up, none of us would have made it out alive."

"We'll have to do as we've always done," said Faro, "and that's be prepared. Never take Indians for granted, if you want to keep your hair."

"They won't be taking my hair, as long as I have a gun in my hand," declared Mamie McCutcheon.

"Nor mine," said Odessa.

Chapter 14

The eight men whom Durham had told of the gold strike wasted no time in making plans.

"If there's gold in southern Utah," said Luke, "who's more entitled to it than us? For sure, not some strangers from Santa Fe. I say we move in and take that claim."

"Yeah," Ebeau agreed, and his sentiment was quickly echoed by the others.

"Then we'd best gather up some grub and ride," said Newsom. "There's another storm buildin', if my rheumatism ain't lyin'."

"We don't necessarily have to ride ahead of the storm," Inkler said. "If that outfit has five wagons, snowdrifts will delay 'em another four or five days. Why don't we wait out the blizzard here, where we'll be warm with hot grub?"

"I'm for that," said Giles.

"Well, I ain't," Kirk said. "If that bunch gets there ahead of us, it'll be us that's claim jumpers."

"He's got a point," said Marklee. "If we got to face ten armed men, then I want to be dug in before the lead starts flyin'. If they get there first, it'll be them that's dug in."

"Inkler," Luke said, "you and Giles can stay here, or you can ride with us. If you stay here, then you don't share in the gold. Which way do you aim to jump?"

"Since you put it that way," said Inkler, "I'll go."

"Then I reckon I'll go, too," Giles said.

"Good," said Luke. "We're all of the same mind. Gather up enough grub for a month, and plenty of shells. I look for us to have a fight on our hands."

"We'll be leavin' our women and kids here alone," Jed said. "I don't like that."

"Neither do I," said Luke, "but we've done it before, and they'll be armed. Some of us may get ventilated and not ride back, but when there's enough at stake, you've always got to gamble."

An hour later, the eight of them saddled up and rode south.

"The part of me that's Injun says there's more snow on the way," Tarno Spangler said. "We got maybe another day to take shelter."

Not more than a dozen miles after crossing the Colorado, the teams had been unhitched from the wagons and the outfit was finishing supper.

"Damn," said Dallas Weaver, "ain't that Injun blood of yours ever wrong?"

"Not as I recollect," Tarno said.

"We don't have to rely entirely on that," said Levi Collins. "The wind's considerably colder than it was this time yesterday. I think perhaps tomorrow we ought to begin looking for some shelter. Otherwise, we might not fare so well. Faro, why don't you ride ahead tomorrow, and let me take over the wagon?"

"Suits me," Faro said, "but you've been through here before. Your judgment might be better than mine."

"I doubt that," said Collins. "All my experience has been with mules and horses. You'll be looking through the eyes of a man accustomed to taking wagons across country."

"Then I'll have a look ahead," Faro said. "I don't know what kind of terrain we may be facing, but this would be a good time to pick up the gait some, if you can. Finding shelter may not be the problem, but it could be a ways off, and gettin' to it ahead of the storm might be difficult. We'll pull out tomorrow as soon as it's light enough to see, and we'll expect a long ride, rather than a short one."

The wagons moved out at first light, facing a chill wind from the northwest. Faro rode far ahead, searching for possible shelter. He viewed the terrain as a teamster, for a wagon had not the mobility of a man on horseback. Drop-offs and steep-sided arroyos must be avoided, often increasing the distance that must be traveled. The river they were following wasn't yet bank-full, but there were no rock or sandbars beneath overhanging banks that might be utilized as shelter. Faro rode south, beyond the river, knowing the terrain would limit them to what the wagons might safely travel. There also had to be a source of firewood, for the temperature might fall to zero or below, trapping them for days. Faro had ridden more than fifteen miles before finding any kind of shelter. Even then, the arroyo was shallow, its rims not exceeding the height of the wagon canvas by more than a foot or two, but there was little hope of finding anything better. The distance the wagons had to travel might already be too great, for as the storm moved in, overhanging clouds would bring twilight two hours early. After resting his horse, Faro mounted, riding back the way he had come. Lest they travel even farther out of their way, he had to reach the wagons and divert them south, away from the river. Riding on, Faro reined up occasionally, listening for the rattle of the wagons. But the wind was at his back, and he had ridden more than ten miles before he finally heard them coming. He galloped ahead, and when Collins—in the lead wagon—saw him coming, he reined up. There was a clearing, and the rest of the wagons were drawn up beside him. It was time to rest the teams, and Faro wasted no time in relaying what he had learned.

"The arroyo's maybe two miles south of the river," Faro said, "and it's still ten miles or more ahead of us. It's not as deep as I'd have liked, but there's nothing else. There is water, maybe a run-off from the river, but no graze, and it'll take some ridin' to drag in enough firewood to see us through. Push the teams as hard as you can, and follow me."

They needed no urging, for the heavy gray storm clouds had come closer, and the winds from the northwest had become much colder. The wagons had traveled less than half the required distance when the sleet began. Wind-driven, it rattled off their hats and the wagon canvas, stinging their cheeks and half blinding them. Wanting to turn their backs to the wind, the mules tried to balk.

"Take their bridles and lead them!" Faro shouted.

Dismounting, Faro tied his horse behind the lead wagon, and seizing the bridles of the first team, forced them ahead. The other teamsters, knowing what must be done, led their teams in similar fashion. As suddenly as it had begun, the sleet ceased, but the wind grew stronger, touching their ears, gloved hands, and booted feet with icy fingers. Just when it seemed they would never reach shelter, they did. Collins and Faro, leading the teams by their bridles, forced the first wagon into the arroyo, and the others followed. Each of the wagons were driven as near the west rim as possible.

"Shanghai, Tarno, Dallas, Collins, and Puckett, saddle your horses and come with me," Faro shouted. "We're going after all the firewood we can find. The rest of you unharness the teams."

As the six of them rode out, the big gray storm clouds seemed only treetop high, as the day became as night. Like a thing alive, the wind moaned through the firs. While there were many lightning-struck and windblown trees, limbs had to be trimmed and their root masses cut away before they could be snaked into the arroyo. The men dismounted with axes and began their race with time. By the time they had snaked in their first loads, there was a fire going, started with dry wood from the possum bellies beneath the wagons. The McCutcheons had the coffeepots on and tin cups ready.

"Here," Mamie shouted, "the coffee's hot."

Gratefully, Faro and his companions took the time to down the scalding brew before returning to their task. By the time they returned with their second load, snow had begun falling, whipping into the arroyo on the wings of the howling wind. Blackburn, Snyder, Withers, and Kritzer had ben busy with axes, reducing the logs to manageable lengths for the fire.

"There's more coffee," Odessa cried.

"No time," said Faro. "We have to bring in another load or two, if we can."

The six men rode out a third and fourth time, ceasing when the storm worsened to the extent that they might become lost, unable to find their way back in the deepening snow. Gratefully they gathered around the fire, warming their hands with tin cups of hot coffee.

Others caught up in the storm hadn't fared so well. Slade had been forced to hole up beneath a riverbank where there was barely room without dangling his feet in the water. He had picketed his horse among some brush, taking the saddle blankets to use with his own, lest he freeze to death.

More than a day's ride to the north, the eight men to whom Durham had revealed the gold strike had been forced to take shelter from the storm.

"I told you we could ride out the storm," Luke said. "This shelvin' rock has its back to the wind, and there's room aplenty for us and our horses. I been across these mountains to California and back. I know where there's shelter and where there's water."

"Yeah," said Ebeau, "this ain't bad. Soon as the

snow melts enough for us to ride, we can find that strike and dig in."

Along the river, a dozen miles west of the arroyo where the wagons had taken shelter, Dog Face, Hueso, and Sangre hunkered before a fire on the lee side of a ridge. In a nearby thicket, their Ute companions had set up their own camp.

"Don't nothin' bother them damn Indians," said Sangre.

"Too bad they ain't more *hombres* like 'em," Dog Face said. "All you an' Hueso has done since you throwed in with me is bellyache about the weather an' th' grub. I'm gittin' almighty tired of it."

His disgruntled companions glared at him, but neither of them bothered to reply.

Along toward dawn, the snow began to diminish.

"Good sign," said Tarno. "This ain't gonna be a bad one. Ought to start warmin' up by tonight."

"There's already deep drifts," Faro pointed out, "and we'll be mud-bound for a while."

"We got plenty of firewood and grub," said Dallas Weaver.

"Yes," Levi Collins said, "and we don't have that much farther to go. There's a chance we can reach the claim before there's another storm."

"But the worst of the winter's ahead of us," said Isaac Puckett. "I think before we do anything else, we'd better establish a permanent camp. Before spring, there'll be storms far worse and more frequent than this one."

"You have the right idea," Faro Duval said. "Not only must we plan for the winter and the snow, we'll have to dig in with an eye to defense."

"Amen to that," said Levi Collins. "The Utes don't seem to observe the seasons."

"Speaking of the Utes," Dallas Weaver said, "wonder how Durham's gettin' along with them?"

"I doubt that he's havin' to," said Shanghai. "He's the kind who'd throw in with them renegades that's been stalkin' us, if they'll have him."

"They won't," Kritzer said. "Slade's with 'em, and he'll see they don't take Durham in."

"They might, long enough to kill him," said Withers, "if they find out he run off with that twenty-five thousand in bank loot."

Collins laughed. "Faro expected that. The saddlebag Durham took was stuffed with old wrapping paper."

That drew a round of laughter, especially from the McCutcheons, but they all became grim when the wind brought the chilling howl of a lobo wolf. It was a vivid reminder of the attack that had seriously wounded Faro and had resulted in the death of the Indian.

"Oh, God," Mamie said, "I hope the wolves don't come after us again."

"We'll have to keep watch day and night," said Faro, "and I reckon we'd better start a couple more fires. This is a shallow canyon, and they can attack from either rim."

Again there was a distant howl, and this time it was answered. Shanghai, Dallas, Tarno, and Snyder began heaping wood for two additional fires, one of which would be near the lower end of the canyon. The mules and horses, already spooked by the distant cries, had moved nearer the wagons. The mules brayed their fear, even as Faro sought to calm them. Collins, Puckett, and Blackburn joined them, and soon the two additional fires flamed high. The men cocked their Winchesters and walked from one end of the canyon to the other, but there was no sign of the fearful predators.

"With the storm dying, maybe we'll escape them this time," Faro said.

Toward late afternoon, the clouds were swept away. Without the wind, the sun seemed warm, and some of the snow showed signs of melting. With the coming of twilight, the first stars bloomed in a vast purple meadow above.

"We'll go with the usual watch," said Faro, "unless we hear from the wolves again. All of you keep your Winchesters loaded and ready, and take off nothing but your hats."

Far to the north—in western Colorado—Hal Durham had taken shelter in a mass of huge boulders where there barely was room for him and his horse. Huddled in his blankets before a meager fire, he was able to boil coffee and broil his bacon. After the snow ceased he waited only until the next morning before riding on.

Gratefully, Slade looked up at the clearing sky. Leaving his cramped position under the riverbank, he managed to break enough dead limbs from a fir to start a small fire over which he broiled his bacon and some much-needed coffee. Concluding his meal, he saddled his horse and rode west, keeping near the riverbank where snow had not drifted. By late afternoon the stream he followed began playing out, and recalling the directions Dog Face had provided, Slade rode due south. Reining up just north of the Sevier River, he dug in for the night.

"We'd better wait another day," Jed argued. "Them drifts will be almighty deep."

"They'll be just as deep tomorrow, and we'll have lost a day," said Luke. "It ain't all that cold, and the sun's up. We'll lead the horses and break trail, if we have to."

So they rode south, dismounting frequently, assisting their horses through deep drifts. But the going was difficult, and come sundown, they were still half a day's ride from their destination. Settling down for the night, they arose at first light and rode south.

The sun was two hours high when Slade reached what he believed was the Sevier River. He rode northwest along it until he reached a bend where it hooked back sharply to the south.

"Damn it," Slade grumbled to himself, "the claim markers, if there are any, are likely under the snow."

Still he rode on, and along the riverbank where the snow had begun melting first, he found what he sought. It was a pyramid of stones. Elated, he continued following the river until he found a second pyramid perhaps a quarter of a mile distant. There would be two more corners, he reasoned, and unless they were on the opposite bank of the river, they would be hidden

among snowdrifts. He debated riding away with what
he had discovered, but his excitement got the better of
him, and he backtracked several miles downriver before he found a place to cross. He then rode west along
the river until he had reached the point where he had
found the stone pyramids on the opposite bank. But
much of the area where he rode was covered with
brush and an accumulation of snow, and it was with
great difficulty that he was able to find the third
marker.

"Well, by God," he cried, "the gold's in the riverbed!"

Slade mounted his horse and rode north. Reaching
the fork of the river he had followed west, he traveled
east. While the snow was slowly beginning to melt, the
resulting mud would easily delay the progress of the
wagons another two or three days, allowing Slade
ample time to reach his companions. When Dog Face
received the information Slade would relay, the teamsters and their wagons could be ambushed at anytime. . . .

Southern Utah, along the Green River.
October 6, 1870.

The wagons took the trail at dawn, avoiding the riverbank where the ground would be softest as it thawed.
Faro again rode the box of the lead wagon, while
Collins had saddled his horse and led out. The sun
seemed unseasonably warm following the storm, and
near noon, Collins returned to meet the wagons. Faro

reined up, the others drawing up behind him. It was time to rest the teams.

"I've discovered something interesting," Collins said as he dismounted. "Perhaps half a dozen miles ahead, I found the remains of several campfires in sheltered areas where some riders waited out the storm. They rode out before the snow melted, but they were following the riverbank, heading west. There were tracks of four shod horses, and tracks of perhaps as many as thirty, unshod."

"Collins," said Faro, "you have the makings of a real frontiersman. I think those are the tracks of the renegades who have been stalking us, and it appears they have a disturbing number of Utes riding with them."

"Their boldness borders on arrogance," Collins replied. "They must have known their trail would be obvious to us, and they don't care. What do you think it means?"

"They've decided they no longer need to follow us," said Faro, "and I think we're in for it. Did you mark your claim in any way?"

"Not before I left for Santa Fe," Collins said.

"We did, before the Utes chased us out," said Isaac Puckett. "We built two pyramids of stones on each side of the river."

"That's it, then," Faro said. "Durham, the varmint, must have told them the claim was somewhere along the Sevier River. One of them has ridden ahead and found the markers."

"Damn," said Felix Blackburn, "they'll get there ahead of us and jump our claim."

"It's more serious than that," Tarno Spangler said. "Them Utes won't care a whoop for a gold strike. They want these wagon loads of supplies."

"That's how I see it," said Dallas Weaver. "We're headin' straight for an ambush."

"My God," Collins said.

"That's about what I expect," said Faro, "and it could come at anytime. If they found the claim markers, they won't figure they'll need us."

"I look for it to come within the next day or two," Shanghai said. "Indians ain't very patient, and them Utes have been holdin' back too long."

"The renegades evidently have armed them with Winchesters, from what I saw while I was in their camp," said Faro, "and that makes it all the more dangerous."

"Starting tonight, I suppose all of us should stand watch," Collins said.

"No," said Faro. "They have us outgunned, and the darkness would give us an edge. I look for them to attack at dawn, while we're on the trail, or near suppertime."

"They'll hit us on the trail, with the wagons strung out," Tarno predicted. "At least half of 'em will attack from behind."

"With their greater numbers, that would be to their advantage," said Faro. "From here on, everyone who is mounted will remain near the wagons. Withers, you and Kritzer will continue riding behind the last wagon, and I want you to keep your eyes on the back trail at all times. Be especially watchful as we pass brushy, thicketed areas. Allow Indians just a little cover, and they'll be all around you before you can blink an eye."

"We'll be watching," Kritzer said.

"I have a horse and a Winchester," said Odessa McCutcheon. "Mr. Collins, if one of your men will take over my wagon, I'll ride with Withers and Kritzer."

"No," Collins said. "I'd prefer that you remain with the wagon."

"I'll go along with that," said Faro. "You've proven yourself a good teamster, and you will be needed when the attack comes. The Utes will be screeching as loud as they can, in the hope of stampeding the mules. All of you rein up, grab your Winchesters, and stay on your wagon boxes. The wagon itself will provide protection from behind. Now let's move on, but be watchful. That bunch ahead of us may have purposely left a clear trail, with intentions of doubling back."

They traveled cautiously on, and before they halted for the night, they came upon the westward trail Collins had found.

"Tracks are two days old," Tarno said, after following them a ways. "I think a couple of us should saddle up and scout north and south. We got to know if they're behind us or ahead of us. The varmints may have doubled back, and the ground's soft enough they got to have left a trail."

"Sorry," said Faro, "we can't afford that risk. A pair of Utes with Winchesters could have fallen back with just that possibility in mind, and we'd be shy two men."

"There is also a chance we might be attacked while you are gone," Collins said.

"That, too," said Faro. "I still think they'll hit us while we're on the move, and in some ways, that's in our favor. Under no circumstances must we become separated with this threat facing us."

"You done good, Slade," Dog Face said, after Slade had told him of the claim markers.

"Now," said Hueso, "when you're done nuzzlin' around over Slade, maybe we kin take over them wagons."

"I know this territory, an' I'll say when," Dog Face snarled. "So far, you ain't contributed a damn thing but your no-account advice, an' I've had enough. How far, Slade?"

"Not more than a day's ride for us," said Slade. "Maybe four days for the wagons."

"*Bueno,*" Dog Face said. "We'll ride out in the mornin' an' start lookin' for a place to take them wagons."

"You aim fer us all to attack head-on?" Sangre asked.

"Why, hell no," said Dog Face. "What kinda fool do you reckon I am? A dozen of them Utes will fan in behind the last wagon an' the rest of 'em—along with us—will attack from the front."

"The Utes attackin' from behind will raise enough hell to give us an edge," Slade said.

"Exactly what I'm countin' on," said Dog Face, "an' them attackin' head-on will all ride ahead of us."

Sangre laughed. "Now you're talkin' sense. We got enough Utes to spare a few."

"Utes or not, you'd better go in shootin' like your

no-account carcass depends on it," Dog Face said.
"That's a salty bunch, or they wouldn't be in these
mountains with their wagons."

"That's the God's truth," said Slade. "They'll take
some killing."

Southwestern Utah, on the Sevier River.
October 7, 1870.

The eight claim jumpers had no trouble finding the
same claim markers that Slade had discovered a day
earlier, but they also found the tracks of Slade's horse.

"What do you reckon that means?" Ebeau asked.

"I dunno," said Luke, "unless one of them rode
ahead to see if the claim's secure. But that don't matter, because we're here ahead of them, and the way
they got the markers set up, it looks like the strike is in
the riverbed."

"Yeah, but there ain't no money in sluice box
minin'," Newsom said. "All you get is a few flakes or
a little dust that's washed down from somewhere else."

"Use your head," said Luke angrily. "You reckon
that bunch is freightin' in five wagon loads of goods
just for a little sluice box dust? I think they've found
somethin' a lot more promisin' than that."

"All right," said Inkler, "suppose there is gold in that
riverbed? See them high banks? I'm bettin' that
water's almighty deep along here. How do we get at
the gold?"

"The *hombres* that put up these markers must have
figured out a way, and we can do as well," Luke said,
"but first we got to nail down the claim. We got to set

up an ambush so's we can rid ourselves of that bunch with the least danger to ourselves."

"Them tracks come west along the river," said Ebeau, "so I reckon we can look for the wagons to come from that direction."

"Yeah," Kirk said, "but there's no cover here. We'd better ride downriver a ways and look for us a better place. We're goin' against ten men, and I ain't wantin' my hair parted with lead."

"Let's ride, then," said Luke. "We don't know how far away those wagons are, or how much time we have."

"I don't like the looks of this," Giles said. "We may be bitin' off more than we'll be able to chew."

"Anytime you feel that strong," said Luke, "you know the way home."

But there was no more argument, and the eight of them rode downriver, seeking their place to arrange an ambush.

Half a dozen miles ahead of the slow-moving wagons, Dog Face had chosen the place for his planned attack. There was a bend in the river, with a profusion of brush that would force the wagons to go around it. The first wagon or two would bear the brunt of the attack, while the screeching Utes would strike from behind the last wagon.

"I don't see how it can miss," Slade said.

"I reckon we can't do no better," said Dog Face, pleased.

"I won't agree till that bunch is dead an' we got the wagons," Sangre said.

"Me neither," said Hueso.

Dog Face said nothing, but he glared at the two in a manner that suggested he might rid himself of them at the first opportunity.

"We're perhaps two days away from where this fork in the river plays out," Collins said. "Beyond that, another day's travel should take us to the claim on the Sevier."

"It seems like we've been on the trail a lot longer than we have," said Dallas Weaver.

"I agree," Faro said, "but we're only nine weeks out of Santa Fe."

"The return trip may be even longer, if everything works out," said Shanghai. "That ore will be heavy."

The balmy weather had continued, and the night passed uneventfully. The wagons took the trail at dawn, rolling westward. A few miles away, along the river, disaster waited. . . .

Chapter 15

"We're ready," Dog Face announced. "A dozen Utes will attack from their back trail, 'an that'll send the rest of 'em hell-fer-leather toward the lead wagon. We'll hold back just far enough fer them teamsters to start returnin' fire. When they do, an' while they're shootin' at the Utes, we move in fer the kill. Any questions?"

There were none. For a change, both Hueso and Sangre were silent. Slade nodded, and they waited for the arrival of the wagons. The Utes who would attack from the rear had doubled back, keeping well away from the river, and they made no move until the last of the wagons was more than a quarter of a mile distant. Withers and Kritzer trailed the last wagon, frequently turning in their saddles to watch the back trail. But the attacking Utes did not ride in direct pursuit. Keeping a good distance to the south, they rode parallel to the last wagon, finally coming at a fast gallop from the side. Like phantoms, they erupted from the brush, taking the ever-vigilant Kritzer and Withers almost totally by surprise. Josh Snyder, jogging his horse alongside the last wagon, was first to see the attackers.

"Indians!" Snyder shouted.

At that moment, Kritzer and Withers cut loose with their Winchesters, and the rest of the Utes broke out of the brush, galloping toward the lead wagon. Levi Collins fired first, killing one of the attackers, but the screeching of the Utes and the roar of gunfire spooked the horse and Collins was thrown. From the wagon box, Faro fired twice, leaving two of the Ute horses riderless. But a slug caught Faro in the left shoulder, pitching him off the wagon box. Rolling under the wagon where Collins had already taken refuge, the two of them continued firing. But the Utes had galloped past the first wagon, only to run headlong into withering fire from the second, third, and fourth wagons, as Shanghai, Tarno, and Dallas cut loose with their Winchesters. Isaac Puckett, riding the box with Dallas, fired as rapidly as he could lever in the shells. But the Ute attack on the last wagon had taken its toll. Felix Blackburn, riding the box with Odessa McCutcheon, fired until his Winchester clicked on empty. At that moment, Odessa was hard hit, and seizing her Winchester, Felix continued firing. Two riderless horses—mounts ridden by Withers and Kritzer—galloped past, only to be spooked by Utes who had attacked the first wagon. On the heels of the Utes, Dog Face, Slade, Hueso, and Sangre rode in fast, their Colts blazing. But the Utes had begun taking fire from the rest of the wagons. Faro and Collins began firing at the four renegades. Slade and Hueso were hit and their horses galloped away riderless. Sangre was flung to the ground when his horse was hit, and he dropped his Colt. Cat-like, he rolled and came to his feet just as Faro's Winchester clicked on empty. Sangre's hand dropped to the sawed-off shotgun swiveled to his left hip, and he was fast. Incredibly fast. Barely in time, Faro drew his Colt and fired, dropping the little gunman as the shotgun blasted its deadly load into the ground at his feet. As suddenly as the attack had begun, it was over, and except for the braying of some of the mules, there was deadly silence. Faro Duval and Levi Collins got to their feet. Faro had a bloody left shoulder, but Collins hadn't been hit. Dallas Weaver and Isaac Puckett still sat on the wagon box, bleeding, Winchesters across their knees. Tarno and Shanghai had not been hit, but Odessa McCutcheon lay beside her wagon, the front of her faded old shirt covered with blood. Mamie stood there helplessly, tears streaking the dirt on her face. Felix Blackburn, blood welling from a wound in his thigh, came limping around the wagon, using his Winchester for a crutch.

"Withers and Kritzer are dead," said Blackburn.

"Damn it," Faro said. "Odessa?"

"She's dead," said Blackburn. "She got two of them before they got her."

Collins had begun tallying the dead, starting with the three renegades, while Faro began seeing to the wounded.

"We accounted for three of the renegades and fifteen Utes," Collins announced, "but we lost Odessa, Withers, and Kritzer."

"Dallas, Isaac, Felix, and me have wounds," said Faro. "I reckon we'll be here a couple of days. Collins, it'll be up to you, Shanghai, Tarno, and Snyder to dig some graves."

"There'll be time enough for that, after we've seen to the wounded," Collins said.

Her face buried in her hands, Mamie McCutcheon sat on the ground beside Odessa. Felix Blackburn sat down beside her, his arm about her shoulders. Thankful for his concern, Mamie spoke.

"She wasn't perfect, and sometimes we fought, but she was all the kin I had."

"You have me," said Felix, "if you still want me."

"Now, more than ever," Mamie said. "You're hurt. We must stop the bleeding."

Tarno already had a fire going, and both coffeepots had been filled with water, which soon was boiling.

"No broken bones and no lead to be dug out," said Faro. "I reckon that's the only good news."

"There could be more," Tarno said. "I think we've busted up this bunch of renegades once and for all, and we cut down enough of the Utes to convince the rest that we're *malo*. Bad medicine."

"My God," said Snyder, "there must have been thirty or more."

"Not more than twenty-five," Tarno said, "and that was too many."

"Half that number is too many," said Shanghai, "when they have Winchesters."

"Speaking of the Utes," Collins said, "hadn't we better dispose of the dead?"

"No," said Faro. "We're overlooking the obvious. Indians always come back for their dead. We'll leave them where they lay. After we've tended our wounds and buried our own dead, we'll move west a ways, before making camp for the night."

*   *   *

Following the death of his three companions and the defeat of the Utes, Dog Face rode west, unsure as to what his next move would be. For a certainty, he had no chance of taking over the gold claim, and little or no chance of exerting any influence among the Utes. His interest in the gold had been no concern of theirs, for they wanted the five wagon loads of goods and supplies. Now, following their devastating defeat, they would likely consider it a bad omen and make no further effort. Gloomily, Dog Face considered his options and found they were few. He could return to California, but that was a good five hundred miles, and he was short on grub. He had counted on the provisions to be plundered from the wagons. Suddenly his horse nickered and he reined up, for ahead of him were the ten mounted Utes who had survived the ill-fated raid on the wagons.

"Buenos amigos," said Dog Face, raising his hands.

The Utes said nothing. One of them fired three rapid shots from his Winchester, and Dog Face was hurled to the ground by the force of the lead. He lay on his back, his blood pumping out of the three gaping holes in his chest. His eyes were open but the soul had departed. Silently one of the Utes dismounted and stripped him of his gun belt and Colt, while another caught up his horse. Finally, without looking back, the band rode south.

Having tended the wounded, Shanghai, Tarno, Collins, and Snyder dug graves for their dead. When the graves were finished and they were ready for the burying,

Levi Collins read the twenty-third Psalm from his Bible.

"There was so little we could do for them," Mamie lamented, as they returned to their wagons. "Is that the best we can expect, a lonely grave a thousand miles from family and friends?"

"It's the luck of the draw," said Faro. "The best you can expect is to be buried deep, so the varmints can't get to you."

"I suppose that's all we can expect in this world," Felix Blackburn said, "but I believe there's another. I once heard a preacher say that it makes no difference where our bones rest, after the soul has gone to its maker."

"Thank you," said Mamie. "That makes me feel better."

"If this gold claim don't pan out," Josh Snyder said, "Felix can always build himself a church and pass the hat ever' Sunday."

"Shut up, Josh," said Levi Collins.

The day had been calm, with little wind, and the shooting a few miles to the east had not gone unnoticed.

"What you reckon was the cause of that?" Ebeau asked. "Indians?"

"Maybe," said Luke, "but that was a powerful lot of shooting for just ten men. Sounded more like twenty, maybe thirty."

"There's a chance the Utes have cut down the odds some," Kirk said.

"We can't count on that," said Luke, "but we got one

thing strong in our favor. They might have been ex-pectin' the Utes, but they won't be lookin' for us."

"We'll still have to make every shot count," Inkler said. "There ain't much cover along this river. Why don't we ride south a ways and attack from that direc-tion?"

"Maybe you got somethin' there," said Luke. "Not much along the river except brush, and that bunch will be shootin' back. Let's fan out and ride south a ways, but don't get beyond rifle range. Look for rock up-thrusts, windblown trees, or anything that'll provide us some cover. We don't have that much time."

"Maybe one of us oughta ride back and see where them wagons are," Giles said. "How do we know they're follerin' this river?"

"It makes sense," said Luke. "The claim's on the river, and they're comin' west. What other direction do you reckon they'd take?"

"I dunno," Giles admitted, "but I just think we oughta be sure."

"Maybe he's right," said Ebeau. "Not only do we need to be sure they're comin' along the river, we need to know when they'll be here. If they was attacked by Utes, some of 'em may be dead or wounded. That could slow 'em up, and we'll be settin' here into some-time next week."

"Then one of you ride back a ways," Luke said. "Find out where they are, and decide when they'll be gettin' here."

"I'll go," said Giles. "I can't abide waitin' for nothin' or nobody."

"Just be danged sure you don't let 'em see you," Luke warned.

Giles mounted and rode east, careful to stay well away from the river.

The wagons had advanced several miles past the scene of the ambush, and there they had remained for two days, allowing the wounded to rest and overcome the ever-present threat of infection.

"I reckon we'll move out in the morning at first light," said Faro. "Dallas, are you up to it?"

"Sure," Dallas said. "I got a leg wound, and that won't bother me handlin' the reins. It was you that was nailed in the shoulder. Are *you* up to it?"

"Not completely," said Faro, "but Collins has agreed to take over the wagon until I'm in better shape."

"I'll take it from here on to the claim," Collins said. "I think we'll be there sometime the day after tomorrow, if there are no delays."

"Maybe I'm still spooked from that last ambush," said Faro, "but I aim to ride ahead and be sure there are no more surprises."

The weather had turned much colder, with a chill wind out of the northwest. Because of their leg wounds, Dallas and Felix had been assigned to the first watch. Following the death of Odessa, Mamie never slept until Felix did, choosing to stand the first watch with him. Collins, Tarno, and Dallas often kept their distance, allowing the two to talk. This night before they resumed their journey, Mamie seemed to have a lot on her mind. Felix kept his silence, waiting for her to speak. Finally she did.

"If the gold claim is all that you expect, what will you do?"

"I'm not entirely sure," said Felix. "Maybe I'll stay in Santa Fe. Would that suit you?"

"Yes," she replied, "as long as you're there. I've always heard that when we have some wealth, it changes us. Will we have a big house, servants, and fancy carriages?"

"Is that what you want?"

"My God, no," she cried.

Felix laughed. "Then I reckon it's safe to tell you there won't be any such. No matter if I'm flush or broke, all I want is a roof over my head, good grub, and a good woman."

"Then I suppose my work is cut out for me," said Mamie. "I'll count on you having a poor memory and try as hard as I can."

"We'll be startin' over," Felix said. "Your past and mine will be exactly that. The past. If we have problems, they'll be the result of whatever we encounter in the future."

"It sounds like you have some in mind," said Mamie. "Do you?"

"I don't know," Felix said. "It depends mostly on you. Bein' honest, I have to tell you that I don't plan on retiring to a rocking chair. A man wasn't meant to do nothing, even if he can afford to. Lay about long enough, your mind decides your life is over, and you die. I don't intend for that to happen to me."

"I haven't decided whether you should have been a philosopher or a preacher," she replied, "but what you've just said makes sense. What do you have in mind for us?"

"I haven't spoken to Levi, Isaac, or Josh," said Felix, "but I'd like to start a freighting business between Saint Joseph, Missouri, and Santa Fe. The frontier's growing, but the railroad's a good twenty years away."*

"I think that's a glorious thing to do," Mamie said. "Perhaps you can join in with Faro and his teamsters. They've proven themselves to be men you can trust."

"They've done that and more," said Felix. "I'd trust any one or all of them with my life. I'll talk to them before we return to Santa Fe."

Southwestern Utah, along the Sevier River.
October 14, 1870.

Faro rode out ahead of the wagons, and soon reached what remained of Dog Face. He wheeled his horse and started back. In the lead wagon, Collins reined up the teams when he saw Faro coming.

"We'll have to take the wagons away from the river a ways," Faro said. "What's left of the last of the renegades is up ahead, and the varmints have been at him. There's not enough of him to bury, but plenty to spook the mules."

"We must have wounded him, then," said Collins.

"Not necessarily," Faro replied. "I didn't see his gun belt, his Colt, and not a sign of his horse and saddle. But I did find the tracks of one shod and ten unshod

---

*The Atchison, Topeka and Santa Fe Railroad reached Santa Fe in 1892.

horses headin' south. I think this *hombre* had the misfortune to run into the Utes who survived their attack on us, and found them no longer friendly."

"A fitting end for him, I suppose," said Collins. "Do you think that means the Utes have given up on us?"

"Maybe that particular bunch," Faro said, "but not necessarily all of them. But at least the rest likely won't be armed with Winchesters."

"Lead out," said Collins, "and we'll follow."

Faro rode a mile south of the river, thus allowing them plenty of leeway to bypass the grisly remains of Dog Face. It was this deviation and pure chance that alerted Faro to the rider who had been stalking them, for the tracks he found had been made the day before. Once the wagons had circled around and again reached the river, Collins reined up, for it was time to rest the teams. Faro wheeled his horse and rode back to meet them: they had to know of the danger ahead. . . .

Picketing his horse and finding high ground, Giles had waited, his eyes on the distant river. He wasn't surprised when he saw the single rider ahead of the lead wagon, but they were following the river, and he was all the more confident. There was virtually no chance of them discovering his trail, as long as he kept to the south of the river. Returning to his horse, he mounted and rode back the way he had come.

"Just like you figured," he told Luke, when he had joined his waiting comrades. "They ain't more than a day away, and they're follerin' the river."

"You didn't leave a trail to warn them, then," Luke said.

"I told you I wouldn't," said Giles angrily. "I kept to the brush, a mile south of the river, comin' back the same way I rode out."

Seeing Faro returning, all the outfit gathered around. Faro didn't waste words.

"We owe that dead renegade for takin' us away from the river. I found tracks of a shod horse leadin' east and returning west. Somebody's stalking us."

"Oh, God," Mamie cried, "not another ambush."

"That or worse," said Faro. "Maybe claim jumpers."

"Claim jumpers?" Collins said. "How would they know of the claim?"

"Durham, the bastard," said Dallas.

"That's as good a guess as any," Faro conceded, "but whatever their interest in us, we won't be nearly as surprised as they will. Tarno, once we've made camp for the night, you and me will do some stalking of our own."

"*Bueno*," said Tarno.

"But you can't see their tracks in the dark," Mamie said.

"We won't have to," said Faro. "They expected us to follow the river, and that's why their rider kept a mile to the south of it. That's exactly what Tarno and me will do, when we go looking for them."

"They'll be almighty confident," Tarno said, "and if we start soon enough, we'll be able to follow the smoke of their supper fire."

"I agree that we must know where and how many there are," said Collins, "but they'll still have the advantage, because we won't know when or where they'll attack."

"We're going to pretend they're Comanches," Faro said, "and in Texas, we had our own way of dealing with them. We'd find their camp, and before they had a chance to give us hell, we'd pay them a visit."

Tarno laughed. "When Faro and me find out where this bunch is holed up, we'll all ride in after dark and deal out some Texas justice."

"You'd kill them all?" Collins asked.

"If they won't have it any other way," said Faro. "Would you rather they kill us?"

"No," Collins said, "but it seems . . . well . . . cold-blooded, to shoot them down without warning."

"I didn't say we wouldn't warn them," said Faro, "but if they've come with killing on their minds, they'll answer with gunfire. Don't forget that."

"We'll give them as much warnin' as a rattler would," Dallas said. "After that, it'll be Katy-bar-the-door."

Nothing more was said. The teams had been unharnessed for the night and supper was over when Faro and Tarno rode out. Collins watched them go.

"Levi," said Felix Blackburn, "they know what they're doing. That last bushwhacking hurt us. We can't stand another."

Collins sighed. "I know, Felix. I know."

It was still light enough for Faro and Tarno to see the tracks that led west, and before dark they had assured themselves that the rider was, indeed, headed in the direction the wagons would travel. He had kept well away from the river to avoid leaving a trail.

"I'd like to get my hands on Hal Durham," Tarno

growled. "This is what we get for not shootin' the varmint when we had the chance. I hope he's with this bunch."

"I doubt he will be," said Faro. "He's too slippery."

Denver, Colorado. October 14, 1870.

Hal Durham reached Denver in the early afternoon, and except for the need of a shave, haircut, bath, and change of clothing, he was no worse for the wear. He had exhausted the grain two days before, and his horse was gaunt. Despite his many shortcomings, his feelings for horses were genuine, and he left the animal at a stable for a rubdown and graining. While he wasn't exactly flush, he had more than three hundred dollars, and he wasted no time in buying himself a new suit of clothes, including a fancy swallowtail coat. He then found a barbershop that offered baths. Afterward he treated himself to a haircut and a shave. Finally he stopped at a restaurant and enjoyed the first decent meal he'd had since leaving Santa Fe. By then it was dusk, and the town had begun to come alive. The saloons were all aglow, and Durham began making the rounds. He paused before one whose gaudily lettered false-front proclaimed it Denver's finest. LAURA'S BAGNIO SALOON. The place was a two-story affair, and through the glassed-in front, Durham could see women moving about and a winding stairway. But most interesting of all was a small sign reading: HOUSE DEALER WANTED. Durham entered, and the fanciest-dressed woman of them all stood behind the bar. Approaching her, Durham grinned.

"Would you be Laura?" he asked.

"I might be," she replied, "depending on who you are and why you want to know."

"I'm Hal Durham, and I want that job of house dealer. I can start tonight."

"Then I'm Laura, and here's the rules. Twenty per-cent and an honest game. You get caught slick dealing, with a shaved deck, or any other way of cheating, and I'll personally see that you go to jail. You are not to so-cialize with the women, and you're not allowed up-stairs. Do you understand?"

"Yes, ma'am," said Durham, "and I wouldn't have it any other way."

She nodded, saying nothing, but Durham thought she looked upon him more favorably. He would shy away from the girls upstairs, because he had his eyes on Laura herself. He could do and had done worse than a fancy woman who owned a prosperous saloon with a whorehouse upstairs. . . .

Southwestern Utah. The Sevier River.
October 15, 1870.

As Tarno predicted, a gentle wind out of the northwest brought them the distinctive odor of wood smoke. By unspoken agreement, they dismounted, picketing their horses.

"They ain't playin' it too smart," Tarno said quietly. "That smokes give 'em away quick as a roaring fire."

"Not if I hadn't seen those tracks," said Faro. "The wagons are still a day away, much too distant for the smoke to betray them."

They progressed on foot, the smell of smoke growing stronger, until at last they could see the wink of a small fire. It was a good distance from the river, offering an advantage to Faro and Tarno, for there was plenty of cover. They crept closer, until they could hear the murmur of voices. In the starlight and in the dim glow of the fire, they counted eight men. Having learned what they wished to know, Faro and Tarno quietly made their way to their horses and rode away. Nearing their own camp, they reined up.

"Identify yourselves," came the challenge.

"Faro and Tarno," said Faro.

They rode in, dismounting, and the outfit gathered around.

"There are eight of them," Faro said. "We'll wait until moonrise, and then we'll ride."

"There are eight of us," said Collins.

"Nine," Mamie said. "You're not leaving me here alone."

"You can go," said Faro, "but you'll remain with the horses."

"Do we dare leave the wagons and the teams unattended?" Collins asked.

"We don't have a lot of choice," said Faro.

"A couple of us may have to ride mules," Tarno said. "We're still two horses shy."

"Not anymore," said Shanghai. "While you and Tarno was gone, two saddled horses showed up, lookin' half starved. Likely they belonged to them renegades."

"*Bueno,*" Faro said. "We can use them."

"How do you propose to handle the attack?" Collins asked. "Will you challenge them with a chance to surrender, or just shoot them down?"

"I'm not as much a barbarian as I seem," said Faro. "While we must be prepared to shoot if they resist, we'll leave them a way out, if they have sense enough to take it. We'll surround them, get the drop, and demand they surrender their guns. If they do, they can ride back to wherever they came from. Any man resisting will be shot. Fair enough?"

"Fair enough," Collins said. "If they're here for any purpose other than attacking us and jumping our claim, they'll go peacefully. Resistance will prove their intentions and their guilt."

There was little more to be said, and they waited until Faro gave the order to saddle up and ride. Slowly the moon crept above the treetops, adding its silvery glow to the light of distant stars. Finally it was time, and Faro gave them last-minute instructions.

"Levi, Dallas, and Josh, you'll be with Tarno, and the four of you will approach their camp from the east. Isaac, Felix, and Dallas, you'll be with me, and we'll circle around and approach from the west. Once we're in position, we'll fan out so we won't all be shooting at the same target. Remember, after I challenge them, any man going for his gun gets the same bitter medicine they're plannin' for us to take. Any questions?"

There were none, and with Faro and Tarno leading, they rode west. Reaching the place where Faro and Tarno had left their horses, they reined up. Without speaking, they all dismounted.

"Mamie," said Faro in a whisper, "stay with the horses."

"I will," Mamie replied. "Do be careful."

Nobody spoke, but Felix squeezed her hand before they were swallowed by shadows.

Quietly Faro led the way around the camp, which was now silent. Reaching the far side of it, Faro positioned his men a few feet apart. In the camp there was a glow as someone drew on a smoke. A voice spoke and another answered, proof enough that some of the men were yet awake. Faro counted slowly to a hundred, and with his Winchester at the ready, shouted his challenge.

"You men are surrounded. Drop your . . ."

But the response was about what Faro had expected, for the darkness blossomed with gunfire and the silence was shattered by the roar of Winchesters. To Faro's right and left, Winchesters barked as men fired at muzzle flashes.

"Don't shoot no more," a voice cried.

"Hold your fire," Faro shouted.

All firing ceased, and the rising wind blew a spark from the dying fire.

"Build up that fire," said Faro, "and stand before it with your hands up."

There was only silence, but the fire flamed up from the coals, revealing five men with their hands up.

"Tarno," Faro shouted, "anybody hurt?"

"No," said Tarno.

"Move on in," Faro replied. "We're comin' in from over here."

Carefully Faro, Isaac, Felix, and Dallas advanced, and soon they could see the shadows of their comrades moving in from the opposite direction. Faro sighed with relief, for it was over, and they hadn't lost a man.

Chapter 16

As the teamsters neared the fire, they kept their weapons ready lest the captives renew the fight, but the five men made no false moves.

"Who are you men?" Faro demanded.

There was silence until Faro cocked his Colt. Finally one of the captives spoke sullenly.

"Ebeau, Jed, Kirk, Newsom, and Inkler. That's Luke, Marklee, and Giles there on the ground."

"That's better," said Faro. "Where are you from, and how did you know about us?"

"North of here, three days' ride," Ebeau said. "Gent name of Durham told us."

"We ought to stampede your horses and make you walk," said Tarno.

"Just give us a chance," Inkler pleaded. "We'll ride out and keep goin'."

"Damn right you will," said Faro. "If any of you show up here again, you'll be shot on sight and without warning. Now saddle your horses, take your dead with you, and ride."

The five wasted no time in saddling all eight horses. The dead were tied belly-down over their saddles, and without so much as asking for their discarded weapons, they all mounted and rode out. The three led horses nickered in protest, not liking their grim burdens or the smell of blood. The sound of their going faded, leaving only the silence of the night.

"Do you suppose they'll keep riding?" Collins asked.

"I think so," said Faro, "but just to be sure they do, I'll ride back this way, ahead of the wagons. One of you put out that fire. Now let's gather up those weapons."

Nearing the horses, they paused. In the silence of the night, the cocking of a Colt seemed loud.

"Mamie," Faro said, "it's us."

"Thank God," said Mamie. "I could hear the shooting. Are any of you hurt?"

"Not a scratch," Faro said, "and the bunch waiting for us are no longer waiting."

"I'm glad," said Mamie, "but how did they know we were coming?"

"Our friend Durham told them," Faro said. "If he followed the Colorado, he could reach Denver a lot sooner than he'd make it to California."

"The sorry, no-account coyote," said Mamie bitterly. "He might have gotten every one of us killed."

"I reckon that's what he was hopin' for," Tarno said. "Once we get back to Santa Fe, remind me to take a ride up to Colorado."

"We'll be a while gettin' back to Santa Fe," said Dallas. "You'd never find him."

"The hell I wouldn't," Tarno said doggedly. "A skunk leaves his smell everywhere he goes."

"Forget it," said Faro. "We came out of it better than they did, and we picked up some extra Colts and Winchesters. Now let's get back to the wagons."

Following the river, they soon reached the wagons. One of the mules brayed as they approached, but there was no other sound. Quickly they dismounted and unsaddled their horses. It was near midnight.

"The first watch will take four hours and the second watch four," said Faro. "That will allow all of us to get a little sleep, even if it means a late start tomorrow."

"I think we deserve that," Collins said.

He took his Winchester from the saddle boot, and Felix, Tarno, and Dallas joined him for the first watch. Less than an hour later, Mamie approached Felix.

"You should be sleeping," said Felix.

"I couldn't," Mamie said. "I was afraid some of you might be hurt, and I was prepared for that. Now I . . . I can't seem to overcome the thought of it. It's like . . . all of you are my family, and after Odessa . . . I can't bear losing any of you."

"You must overcome that fear," said Felix. "I believe our troubles are over, except for a possible clash with the Utes, and they shouldn't have rifles."

Nothing disturbed the tranquillity of the night, and with Mamie helping, Felix soon had breakfast ready.

"I believe we can reach the claim today," Collins said.

"Maybe," said Faro, "but we'll have to step up the gait some."

"Then let's do it," Josh Snyder said. "It seems like we've been on the trail forever."

"Levi," said Faro, "I'll want you to take the first

wagon the rest of the way. While I don't expect those *hombres* to return, we can't take the risk. They may have had extra Colts and shells in their saddlebags. I aim to ride well ahead of the wagons."

"We should have searched their saddlebags before we let 'em go," Shanghai said.

"I don't expect any more trouble from them," said Faro. "Not after they saw three of their friends die before their eyes."

"It does have a way of driving home the finality of a man's own mortality," Felix said.

While the teams were being harnessed, Faro rode out. Since Odessa's death, Felix had taken responsibility for her wagon. Today, instead of riding alongside the wagon, Mamie had tied her horse behind and sat beside Felix.

"I hope you don't mind," said Mamie. "I think they all know about us, by now."

"I daresay they do," Felix said, with some humor.

"Sometimes I wonder what they're thinking," said Mamie. "After all, they know what fools Odessa and me made of ourselves over Hal Durham. My God, the proper folks back in Amarillo . . ."

"Have become too civilized for the frontier," Felix finished. "Faro, Shanghai, Dallas, and Tarno are frontiersmen, and I like to think the rest of us are becoming like them. I know I am, and I don't expect any less of Levi, Isaac, and Josh. I'd gamble my share of the gold there's not a man among us who's not guilty of some things he can't recall with pride. I knew several men in New Orleans who later came west and married women right out of whorehouses."

Mamie laughed. "At least you didn't sink quite that low."

Southwestern Utah. The Sevier River. October 17, 1870.

Faro rode west along the river until he reached the first of the pyramids marking the claim. Since they had to establish a camp for many months, he sought some kind of shelter that might also afford protection against possible attacks by the Utes. But he rode all the way to the bend in the river, well beyond the claim, without finding any natural shelter. Finally, convinced there were no unseen dangers, he rode back to meet the wagons. They stopped to rest the teams so that they might learn what Faro had discovered.

"No tracks except what that bunch made when they rode out last night," Faro said. "I rode west along the river, well beyond the claim, without finding anyplace we might use as shelter and maybe defense against Indian attacks."

"There is no shelter and no cover along the river, near the claim," said Collins.

"No," Felix agreed. "That's how the Utes made it so hot for us, we had to run for it, instead of waiting for Levi and the supplies."

"One thing I noticed that might work in our favor is the high banks of the river, half a mile or so beyond the claim," said Faro. "There's a considerable overhang that can shelter us from rain or snow, and would make attacks by the Utes difficult."

"There's just one problem," Isaac said. "There's

water from bank to bank, and I'd say it's deep. There's no place even for us to hunker down there, and certainly no protection for the horses, mules, and wagons."

"Nobody's said anything about the location of the gold," said Faro, "but from where the claim markers are located, I'd say it's in the riverbed. Am I right?"

"One hundred percent," Collins said, "and that's why we have dynamite in all five of the wagons. There's a canyon—Devil's Canyon, we call it—that parallels the river. In fact, the river flows into it several miles east of our claim."

"I noticed that," said Faro, "and you have plans for blasting the river into a new path, so that it flows into the canyon somewhere beyond the claim. That would leave the portion of the river's bed dry where your claim's located."

"Exactly," Collins said. "You are an observant man."

"Then let me offer a suggestion," said Faro, "since you intend to divert the river anyway. Devil's Canyon runs alongside the river for maybe two miles beyond the claim, all the way to the bend in the river. Suppose, just this side of the bend, the river was diverted into the canyon there, instead of just barely beyond the claim?"

"The river's original bed would then be dry well beyond those high banks," Collins said excitedly. "Those high riverbanks would become our shelter and fortification."

"That's what I'm thinking," said Faro. "Our only difficulty might be in finding a place where the banks are low enough to get the wagons down there."

"More dynamite," Felix said. "With that and some shovel work, we can build ourselves a road. After all, we built a bridge, didn't we?"

"For needed shelter and defense against the Indians, it would be worth the extra work, I think," said Faro.

"There's more advantage than that," Dallas added. "When you're dealin' with gold in a riverbed, how can you be sure where it starts and stops? Blasting the river into Devil's Canyon a mile farther upstream instead of doin' it right next to the claim might produce even more gold. How do we know gold can't be found farther up the river, beneath those high banks?"

"We don't," said Collins. "In our excitement, we overlooked the obvious."

"Didn't we, though?" Felix said. "We ought to follow Faro around and learn from him, if we can."

"Oh, hell," said Faro, embarrassed. "I wasn't thinking of the claim extending upriver beyond your markers. When I couldn't find any shelter and no decent place for defense, I was only thinking of a way we could use those high banks and their overhang in some way. Even if there's more gold upriver, it won't be worth as much to us as shelter during the coming winter and as a defense against Indian attacks."

"Amen to that," Felix said. "Let's get rolling. I want to have a look at Devil's Canyon up there beyond the claim."

The wagons rolled on, and before sundown they reached the point on the Sevier River where the claim had been marked.

"Too late to accomplish anything today," said Collins, "but I think we should perhaps plan on doing some blasting within the next day or two, if it turns out that we can use the old riverbed for shelter. I look for some serious snowfall, and it may be soon."

"Isaac's had considerable experience with dynamite," Josh Snyder said, "and I've had a little, myself."

"I'm counting on that," said Collins. "In the morning, after breakfast, I'd like for both of you to accompany Faro to the place he feels we ought to blast the river into Devil's Canyon. Then if you feel there are possibilities, decide where the charges should be set, and get on with it."

"I'm almighty tired of snaking in tree trunks for firewood in the midst of a blizzard," Dallas said. "Once we're sure where the permanent camp will be, I'd favor all of us that's not involved in the blasting startin' to drag in firewood."

"Not a bad idea," said Faro. "If we're able to divert the river and set up camp in the old riverbed beneath the overhang, there's no reason we can't work the claim in the worst kind of weather. But we'll need plenty of fuel, and I don't see a lot of timber close by. I reckon we need to follow your advice, Dallas, and I'd be obliged if you'll take charge of gathering as much wood as you can. If the claim is anything close to as rich as we think, then I doubt any of us will want to take the time to drag in fallen trees to feed the fire."

"Right," Dallas said, "but I'll need help. Who'll go with me?"

"I will," said Collins. "Faro, Isaac, and Josh will decide where to set the charges for the blasting."

"Tarno and me will go with you," Shanghai said.

"So will I," said Felix.

"If the blasting works out," Faro said, "our next step will be to find a place where the wagons can be driven down into the old riverbed."

"Let's just hope the old riverbed is solid," said Dallas. "If there's mud, we may have to wait a week or two for it to dry."

"We have reasons to believe it's solid," Collins said. "At least it was in the shallows from which we first took ore samples."

Mamie and Felix had supper ready well before dark, and the fire was doused. The sun set behind a cloud bank, shooting glorious arrows of crimson far into the evening sky.

"I hope there ain't too much mud in that riverbed," said Tarno. "The Injun in me says there'll be more snow. After the light one we had last time, the one that's comin' may be neck-deep."

"I wish the damn Injun in you wasn't always right," Shanghai said. "The varmint can take his turn with an ax, choppin' wood."

The night passed quietly, and when breakfast was over, Faro, Isaac, and Josh saddled their horses and rode up-river to further investigate the possibility of diverting the river where Faro had suggested. Dallas and the rest of the outfit, armed with axes, rode out in search of windblown and lightning-struck trees that could be snaked in for firewood. A Winchester by her side, Mamie had remained in camp to clean up the breakfast fixings.

"Along about here," Faro said, reining up his horse. "Let's see how much of a path we'll have to blast," said Isaac. "The only problem I can see would be that the distance from the river to the canyon rim is too great, or that there is solid rock in the way."

"We don't have to blast at any certain place," Faro said, "as long as we're far enough upriver to free part of the riverbed for the shelter we need. First we must find a place in the bank that's low enough for us to cross to the other side of the river."

"We could have crossed downstream," said Felix, "but it's a long way. That's where we crossed to set up the claim markers."

"We'll ride on a ways," Faro said. "Then we can work our way back, looking for the best place to blast. How far upriver does the canyon go?"

"I have no idea," said Isaac. "Once we set up the claim markers, we didn't concern ourselves with the canyon beyond there."

"I don't see a far canyon rim from here," Josh said. "Could be a box canyon. That or it veers away from the river along here."

"We won't know until we're able to cross," said Faro.

They had ridden what Faro estimated to be five miles before finding a place where they could lead their horses down one steep bank and up the other. Reaching the far bank, they stopped to rest the animals.

"I think we'll have to find a place somewhere downstream to take the wagons into the riverbed," said Josh. "We'd never level those banks where we just crossed. There's too much rock."

"That won't make any difference, if Devil's Canyon

plays out somewhere below here," Isaac said. "Before we make any plans for getting the wagons down to the riverbed, we'd best be sure there's a canyon where the river can go."

With that in mind, they rode away from the river, to the north, only to find there was no canyon paralleling the river.

"It's a blind canyon at this end," said Isaac. "We'll have to ride downriver until we find the head of it. From there we'll look for a place where it's closest to the river."

"That's something I didn't consider when I suggested going even farther beyond the claim before diverting the river," Faro said. "We may be limited by the distance between the river and the canyon."

They rode almost three miles before they could see the north rim of the canyon ahead of them. Dismounting, they led their horses closer, and by the time they reached the box end of the canyon, they could barely hear the roar of the river.

"Too far from the river," said Felix. "We'll follow it until we find a place where it's nearest the north bank."

They continued along the canyon rim until they could again hear the surge of the river.

"There's piles of loose dirt and rock down there in the canyon," Josh said, "and I'd say that's proof enough it ain't solid rock between here and the river."

"It's encouraging," said Isaac, "as long as there hasn't been a slide serious enough to block the canyon."

"It's plenty deep," Faro said, "unless it becomes too shallow too soon."

Suddenly Faro went closer, peering into the canyon. "What is it?" Josh asked.

"I thought I saw something down there," said Faro. "There it is again."

Amid a pile of dirt and rock that had tumbled down from the rim, the sun shone on a bright object.

"Gold," Josh said. "We're about to flood Devil's Canyon, when there's gold in it."

"Maybe not," said Faro. "The sun might reflect off any kind of metal."

"Other kinds of metal would rust, but gold wouldn't," Isaac said. "One of us will have to go down there."

"I'll go," said Faro, "but we'll have to knot a pair of lariats together. One wouldn't be long enough."

Taking a lariat from his saddle and one from Isaac's, Faro knotted them together. He then tied one end to the horn of his saddle, and taking a strong hold on the rope, stepped over the canyon rim. Keeping the rope taut, he walked down the canyon wall, loose rock and dirt tumbling down ahead of him. Reaching the canyon floor, it took a moment for him to locate the object that had first attracted his attention. Kneeling, he scooped away the loose dirt to reveal a golden cross on a gold chain.

"It is gold!" Josh shouted from the rim.

"Yes," said Faro, "but not the kind we're looking for. It's a gold cross attached to a gold chain, and the chain's caught on something."

"I brought a pick and shovel," Isaac said. "Which do you want?"

"Drop me the shovel," said Faro. "It's mostly loose dirt from the canyon rim."

With the shovel, Faro began removing the dirt a little at a time. Eventually the shovel clunked against something solid, and laying the shovel aside, Faro began scooping away the dirt with his hands. He then found himself looking into the empty eye sockets of a skull, and digging further, he found the gold chain was around the skeletal neck. Carefully, so as not to dislodge the skull, he removed the chain. He then held in his hands a gold cross that was some six inches in length, with a cross member of two-thirds that. Brushing the dirt away, Faro could read an engraving that had been etched into the cross member:

Padre Esteban Borrego 1759.

"Spanish gold," Josh shouted excitedly.

"Looks like it," said Faro, "and this gent's been here awhile. There's engraving on the back of the cross."

Faro read the title, the name, and the date.

"A priest," Isaac said. "Do you want one of us to come down and help you uncover the rest of him?"

"I can do it," said Faro. "The dirt's loose. I think he was lying here all the time, and the dirt slid off the canyon rim and covered him."

Carefully Faro shoveled away the dirt and found only the upper torso of the skeleton intact. The bones of the legs and feet were missing, and there was nothing else beneath the pile of dirt that might help to identify the long-dead priest. Faro shoveled dirt over the remains until the skeleton was completely covered.

"That's it," said Faro. "I'm sending up the shovel and the cross. Then you can throw the rope back to me."

Josh backstepped the horse, drawing Faro up to the canyon rim. Isaac helped him to climb over the edge.

"The river ain't more than fifty yards away," Josh said. "It may not get much closer to Devil's Canyon than that."

"But it won't hurt to go a bit farther," said Isaac. "We're still nearly two miles above the claim, and the shorter the distance between the canyon and the river, the less blasting we'll have to do."

"That's good thinking," Faro said. "If the distance increases as we continue, then we'll still be able to come back here."

The three of them mounted their horses, and within half a mile they found what they were looking for. There was a bend in the canyon, bringing it nearer the river. There was only a narrow strip of land separating the two.

"We won't find a place more ideal than this," said Isaac. "I think the only reason the river hasn't already broken through into the canyon is that there's too much rock. We're still more than a mile above our claim, and if we can divert the river here, we'll have all the riverbed we'll need for shelter and defense."

"Then we'll do our blasting here," Josh said. "Does that suit you, Faro?"

"Yes," said Faro. "We have dynamite, and even a few feet of solid rock can't stand up to that. It's better that we open a channel through rock. If there was only dirt, the force of the water might cave in the banks farther down."

"Then let's return to camp and make plans for the blasting," Isaac said. "Maybe we'll be able to do it today. But first we must talk to the others and get their approval."

Mounting their horses, they rode upriver, where they crossed to the south bank. When they reached the wagons, the rest of the outfit was there, having just snaked in their first logs for firewood. First, Isaac showed them the golden cross and chain Faro had found.

"Let me see that," said Felix excitedly.

Isaac passed it to him and he studied it intently. Finally he spoke.

"I've done some reading about the early days, when Spain owned most of the territory from Texas to California. The gent who owned this may have been on his way to Santa Fe from California. There once were Spanish missions all over the Southwest."

"There's a date, 1759," said Faro. "What do you think it means?"

"I can't tie that date back to any particular event," Felix said. "It might have been the year he was ordained, or maybe his birth date."

"Solid gold," said Josh Snyder. "Wonder what it's worth?"

"Not as much for the gold content as it's worth historically," Felix said.

"Faro found it," said Isaac, "so it will be up to him what becomes of it."

"Consider it yours, Felix," Faro said. "I agree that it's a piece of history, and that it deserves better than just being sold. We're here to mine gold, and I believe we've found the place to blast through the riverbed into Devil's Canyon."

"He's right," said Josh, "but it'll be through almost solid rock."

"That's why we brought plenty of dynamite," Collins said, "and thanks to Faro, we'll be diverting the river and at the same time, creating a shelter from the elements as well as Indian attacks. How soon can we begin blasting?"

"Maybe today," said Isaac, "unless some of you think otherwise."

"All of you heard," Collins said. "Are there any objections?"

There were none, and Collins continued.

"Isaac, since you, Josh, and Faro began this, why don't you finish it? You can have as many of us as it takes, if you feel that you need help."

"The three of us can handle it," Isaac said, "and the sooner we divert the water into the canyon, the sooner the riverbed can begin to dry."

"Then we won't bother chopping these logs down to firewood length," said Collins. "If the blasting accomplishes what we expect, we can just roll the logs over the riverbank and take axes to them later."

Collins and his companions rode out for more firewood, while Faro, Isaac, and Josh began unloading dynamite from one of the wagons.

"I feel awful useless, hanging around the wagons while the rest of you are working," Mamie said.

"You'll be doing more than your share, if you'll fix us some noonday grub," said Faro. "The wind's gettin' a mite cold and some hot coffee will be welcome."

"I'll start right now," Mamie promised.

Having broken open the wooden case, Isaac and Josh had begun capping and fusing the dynamite.

"I reckon a case of it will be enough," said Faro.

"Unless it's solid rock to the center of the earth," Isaac said, "this should be enough to blow up all of southern Utah."

As the explosive was made ready, Faro began placing it in the saddlebags of their still-saddled horses. Finally the three of them mounted and rode upriver, again crossing to the north bank.

"We'd better leave the horses a good distance away, and continue on foot," Faro said, "or the blast will spook them and we'll end up walking back to camp."

"I figured we'd leave them up-canyon about where you discovered the gold cross," said Isaac. "That's maybe half a mile. All the dynamite has a long-burning fuse."

They dismounted, picketing the horses where there were some patches of graze along the river. Isaac removed four sticks of dynamite from his saddlebag.

"We'll start with a small charge, increasing it if we need to," Isaac said. "If the charge is too heavy, you lose control of it."

"I can believe that," said Faro. "Do you begin blasting at the riverbank, or at the rim of the canyon?"

"At the canyon rim," Isaac said. "We must be sure the channel from the river to the canyon is deep enough and that the elevation is right for the water to flow, before we bust through the riverbank. We need just enough of a retaining wall to hold the water back, but not so much that a final blast can't finish the job."

"I reckon," said Faro. "I can't imagine lighting a dynamite fuse under water."

Expecting some rock, Isaac had kept the pick and shovel. When they reached the area where the distance was shortest between river and canyon, he swung the pick hard, driving it into the canyon rim. As expected, he struck rock, and quickly determined that most of the area between riverbank and canyon rim was equally obstructed.

"Well," said Isaac, "that explains why the river never broke through into the canyon at this particular place. We may need a sledgehammer and drill."

"Maybe not," Faro said. "That's why I brought a lariat. If the two of you can lower me over the rim a ways, maybe I can dig far enough into the canyon wall to set a charge. That should blast away enough of the rock for us to continue to the riverbank."

"That should work," said Isaac, "but it's a pretty good drop to the canyon floor, and I think we should go back for one of the horses. Josh?"

"I'll bring one of 'em," Josh said.

When Snyder returned with his horse, Faro tied one end of the lariat to the saddle horn. In the other end, he made a loop that he brought over his head and tightened about his waist.

"That'll cut you in half," said Isaac.

"All the more reason for me to do it *pronto*," Faro replied.

Chapter 17

Josh backstepped the horse, bringing the lariat taut until Faro was over the edge of the canyon rim. A dozen feet down, there was a hump in the wall on which Faro was able to rest his feet, easing the strain of the rope around his middle. With all the force he was able to muster, he swung the pick, driving it deep.

"More rock?" Isaac shouted.

"Not yet," said Faro.

He drove in the pick again and again, dirt and loose stones cascading over him to the canyon floor below.

"Don't try to dig in too deep," Isaac said. "Just enough to set a charge."

"Then haul me up," said Faro wearily. "I can't last much longer."

By the time they helped Faro over the edge, he was having trouble breathing. When he was at last free of the lariat, he lay there wheezing.

"That's the most difficult part," Isaac said. "Josh or me can go down long enough to place the charge."

"There's barely room enough, I reckon," said Faro, "but maybe it'll be enough."

"I'll go down there and set the charge," Josh said, "and once that fuse is afire, haul me up fast."

He tightened the lariat around his middle and took the four sticks of capped and fused dynamite that had been bound together. Faro backstepped the horse, tightening the rope as Josh stepped over the canyon rim. When he was in position, he shoved the dynamite into the crevice with as much force as he could. In his teeth he gripped three matches, and popping one of them aflame with his thumbnail, he lighted the dynamite fuse. Belly-down at the canyon rim, Isaac had been watching his progress.

"Haul him up," Isaac shouted.

Quickly Faro backstepped the horse. When Snyder reached the canyon rim, Isaac was quick to help him to safety.

"Help him mount his horse," Faro said. "We may not have time for him to get his wind."

Quickly Isaac boosted Snyder into the saddle and the trio retreated to where they had left the horses. Still the charge didn't blow.

"Damn it," said Snyder, "the fuse may have flamed out. I should have waited a little longer, bein' sure of it."

But at that moment the earth shook with the force of the explosion, and the horses nickered in fear. Once the horses were again calm, Isaac took another four sticks of the dynamite from his saddlebag, and the trio set out for the scene. Reaching it, they found the blast had dislodged an enormous boulder, which now lay on the canyon floor.

"Except for the one big rock, it didn't accomplish much," Faro said.

"That's enough," said Isaac. "While we've gained less than half a dozen feet, that'll be all we'll need to set another charge."

"If I'm any judge," Josh said, "we'll have to go a lot deeper than that."

"I agree," said Isaac. "Without enough elevation, the river won't empty completely, but I think we ought to continue this channel on to the riverbank. That will give us some idea as to how much deeper we need to go. Then we'll come back to this end and shoot for the proper depth."

"We may not finish today, then," Faro said.

"Probably not," said Isaac. "When you're blasting through rock, you have to take it a little at a time, like the calf ate the grindstone."

Faro laughed. "This is the first time I've heard that expression since leaving Texas."

"Let's set another charge," Josh said. "That should give us some idea as to how tough the rest of it will be."

The second blast dislodged more rock, advancing their channel another three or four feet. A third and fourth blast provided further proof of what they already suspected. Their progress was going to be agonizingly slow.

"Looks like I was wrong," Isaac said. "We'll need more dynamite before this day is done, so we might as well ride back for some of that grub Mamie's making ready."

The food was ready and the rest of the outfit was eating.

"We waited for you as long as we could," said Dallas Weaver. "Three minutes."

"That's better than I'd expect," Faro said. "I reckon you've been hearin' our progress. I hope the lot of you have hauled in enough wood to last the winter."

"I expect we will have, before you gents get the river diverted," Dallas said. "Looking down there, I still see water."

"You'll probably be seeing it for a while," said Isaac. "While there doesn't seem to be much separating the river from Devil's Canyon, what there is appears to be mostly rock."

"That's why we brought plenty of dynamite," Collins said.

"There may not be any left over," said Felix. "We were lucky, being able to dig some ore from the riverbank. For all we know, we may end up blasting the rest of it loose."

"We may need as much as two more cases of dynamite to blast the channel from the river to the canyon," Isaac said.

"Perhaps you should increase the charge," said Collins.

"I doubt it would help that much," Isaac said. "Blasting through rock, you can only get so far with a single charge. We're using four sticks at a time. Too much force might only widen the channel, rather than lengthening it."

"Then continue as you and Josh see fit," said Collins.

"Yeah," Tarno said, "just as long as you have that riverbed dry in another day or so. The wind's gettin' colder, and the Injun in me says we're due for another storm, and we'll be needin' shelter."

"Then if you can find a piece of ground that's not solid rock," said Faro, "you'd better dig a hole big enough for you and that Injun in you to crawl into. Blasting this channel to Devil's Canyon from the bank of the river is some devil of a job, and it may run right on into next week."

Taking a second case of dynamite from one of the wagons, Isaac and Josh capped and fused it. The three of them then rode back to continue what they had started.

"At least another fifty feet to the riverbank," Isaac observed, "and even then we won't have the depth we'll need."

"No," said Josh, "but when we begin blasting on a second level, there may not be so much rock. Then we can increase the charge."

"Seems to me we'll have to blast this new channel even lower than the riverbed," Faro said. "Otherwise, we may divert only some of the water, with the rest flowing along the original bed."

"That's exactly right," said Isaac. "Water always seeks the lowest level, so we may have to drop this new channel several feet below the original riverbed."

As the afternoon wore on, they placed six more charges, each advancing their channel a few more feet.

"There's enough dynamite for four more charges," Josh said. "That should get us to the riverbank on a first level, and will be about as much as we can do today. Tomorrow we can begin deepening the channel."

The last charge advanced their channel all the way to the riverbank, but still far short of their goal.

"Now we'll have to back up to the canyon rim and shoot for depth," said Isaac. "We're still a dozen feet away from water level, and depending on the depth of the river, we may have to go down another sixteen to twenty feet."

"Tarnation," Faro said, "I hope we'll have enough dynamite."

"We will," said Isaac. "Josh and me figured on something like this, before Levi went to Santa Fe. There's a good chance, as we go deeper, there'll be less rock. In that case, the force of the river will work for us."

They reached camp an hour before sunset. The rest of the outfit was already there, and Felix was helping Mamie prepare supper. An enormous pile of logs had been dragged in for firewood. While they waited for supper, Isaac told them what progress had been made. Collins expressed some doubt.

"Will we have enough dynamite? Where we had originally planned to divert the river—just above the claim—the banks were much lower."

"Yes," Isaac agreed, "but there was a greater distance between Devil's Canyon and the river, so it should even out."

"Isaac and me went a little heavy, orderin' the dynamite," said Josh. "We're seven hundred miles out of Santa Fe, so it's better havin' too much than not enough."

"I don't believe we'll have too much," Isaac said. "We're considering the possibility that we may have to blast some of the ore loose, once the river's been diverted. For all we know, the vein may run through solid rock."

"If it does, it'll be worth the extra effort," said Dallas Weaver. "I've had some experience with mining, and when you find rock shot with color, it's almost always pure gold."

"I've heard talk about that," Felix said.

"This is all so exciting," said Mamie. "It'll be hard to wait."

With the dawn came a cold wind from the northwest that had the feel of snow. Along the western horizon stretched a band of gray clouds.

"Before we do anything else," Faro said, "I think we'd better position four wagons and get our canvas shelters in place."

"Leave that to the rest of us," said Dallas. "You, Josh, and Isaac continue blasting."

"I believe that's a worthy suggestion," Levi Collins said. "When the canvas is up, we'll continue the search for firewood."

So Isaac and Josh capped and fused another case of dynamite, and with the explosive in their saddlebags, they returned to the scene of the blasting. Dallas and Collins lined up the first and second wagons side by side, a dozen feet apart, their sides facing west. Shanghai and Tarno brought wagons three and four into a similar position. With all four in a line, canvas was stretched from the bows of one wagon to the bows of the next, secured with rawhide thongs. Finished, there was adequate shelter between wagons one and two, two and three, and three and four. On the outside of the fourth wagon—facing west—canvas was secured to the wagon box, stretched tight, and pegged to the ground. It would be an effective windbreak as well as protection from blowing snow.

"That's about all we can do," said Dallas, "but it's helped us survive blizzards on the plains in Kansas, where there wasn't a hill, or even a rock."

"It's a touch of genius," Felix said. "Who came up with the idea?"

"Faro, mostly," said Dallas. "Freighting ain't a fair-weather business. To survive, you can't let an occasional blizzard discourage you."

"I suppose not," Collins said, "but there's the melted snow, the rain, then the mud."

"Yeah," said Tarno. "We been suggestin' that Faro come up with a way to beat that, but so far he ain't done a damn thing."

By the time the rest of the outfit had prepared for the expected storm, there had been two more explosions upriver.

"It's looking better than I expected," Isaac said, as he viewed the results of the last explosion. "A lot of the rock is near the surface, and we're already below that. I believe we'll make better progress from here on."

"Maybe we should increase the charge," said Josh.

"Eventually," Isaac said, "but let's continue the way we're going for at least today, so that we know we're through most of the rock."

"We should have time to fire another four charges by noon," said Faro. "Then it'll be time for grub."

"I expect we'd better make good use of this afternoon," Isaac said, "from the looks of those clouds."

"I expect you're right," said Faro. "If I'm any judge, there'll be snow sometime tonight or early tomorrow."

They fired four more charges, exhausting their supply of dynamite, and rode back to camp for the noon meal. After erecting the shelters, the rest of the outfit had been busily chopping wood, and there were piles of it beneath each of the wagons.

"We got more than enough wood to see us through the storm," Dallas said, "so we just went ahead and chopped a bunch of it firewood length. It's hell, choppin' with your hands half froze, and this time we shouldn't have to."

"*Bueno,*" said Faro. "Every once in a while, you use your head for something besides a place to hang your hat."

The meal finished, Faro, Isaac, and Josh took another case of dynamite and continued blasting, while the rest of the outfit began dragging in more logs for firewood. Long before sundown, the sun disappeared behind the gray storm clouds gathering in the west, feathering the sky with crimson. The wind grew colder.

"One more charge," Isaac said, "and we'll give it up until after the storm."

When they reached the wagons, the rest of the outfit had just dragged in more logs for firewood.

"Hang it up until after the storm," said Faro. "Everybody deserves some rest."

Felix and Mamie had devoted one of the canvas-enclosed shelters to a cooking area, and there was still plenty of room for them all to gather and eat. It would serve as an all-night rendezvous for the men on watch, with a warm fire and plenty of hot coffee. After supper, Isaac spoke of the progress of the channel between the river and Devil's Canyon.

"I think maybe another week, and we'll break through."

"That's if we don't end up neck-deep in snow," said Tarno.

"We won't let that slow us up," Faro said. "When the storm blows itself out, we'll break trail for the horses, shovel the snow out of our way, and get on with the blasting."

"Excellent," said Collins.

Nothing more was said, for supper was ready and everybody was hungry. Since there was little graze, the horse and mules would have to be fed grain, and the lot of them had been secured in a nearby rope corral. They were down to last cups of coffee, when Faro spoke.

"The usual watch, unless there are wolves. If the varmints show up, nobody sleeps. Unless wolves come, those of us on watch shouldn't have to go out into the storm, for we can see the horses and mules from here. For their sake, let's build another fire—a big one—outside the wagon enclosure, nearer the animals. Snow or not, we won't have to tend it more than two or three times during the night."

"A commendable idea," Collins said. "Without horses and mules, our cause is lost."

The snow began an hour after dark, borne in on a

howling wind. With Collins, Felix, Tarno, and Dallas taking the first watch, the rest of the outfit retired to another of the wagon shelters and rolled in their blankets. With all the first watch gathered in the same area, there was little opportunity for Mamie and Felix to talk, but Mamie remained with them, nodding occasionally. After a while, all conversation lagged, and the men contented themselves with hot coffee. At midnight, Faro, Shanghai, Isaac, and Josh took over for the second watch. The storm continued to roar, and only by Faro's pocket watch were they able to determine when the dawn came. There was already hot coffee, but a second pot was put on the fire, as Felix and Mamie began breakfast.

"Everybody not involved with cookin' breakfast gets to help me fill feed bags and feed the horses and mules," Faro said.

The animals had their backs to the storm, and seemed grateful for the grain, but the force of the wind threatened to rip the bags from the numbed hands of the men. Finally they were able to return to the shelter for more hot coffee.

"This may be the worst storm yet," Tarno said. "Last one was a mite short."

"It won't matter," said Faro. "When it's done, we'll start the blasting."

"Then we might have all the ore we can haul, and be ready to start for Santa Fe by the last of April," Collins said.

"That may be good or it may not be so good," said Felix. "Suppose it's a rich strike, and we have to leave most of it behind?"

"I've considered that," Collins replied, "but our deal called for Faro and his outfit to freight in supplies and take out loads of ore. Beyond that, I don't know."

"But that was before we owned half the claim," said Dallas. "If we came in here once, we can do it again."

"That's my thoughts, too," Faro said, "but I won't draft anybody. It would have to be strictly voluntary."

"Then consider me volunteered," said Dallas.

"Me, too," Shanghai and Tarno said, in a single voice.

Collins laughed. "I don't see how we could do any better than that."

"I do," said Felix Blackburn. "It's not my style to hunker in town and spend money. I find the freighting business appealing, and I'm thinking of investing in some wagons of my own. Every man of us can drive a wagon, which means we can bring three more the next time."

"If you feel that strong," Faro said, "why don't you just throw in with us? We can't promise you a bed of roses, but I can promise you that you'll never be bored. In years to come, Santa Fe will be booming, and until there's a railroad, they'll be depending on our wagons and others like them."

"I think I'd like that," said Felix. "From what I've seen of the four of you, I like your style."

"No more than I do," Isaac Puckett said. "Is this a closed game, or can I play?"

"You're in, if that's what you want," said Faro. "In fact, I think all of you've proven yourselves men who can be depended on."

"I wouldn't be opposed to such an alliance," Levi

Collins said. "I must say that I have learned a lot, and I have nothing but admiration for you men and your knowledge of the frontier. I believe this is a challenge I would welcome."

"*Bueno,*" said Faro. "There's a chance, then, that we can do our own freighting from here to Santa Fe, without risking the hiring of outsiders. Josh, where do you stand?"

"With the rest of you," Snyder said. "I'd rather wear out than rust out."

"Storm and all," said Faro, "this is a good day."

"I agree," Collins said, "and after all we've been through together, I can't see anything but good coming of this."

"I'm so glad," said Mamie. "I think of all of you as family."

The day wore on and the storm continued, and not until sometime during the second night did it appear to be subsiding.

"The wind's not quite so fierce," Faro said. "This one may be winding down."

"I think so," said Shanghai. "It don't seem quite as cold."

"Before there's another storm, we'll have the river diverted and permanent shelter set up," said Isaac.

By dawn the snow had ceased, and by noon the clouds had cleared, making way for the sun. It shone on a blinding white mass as far as the eye could see. The horses and mules stood belly-deep in it, the snow answering their need for water.

"The drifts aren't so deep along the riverbank," Faro

said. "I think we should take shovels and a case of dynamite and go on with the blasting."

"I'm game if you are," said Josh.

"So am I," Felix said.

"That doesn't seem fair to the three of you, while the rest of us sit here by the fire, doing nothing," said Collins.

"I don't know what you could do that would make it go any faster," Faro said. "Isaac and Josh are doing the blasting, and they don't have all that much need for me. I reckon I can help break trail."

"We won't be exactly wasting our time," said Dallas. "Just because we haven't heard wolves don't mean there's none around. When the snow gets deep, they always go huntin' grub, and we'll need to keep watch over our horses and mules."

So Isaac took another case of dynamite from one of the wagons, and Josh joined him in capping and fusing the explosive. With Faro leading out, the three of them set out along the riverbank. Mostly they led their horses, going ahead and breaking trail. Each of them carried a shovel, and there were times when they were forced to shovel their way through heavy drifts. It took them more than an hour to reach their position, and then they had to shovel snow from the channel they had begun blasting. They were again working their way from the canyon rim to the river, and their first charge was encouraging.

"It's blowing deeper," said Isaac. "I think it's time we increased the charge."

He added a fifth stick of dynamite to the next charge, with a marked improvement in the results.

"It made a considerable difference," Josh said, "but we won't have enough dynamite to last more than a couple of hours."

"Don't let that bother you," said Faro. "I'll ride back for another case of it."

Faro returned to the wagons, taking the case of dynamite, along with enough caps and fuse. Before he returned, there were two more explosions.

"We made some progress while you were gone," Isaac said. "The stronger charge will probably finish this in two or three more days."

"*Bueno*," said Faro. "Instead of ridin' back for grub, let's just use up the rest of this dynamite and call it a day. It'll be almighty cold up here, late in the afternoon."

Well before they had finished, the wind rose. The sun sank below western peaks, and the cold seemed all the more intense, as Josh lighted the fuse to the last charge.

"Well," Isaac said, following the explosion, "do we go back and have a look, or wait until tomorrow?"

"Let's wait until tomorrow," said Faro. "My feet are so numb, I don't know if my toes are still there or not."

"I agree," Josh said. "We could have set by the fire and lost two or three days, waitin' for it to warm up, but we didn't. I feel like we're ahead by that much."

"That's how you have to think on the frontier," said Faro. "Never put off anything until tomorrow, because you're likely to have a whole new set of problems by then, piled up right on top of the old ones."

When they reached the wagons, Felix, Shanghai, and Tarno took their horses.

"We'll unsaddle and rub them down," Tarno said. "Get some hot coffee and get next to the fire."

"We saved you some food," said Mamie, "if you don't think it'll spoil your supper."

"We'll risk it," Faro said.

The three of them sat cross-legged before the fire, drinking hot coffee and eating. By the time they had finished, Felix, Tarno, and Shanghai had returned. Isaac then reported their progress.

"Wonderful," said Collins. "The three of you are to be commended for fighting your way through the snow to continue your work."

"We aim to get an early start in the morning," Faro said. "It's bearable with the sun, but later in the day, when the wind picks up, it's almighty cold."

The following morning, Faro removed two cases of dynamite from one of the wagons, and when it had been capped and fused, Faro, Isaac, and Josh set out for their day's work.

"Without more snow, it'll be some easier going today," Faro predicted. "The trail we broke yesterday should be enough."

And it was. They were able to remain mounted until it was time to cross the river, and there, because of the steep banks, they had to lead their horses.

"We made some progress with that one," said Isaac, viewing their last blast of the day before. "Since we brought enough dynamite, let's increase our charge to six sticks. If it's not all that much improved, then we can go back to five."

But their first blast using a heavier charge encouraged them to continue it, and when they had exhausted their supply of dynamite, they observed the deepening channel with satisfaction.

"Maybe another ten feet," Isaac said, "and we can blast through to the river."

The following day, after a third day of sun, the snow began to melt and the once cold wind turned almost balmy. Again Faro, Isaac, and Josh took two cases of dynamite, setting the heavier charge, and by the end of the day, Isaac judged the end of the channel next to Devil's Canyon had reached the desired depth.

"Now all we must do is reach that same depth all the way to the river," Isaac said.

"I figure another three days," said Josh.

Faro said nothing, preferring to wait and see.

With the melting of the snow, Dallas and his companions took to snaking in more logs for firewood. Once they had an enormous pile, they attacked it with axes, chopping it into convenient lengths.

"My God," said Felix, rubbing his blistered hands, "instead of a teamster I'm beginning to feel like a wood chopper who does a little hauling just once in a while."

Shanghai laughed. "In the winter months, that's what most teamsterin' consists of, just tryin' to keep from freezin' to death."

Finally the day came when the channel between the Sevier River and Devil's Canyon had been blasted deep enough and far enough that only half a dozen feet separated the river and the canyon.

"One more blast ought to send the river through to the canyon," said Isaac.

"Good," Josh said. "We have enough dynamite for one more charge."

"Then let's set it off and see what happens," said Faro. "We've waited long enough."

The blast seemed to shake the earth, and before the excited trio could reach the scene, there were three shots from a Winchester, downriver.

"There must be trouble at camp," Josh said.

"I doubt it," said Faro. "I think they're tellin' us we've been successful."

When they reached the scene of the blast, the channel on which they had worked for so long was full of rushing water, and there was the sound of a waterfall as it poured into Devil's Canyon. Eagerly they ran to the riverbank, where the original bed now contained only puddles of water.

"Very little mud," said Isaac. "It looks like solid rock."

"God Almighty," Josh said, "I hope it ain't like that all the way, with the gold underneath it."

"So do I," said Isaac. "We still have plenty of dynamite, but not *that* much."

Chapter 18

Triumphantly Faro, Isaac, and Josh rode back to camp. There, with the exception of Felix and Dallas, they found the rest of the outfit gathered along the riverbank. Felix and Dallas, armed with picks and shovels and using lariats, had lowered themselves down to the riverbed.

"All right," Faro shouted, "what's the verdict?"

"It's not solid rock," said Felix, "but we haven't found any gold yet."

"Don't tell us that," Isaac said, "after all this work. Why don't you go back to where we found the first ore?"

"We're just testin' the riverbed to see how solid it is," said Felix. "I think we'll need to let it dry for a couple of days. By then, we should be able to bring the wagons down."

"By then," Faro said, "maybe we'll have found a place to get them down the bank."

"We'll begin that project tomorrow," said Isaac, "and I expect we'll have to level the bank with picks, shovels, and maybe dynamite."

"Then let's celebrate with an early supper and a good night's rest," Collins suggested.

Much of the snow had melted, and the cold wind that had plagued them daily since the storm had subsided. While Felix and Mamie prepared supper, the rest of the outfit filled feed bags for the horses and mules.

After breakfast the following morning, Collins, Faro, Isaac, and Josh rode downriver to the place Collins wished to investigate. Isaac and Josh had brought picks and shovels.

"The bank here is not more than half as deep as the bank upriver," Collins said, "and we're only about two miles below the claim."

"Let's find out just how solid that bank is," said Isaac. "Come on, Josh."

They dismounted, and with picks they attacked the riverbank. The picks went in deep, and withdrawing them, Isaac and Josh tested the ground in several other places, with the same result.

"Unless there's rock deeper down, we can level this bank in a day," Isaac said.

"It sure looks better than what we've been blasting," said Faro. "Eight of us with picks and shovels should make short work of it. Why don't we start today?"

"There's no reason why we can't," Collins said, "but I'm a bit nervous when all of us are away from camp at the same time. Suppose four of us work half a day at a time, with the others watching over the horses, mules, and wagons?"

"That's likely a good idea," said Faro. "Josh and

Isaac already have picks and shovels. You and me can ride back for ours, and tell the others what we have in mind."

They rode back to camp and Collins told the rest of the outfit what he and Faro had decided.

"Dallas, you're in charge here," Faro said. "If there's trouble of any kind, three quick shots will bring us on the run. When we ride in and the noon meal's done, then the rest of you can ride downriver and pick up where we leave off."

Taking picks and shovels, Faro and Collins rode back to join Isaac and Josh, and found them using shovels instead of picks.

"Saves time," said Isaac. "Unless we hit rock, we may not need the picks at all."

"You've started back far enough for a decent slope," Collins observed. "That should be sufficient."

"One thing we must keep in mind, and what we must tell the others," said Isaac, "is that none of the dirt from our digging is to be thrown into the riverbed. We don't yet know where we'll be mining for gold, and I can't see moving this dirt again."

They spent two days leveling the riverbank to the extent that the wagons could safely be taken down to the now dry riverbed.

"It should be packed hard," Faro said, "and the mules can take care of that."

All the mules were brought downriver on lead ropes and were led repeatedly up and down the newly dug slope until the surface was packed hard.

"Now," said Faro, "we're ready to move the wagons

down here, into the riverbed, and back upstream near the claim."

"I don't want to get in the way of progress," Collins said, "but shouldn't we first be sure the riverbed's solid all the way, and that there's no pockets of deep mud?"

"That might not be a bad idea," said Faro. "Let's you and me find out. We'll ride up there as far as we aim to take the wagons."

They did so, and while there was some remaining mud, the riverbed beneath it seemed solid enough. Collins was satisfied, and within an hour the five wagons were making their way along the former bed of the river, toward the gold claim. Faro positioned his wagon well under the protective overhang and the rest of the wagons were drawn up in similar fashion.

"All we'll need is a rope from bank to bank," Dallas observed, "and we'll have a corral for the horses and mules, and when there's snow, there's plenty of overhang where they can take shelter."

"I suppose it's time to drop all those logs over the edge," said Collins. "Then we can take turns working the claim and chopping wood."

"Yeah," Dallas said. "Them that's takin' a rest from working the claim can chop wood while they're resting."

"Just a damn minute," said Tarno. "If you're the *segundo*, I quit."

Faro laughed. "I think we'll all work the claim for a few days. It's time we had a taste of the reward that brought us here in the first place."

"I'm in favor of that," Felix said.

The rest of them quickly shouted their agreement.

"I see I'm outvoted," said Collins in a jovial manner. "Tomorrow we'll begin working the claim."

After breakfast, eagerly seizing picks and shovels, they followed Collins to the place from which the original ore samples had been taken.

"Because of the river's water, we only had a small area in which we were able to dig," Collins said. "Now we have the entire riverbank. Felix, why don't you do the honors?"

Felix Blackburn swung his pick, and driving it deep into the riverbank, brought forth a small landslide of earth and rock. The rock came loose in flat chunks and the surface of it was honeycombed with thin threads of gold.

"My God," said Dallas Weaver, "I've had a little mining experience, but I've never seen anything the equal of this. That'll assay at ten thousand dollars a ton."

"Let's see if it continues," Felix said, swinging the pick at a different portion of the riverbank.

There was more of the brittle rock, with threads of gold becoming visibly wider.

"Maybe we can find it somewhere else," said Dallas, seizing a pick.

A dozen feet beyond where Felix had begun digging, Dallas drove the pick deep into the riverbank. There was more of the strange rock, crisscrossed with threads of gold. Aflame with excitement, the others began driving picks into the riverbank, with the same astounding results. So frantic were their efforts, they were soon exhausted, and when they sat down to rest, they stared at their discovery with unbelieving eyes.

"I believe this may be one of the lost treasures I've read about in history books," said Felix. "Some of them were supposed to be so rich, threads of gold could be broken loose from the ore by hand. There have been legends of strikes such as this, back in the days when Spain owned this territory."

"I've never heard of such a strike in Utah," Faro said. "What in tarnation possessed any of you to look for gold here?"

"Felix believed there was a rich strike here somewhere," said Collins, "and he persisted in looking for it, long after the rest of us were convinced we were wasting our time."

"It's a lot like salvation," Felix said. "It never comes to you, unless you believe that it exists. Only then can a dream become reality."

"I just wish you'd dreamed it was closer to Santa Fe," said Josh.

"This would be worth the effort if it was a thousand miles from Santa Fe," Isaac said.

"This claim should have been registered with the assayer's office in Santa Fe," Faro said.

"We thought of that," said Collins, "but we were fearful of starting a gold rush before we knew exactly where the gold was."

"That," Isaac said, "and the fact that we just didn't know if our claim would be legal, since it's in Utah Territory, and we would have had to register it in New Mexico."

"Utah Territory is part of the United States," said

Faro, "and someday Utah will be a state. Federal law should protect you here."*

"I'm not too sure of that," Dallas said. "Remember the renegades who ambushed us, and them eight varmints Durham put on our trail? They didn't care a damn for the law, and all that protected us was our loaded guns. I reckon the time's comin' when a man won't be allowed to protect himself, when the world becomes civilized and law-bound. Then the men we pay to protect us will nuzzle up to the politicians, and the lot of 'em will sell us out to the very varmints who want us dead. I hope I don't live so long that I can't load my gun and stomp my own snakes."

"I reckon you're right," said Faro, "but I still think this claim should be registered in Santa Fe."

"We might as well register it when we return," Felix said. "Once we roll into town with four wagon loads of the wealth we're lookin' at, there'll be no keeping this claim a secret. We'll have men following us day and night."

"I don't doubt that," said Faro, "but we'll defend what's ours as we have so far. With guns, if there's no other way."

"We'll cross that bridge when we get to it," Shanghai said. "Right now, I reckon we're lookin' at another problem. Loadin' this ore into the wagons will be something different. Barrels and crates, sides of bacon and the like is one thing, but wagon beds ain't deep enough for the ore we aim to haul. Pile it too high, and

*In 1896, Utah Territory became the forty-fifth state.

we'll lose a lot of it along the way, and if we don't pile it high, it means we can't haul near as much."

His companions looked at Shanghai and then at one another. Faro spoke.

"It's something we should have considered before leavin' Santa Fe, I reckon. There we could have bought lumber and built sideboards for the wagon bed."

"But we had no idea the strike would be this rich, or that we'd be hauling so much ore," said Dallas.

"Perhaps we'll just have to make the best of it, and haul what we can," Collins said.

"Do we?" said Felix. "After all the challenges we've met, there has to be a way to add to the depth of those wagon beds, using materials that we have."

"Maybe there is," Faro said. "There's the wagon canvas."

"The bows ain't strong enough," said Tarno. "Throw the weight of that ore against 'em and they'll snap like matchsticks."

"We won't be depending on the wagon bows," Faro said. "We'll have to cut uprights maybe five feet long, using available timber, and spacing them three feet apart, anchor them to the wagon beds. The wagon canvas is less than six months old, and when it's taut against those uprights, it'll hold as much ore per wagon as the teams can pull."

"That'll take some time," said Josh Snyder. "It'll delay work on the claim."

"No matter," Levi Collins said. "Without the extra depth to the wagon beds, the time saved to work the claim won't mean anything. For that matter, with all the firewood we have, we can build enough fires to work on both the wagons and the claim at night, if we have to."

"*Bueno*," Faro said. "That's the kind of thinking that leads to success."

"Then we'd better put our heads to it and figure some way to increase the depth of the wagon tailgates, and to build a barrier behind each wagon box," said Dallas. "Them canvas puckers won't do a thing to keep the ore from slidin' over the tailgate at the back, or from comin' down on the wagon box like an avalanche, when we go down a slope."

"I reckon we can solve that problem, too," Faro said. "We have the canvas that served as shelter between the wagons durin' storms, and we can use as much of that as we need. We'll have to add some of those wooden uprights to the tailgates of the wagons and stretch canvas tight over them. A similar barrier will have to be built behind each wagon box, too. We still have plenty of those spikes, don't we, Dallas?"

"Yeah," said Dallas. "They'll work, if we cut only three- or four-inch firs and flatten the ends where they're to be anchored to the wagon."

"We know the ore's here," Collins said, "and I believe we should devote our time to modifying the wagons. Now that we have shelter, they must be unloaded."

"Yes," said Faro. "We'll need several of them to haul in the timber for the uprights."

So they set about unloading the supplies from the wagons, piling them up against the riverbank, under the protective overhang.

"It occurs to me," Felix said, while they rested from

their efforts, "that we may have too much of this grub left, when it's time to return to Santa Fe."

"I've thought of that, myself," said Collins, "but our original plans called for us to be here for at least a year, and we would have needed the extra supplies."

"But when we joined your outfit," Dallas added, "you had eight men to work the claim, and that cuts the time in half. But we'll need grub for the return to Santa Fe, so at least some of our wagon space will be needed for that. Why don't we go ahead and build sideboards for all the wagons, but count on using one of them as a supply wagon?"

"That's a practical solution," said Collins. "What do the rest of you think?"

"It makes sense to me," Faro said. "From what we've already learned, there's no way we can take as much of this ore as we'd like, even if we were able to use all five wagons. The best we can do is load four of them as heavily as we safely can, and like Felix has suggested, add more wagons when we return."

Quickly they all agreed to the proposal, and finished unloading the wagons. Early the next morning, Faro told them how he believed their plan should proceed.

"Four of us will take two of the wagons and begin cutting timber for the uprights. I think I've figured pretty close to how many we'll need. A couple of days and we should have all we'll need. Shanghai, Isaac, and Josh will go with me today. Tomorrow, the rest of you will finish the job."

"I like that arrangement," said Collins. "Those of us remaining in camp can continue to work the claim."

"So do I," Josh said.

The others quickly agreed. Faro and Isaac took one wagon while Shanghai and Josh took the second, and they set out to begin cutting the necessary timber.

Cutting, hauling, shaping the timber, and shoring up the wagons took them a week, and then they began working the claim in earnest. So that Felix might work with the rest of the outfit, Mamie took over cooking for them all.

"Tarnation," said Dallas, one night during supper, "at the rate we're goin', we'll have these wagons loaded and ready to go, long before April."

"Yes," Collins said, "but the deadliest part of winter will probably be during January, February, and March. We could be laid up on the trail for days at a time, because of snow and the mud that follows with the thaw."

"We won't have any shelter on the trail," said Shanghai. "We used most of the shelter canvas to help shore up the wagon beds. I favor stayin' right here until April. God knows, we have plenty of grub and supplies. If we start back too soon, we'll need more than one wagon for supplies."

"Normally I wouldn't agree with such a delay," Faro said. "A teamster can't allow the winter to delay him, but this time, I reckon we ought to make an exception. I won't be surprised if we have snowdrifts by Christmas that may still be there three months later."

"I believe that's a wise decision," said Collins. "On the return trip, we'll be better able to plan what we should do."

They all understood and quickly agreed.

**Southwestern Utah, on the Sevier River.
December 25, 1870.**

"Today," Dallas Weaver said, "I don't aim to do a blessed thing but eat and sleep."

"Go ahead," said Faro. "It's about all the Christmas a teamster ever gets."

The entire outfit enjoyed a day of leisure, except for Felix and Mamie, who did all the cooking.

"I feel a mite guilty," Shanghai said, "layin' here doin' nothin', while Felix and Mamie do all the work."

"If it will ease your guilt," said Felix wryly, "you can always pitch in and help."

"I don't feel *that* guilty," Shanghai said. "Besides, my cookin' would spoil Christmas for the rest of you, and I just ain't that mean."

"If there ain't nothin' else," said Tarno, "we can always give thanks for this shelter. I look for snow sometime tonight."

Tarno's prediction proved all too true, and by midnight there was a howling blizzard in progress. Several extra fires were built, and the horses and mules huddled gratefully under the protective overhang of the riverbank.

"Ain't often a bunch of teamsterin' mules gets this kind of shelter," Dallas said.

"Teamsters neither," said Shanghai.

The new year arrived just hours before another storm, piling snow atop drifts that had not only not melted, but were frozen solid. The temperature fell below zero and remained there for days. Two weeks passed before they again saw the sun, and the cold continued. While there was plenty of food, warm fires, and shelter, the camp wasn't wolf-proof, and one frigid day after the worst of the storms had blown itself out, the silence was broken by the fearful howling of wolves.

"We can manage with our normal watch," Faro said, "but we'll all have to be ready for them. We'll keep our Winchesters ready. Thanks to the overhang of these riverbanks, I'd say they'll have to come after us along the riverbed."

"We can build up a roaring fire at each end of the camp, durin' the night," said Dallas, "and that should help."

"It will," Faro said, "but with everything frozen solid and the scent of fresh mule, they won't be waitin' for night."

The predators came, a dozen strong, but as Faro had predicted, they ignored the high riverbanks. Instead, they came from two directions, skulking along the riverbed. Collins, Felix, Dallas, and Josh were standing watch on one side of the camp, while Faro, Isaac, Tarno, and Shanghai watched the other side. As though by prearrangement, the wolves came at them from both directions. Winchesters roared, while horses nickered and mules brayed, but the wolves were quickly gunned down.

"We'll have to rope the varmints and drag them far enough that they don't spook the mules and horses," said Faro. "A little more, and we'll have a stampede on our hands."

*   *   *

Time passed slowly, for the sun seldom shone, and it was difficult to tell when one day ended and another began. Dallas Weaver tied a knot in a leather thong, marking the dreary passing of each day.

"Accordin' to my count, it's the first day of March," Dallas announced.

"We already have enough ore to load all the wagons," said Felix. "Looks like we'll have plenty of time to rest before we leave for Santa Fe."

"I think we'll see what March brings," Faro said. "If there's a break in the weather, we may not wait for April."

But there was no break, and the snow from previous storms had more piled on top of it. Each day they looked at the dreary gray skies, impatient to be on the trail to Santa Fe, yet knowing they dared not risk it. Not until the second day of April did the skies begin to clear. The temperature rose dramatically, and the west wind came in with a warmth they hadn't enjoyed for months.

"Soon as the snow melts and the mud's had a chance to dry, we'll pull out," said Faro.

A week later, they set out for Santa Fe. Four of the wagons were loaded with all the ore the teams could pull, while the fifth wagon was overloaded with supplies. The warm weather continued, and the worst they had to contend with was rain and the sea of mud that followed.

"I'm surprised the Utes haven't bothered us," Collins said.

"The kind of winter we've had," said Faro, "I

wouldn't be surprised if they drifted to the south, where it's a mite warmer and there's game to be had."

"We wiped out half that bunch that ambushed us," Tarno said, "and that's enough to convince them we're *mala medicina*. Bad medicine."

The Colorado River. April 25, 1871.

"At least the bridge we built is still here," said Collins. "I'm surprised the Utes didn't somehow destroy it."

Tarno laughed. "Too much work. Indians avoid that, whenever they can. They might have set it afire, if the wood hadn't been green."

"We'll still have to inspect it," Faro said. "The ground's been frozen, and the stakes we used to anchor the stringers may have worked loose."

But the bridge remained solid, and using blinkers to stay the fear of the mules, they led the teams across. Still they saw no Indians, and with each passing day, spring seemed a little closer.

"Looking back," said Mamie, "it all seems unreal."

"In a way it does," Felix agreed.

They sat beneath starry skies, and a gentle wind whispered through fir trees. The first watch ended at midnight, and as they took to their blankets, Faro, Shanghai, Isaac, and Josh took over.

Southwestern Colorado. May 10, 1871.

"Damn," said Faro, as he viewed the sagging rear of the supply wagon.

"A busted axle ain't no fun," Shanghai said, "but it

could be worse. It could have been one of the wagons loaded with ore. This one won't be half as heavy."

"No," said Dallas, "but it'll take just as long to chop down a tree, make a new axle, and replace the broken one."

"Now that we're goin' to have money," Tarno said, "let's make good use of some of it. Every wagon carries a spare wheel, so why not a spare rear axle?"

"I'll go along with that," said Faro, "but that's no help to us now. Who wants to ride out and find a tree for a new axle, while I jack up the wagon?"

"I'll go," Dallas said. "Just don't tell me all the axes are at the very bottom of all that load in the supply wagon."

"They are," said Tarno with a straight face. "Ever' damn one. I put 'em there myself."

Just for a moment, Dallas took him seriously, and they all had a laugh at his expense.

"Just for that, Tarno," Faro said, "you can go along and help him. While we haven't had any Indian trouble, nobody rides alone."

An hour later, Dallas and Tarno returned, dragging the trunk of a fir of sufficient size to replace the broken axle. Faro had the rear of the wagon jacked up, and by the time the new axle had been fashioned and put in place, the sun was less than an hour high.

"There's water," Faro said, "so we'll stay here for the night."

"This stream will take us to the western foothills of the San Juan Mountains," said Levi Collins. "We ought to reach Santa Fe by the first week in June."

Felix and Mamie set about preparing supper, while

the rest of the outfit grained the horses and mules. While they were eating, talk turned to the nearness of Santa Fe.

"I hope we'll be there in a few days," Mamie said. "I need clothes."

"We'll have to be there a while," Faro said. "It won't be easy finding more wagons and mules, and we must have some decent sideboards built for all these wagons to replace the makeshift ones."

"Then we'll be there long enough for Mamie and me to find a preacher," said Felix.

Josh laughed. "I thought you was plannin' to become a teamster, spendin' all your time on the trail, sleeping on the ground."

"He may be sleeping on the ground," Mamie said hotly, "but he won't be sleeping alone. What about you?"

Snyder was visibly embarrassed and finally he grinned. "I reckon I deserved that."

"You did, for a fact," said Felix. "Mamie can shoot and she can cook."

"Amen," Shanghai said, "and that's fifty percent better than most teamsters can claim."

"That's true," said Dallas. "You oughta try some of Shanghai's biscuits. I swear they could be used as cannon fodder."

"All right," Shanghai growled, "I admit I can't cook. Don't rub it in."

With the dawn, they again took the trail, and ten days later they reached the western foothills of the San Juans.

"It's the first day of June," Dallas announced, consulting the rawhide thong in which he had tied a knot for each passing day.

"Another week, at most," said Collins.

They moved on, the elevation decreasing as they progressed.

Northwestern New Mexico. The Chama River. June 8, 1871.

"I remember this river flowing right into Santa Fe," Mamie said, when they stopped to rest the teams.

"That it does," said Collins. "Looks like my prediction for the first week in June will be shy, but we'll arrive within two or three more days."

Santa Fe, New Mexico. June 12, 1871.

The sun was noon-high when they reined up to rest the teams. Somewhere just ahead, a dog barked.

"I think some of us had better ride in and learn how we're to dispose of this ore," said Faro. "Maybe we can get it off our hands without all of New Mexico knowing about it."

"Come on then," Collins said.

When Collins and Faro returned, the outfit rode triumphantly into Santa Fe.

"Now," said Faro, "hadn't we better register our claim?"

"Faro and me already have," Collins said, "and we know where to take the ore."

"Thank God," said Mamie. "I can't wait to sleep in a real bed."

"Not until we find a preacher," Felix said.